Ward Nine

This book is dedicated to all the heroes nursing family members with mental illness.

Ward Nine

Emily Khalayi Wekulo

Worlds Unknown Publishers

Prologue

"You know I'm of royal standing here, right?" Elima's Spirit floated away from Ploutus's.

"Yes," Ploutus replied. "That's why I took my life for you. I will be your king in this realm . . . and you will be my queen."

He tried to catch up with her.

Elima turned around angrily, throwing pig bile in his face.

Ploutus screamed in agony as the pig bile immersed his spirit in excruciating pain. The uproar drew more spirits toward him. They swarmed around him, ready to attack. Ploutus's spirit was trembling, begging, pleading for Elima to save him.

All spirits carried pig bile in their porous palms, dripping through their bony fingers. So many spirits were seeking revenge. For the first time, he realized just how many people he had killed in his life. That fact alone shook him to the core . . . more than the pig bile.

Then he saw Nysa taking her aim with the bile. Her hollow eyes were dark and angry.

"Nysa, my daughter!" he begged. "I know what those Blue Brutes did to you. We will avenge you together. Help me lose these monsters on my tail!"

"You are the monster here! "Nysa responded. "You openly denied me in life. You chose your bastard son over me. You should have sent him here first to pave way and deal with your enemies before falling for Elima's tricks. To imagine that my mother loved you . . ."

Pig bile came splashing from all corners.

"Please. Please!" Ploutus howled as his spirit disappeared in bile. "Somebody, help! Anyone I served in life. Please help me . . . help me, Elima. Forgive me. Help me . . ."

Elima laughed in pleasure for a while. Then she raised her royal cat's tail to call the spirits to attention and whisked them away with the tail. They left Ploutus alone, squirming in pain.

"I have to go see my daughter," said Elima. "Najma needs me. She might be in danger . . ."

"Can I come?" Ploutus asked, almost begging.

She summoned mimosa bushes in a flash and bound Ploutus's spirit. He could not move. Neither could any other spirit find him when she was among the living. Not even Cosmos . . .

Monday Morning – THE SACRIFICE

Najma's eyes froze between blinks when she saw her mother. Her heart sunk, and her breath was reduced to inadequate gasps. Najma thought she would faint.

She heard the crunch of shoes against gravel—someone approaching—before a hand gripped her elbow. She tried to pull away but it held on even tighter. Najma thought against resisting harder. The sight before her had drained her fighting spirit.

A strong masculine scent floated towards her nose, overpowering her mother's smelly guts, which lay strewn on the pavement next to her limp body.

It was a scent she knew too well.

"We will take care of it. I am sorry Najma".

Silence.

"The police will be here soon."

Silence.

What does he mean . . . take care of it? she wondered, Does it mean tracing where half of my mother's hair, breasts, and tongue have disappeared to? What would the police do? Revive my mother? Who does this man think he is?

She wanted to turn and look into his face, but her neck could not move. Her eyes refused to blink, and suddenly, her throat was dry and her tongue missing like her mother's. She could not speak, even when she opened her mouth to do so. No sound fell from her quivering lips.

She wanted to ask how he would take care of it. She wished she could turn around and look him in the face. She wanted to ascertain that he really knew what he was talking about.

The mutilated body of Najma's mother lay on the concrete, dead and naked. Her breasts were neatly chopped off and her tongue had been pulled out.

"Take that girl away," a woman shouted from the gathering throng of people.

There was a scream here, a gasp there . . . someone was gagging in a trench nearby.

A man whistled in shock and more screams filled the quiet air, shattering the silence. Najma continued to stare, her eyes fixed on her mother's body.

"Someone take that child away from here, for heaven's sake. She is going into shock!" another woman said empathetically.

But Najma wanted to be there. She wanted to be there with her mother, even in death. That was what she had done all her life, and no one had cared to take her away from her mother.

She let out a low painful mourn as blazing fire consumed her belly.

She didn't want to go anywhere.

"Don't you dare touch her," the person holding her hand commanded.

The woman in the crowd who tried to touch Najma to take her away stopped, turned away, and left.

Najma knew that voice; she knew the mouth that spoke. Her eyes moistened, moving from her mother's body to the feet that stood by her side. She knew the shoes they were wearing. Those shoes were in her house the previous night. What was he doing here? How did he know about her mother? Who was he?

"Who are you?" Najma demanded as she turned toward him.

A sharp pain shot through her shoulder as she twisted her arm free.

"We need to get you out of here, Najma." He said to her face. She saw tears dancing in his eyes but he pushed them back with quick blinks.

"Who are you?" she asked again, this time willing the tremor in her heart to accompany her voice.

The crowd fell silent. The screams died. The retching man slowly walked back to the gathering. The woman who had just spoken pursed her lips tightly.

The sudden silence lingered for only a second and was followed by a soft murmur from within the crowd.

"Have you ever seen him?" one asked.

"No," another said matter-of-factly. Most just shook their heads in disagreement.

"Najma, let's go to the house please," he pleaded with her. "The police will be here soon."

No one dared raise his or her voice to speak. They just looked at the pair, the young man holding onto the arm of the teary, bewildered girl.

Najma sunk the grip of her feet deeper into the ground and clenched her teeth. No one was going to peel her away from the scene. Her mother had been brutally murdered and her body mutilated. She was going to wait for the police and tell them what she knew.

"Who are you, young man?" asked a mature man in neatly pressed navy-blue trousers, his white shirt perfectly tucked in. "We have never seen you in Corner Street."

Najma looked up toward the face of the speaker. He wore a red tie, and his lips were strangely symmetrical. She'd never seen such a mouth before, with lips perfectly even. Najma was taken aback. She could have sworn they looked the same, like having two lower lips or two upper lips on one face. He stood tall above the rest, his shoulders heavy set and widely spread beneath his stout neck. He carried a newspaper and a phone. His eyes seemed clear and transparent, like crystal, creating the impression that one could see right through them, into his skull.

"Why don't you tell the girl who you are?" he continued. "Perhaps then, she'd consider following you."

Najma had to force her eyes away from his lips to look at the younger man beside her.

"I'm her brother," said the man with the familiar shoes matter-of-factly.

Najma was shocked at first; and then she laughed. Her laughter was loud enough to overpower the siren of the approaching police van.

What did he mean . . . brother?

I have no brother, she thought. This must be the man behind my mother's death, and now he wants to kill me too. If not that, then he knows the reason and the people behind her death. How can I trust him?

"Najma," he begged again, "I can explain in the house. Please let's go before the police arrive."

Ooh, she thought, now he wants to hide from the police.

The crowd reacted upon hearing the word "police," dispersing as quickly as they came, pretending to watch from a distance. Only the man with strangely matching lips remained behind.

No one wanted to be involved in a homicide, especially on a Monday morning. Dwellers of Corner Street knew how the police could turn things around. They knew that anyone looking like a suspect would be shoved into the police Land Rover and locked in a cell. If an important person was involved in the murder, anyone else could be picked up and framed for the murder. The case would be dropped after a month or so when a new subject of interest came up.

"Najma, please," the man by her side begged again.

"Go with him, young girl. He is a good person," the man with strangely matching lips said and began to walk away.

Najma would see those lips again, a few months later.

Good person indeed, Najma thought. How could he be a good person yet he was hiding from the police? But I doubt I have anyone else, so I'd better go with him.

"Who could have done such a thing to an innocent, mentally unstable woman?" Najma heard the woman who insisted that she should be taken away say to another. They were already gossiping about her mother.

She wanted to go back and scream at them but thought against it. Had they not always talked about her? Had they not branded her the mad woman who sang songs to an imaginary baby on the streets? The mad woman who ran from one shop to the other like one running away from spirits? The mad woman who would sometimes walk around Corner Street, back and forth, till her feet bled?

Najma walked away, like she always did when people whispered about her and her mother. She walked away like she had done before, when her fellow pupils refused to play with her in school.

As she walked away with the young, familiar man, she finally allowed herself to cry. She wasn't sure whether they were tears of sadness for the loss of mother, or tears of pain because people who knew nothing about her mother assumed that she was mentally unstable and gossiped about it.

Mentally unstable! Najma thought. My mother was not a mad woman. She was just depressed. If only I could have helped her.

She should have been patient for me to finish school, so that I could stay with her every minute till she got well.

"Don't cry. You'll be okay," the man said, slowing down so that they could walk together. He reached out to her and held her hand.

"You need to be strong for her," he said, locking his fingers into her slender ones.

There was a sudden sense of comfort in Najma's heart. It made her angry. She wanted to feel the pain. She did not want to stop crying.

"My mother is dead. I can't help it," she snuffled.

Anger choked her. Who did he think he was, telling her what to do? Did he understand her pain? She wanted to turn around and run. What if her life was in danger? The man didn't look like he would harm her, though. He had come to their house so many times, and she knew if he had wanted to harm her, he would have done it already.

But I need to be angry at something, she thought again. It has to be him. I don't want to be comforted just yet.

"You are sixteen, Najma," he said. "You will survive. I will not let anyone or anything hurt you." He squeezed her hand gently as he spoke.

She wanted to pull away, but he held on tighter. She knew he meant everything. For the first time, Najma lifted her eyes to his face. She looked away when their eyes met. She thought she saw tears in his eyes.

They walked to her house. She noticed a dark car parked in the distance. She knew it was his. She had seen it before. She let him walk into the house first, then followed in and locked the door behind her.

The midmorning sun was extraordinarily hot, its rays licking the dew from the grass like a thirsty cat lapping milk from a pot. The trees stood still on Corner Street. A heavily pregnant cloud sat on the sky precariously, like it would let go of its fat babies any minute. The air was strangely humid and warm, and Najma felt her nose get stuffy.

On a normal day in October, trees would be swaying in the wind, letting go of dead leaves that would carpet the sidewalks. A bird would be chirping here, a dog barking there and a woman shouting at a child from a distance. The hawkers would call out for buyers, shouting the names of their goods louder as they approached Corner Apartments. A door would crack open here, then click shut. Another would swish in a wide wave as others remained totally shut. Clothes, pegged still on wirelines would be lazily flapping in the air, filling it with the fresh smell of detergent and lavender fabric softeners.

A neat pavement separated the residential area from the market square. On one side of the street lay a set of neat, Lego-like buildings that were salons, butcher shops, and drug stores. Many were recently painted and renamed. A person who had been raised in Corner and left for ten years or so would certainly be confused by the new set-up on return.

Most of the buildings were whitewashed and weather-beaten the whites were now greys and greens covered in moss. There was one new major shopping mall, Corner Mall, holding a fancy restaurant, a supermarket, a clinic, and a few offices. There were two banks in the new skyscraper as well.

At the far end of the street was a small dispensary linked to a drug rehabilitation center, built by the town council and the state of West Valley. The schools were built close to the dispensary and connected to a private road from the residential side. From an aerial view, Corner Street looked like a sharp-edged trapezium stabbing into the belly of West Valley. It was set apart from the rest of the other small towns and villages. It looked like a favored child in the West Valley family of towns—fat and spoiled.

On the other side of the street were houses with uniform architectural designs—a mimicry of Old English mansions. Each home had a parking square next to the front porch and a tiny veranda adjacent to the front rooms. Most houses were a shade of yellow and brown, with white rafters and corrugated iron roofs. Most were either owned by or rented out to families that could afford the hefty prices.

At the far end, away from market square, were the common people's apartments. Those who had no homes rented there. These were mainly the mall staff, blue-collar workers from the dispensary, school faculty members, and single adults.

The apartments were connected to the main road that connected Corner Street to West Valley at the sharpest end of the trapezium. This is where Najma grew up—where she never made friends and where everyone looked at her sick mother with suspicion and gossiped about her. Some of the neighbors would openly flee when they saw her sitting outside with her mother. They would grab their children and shrink away in horror.

This was where Najma first learned to hate the people around her and love her mother deeply at the same time. In this neighborhood, she had learned to separate those who were for her from the rest . . . from who had been against her at a very tender age.

As the clouds let loose fat droplets of rain, which hammered the corrugated iron roof, the noise filtered through the plywood ceiling of her house, and she thought of her life without her mother. It dawned on Najma then that her mother was the reason she wanted to see new days. The humming rain reminded her of the days they cuddled on the streets—days when her mother refused to set foot in the house. It reminded her of the fear she had as a child when thunder struck. She remembered how her mother would hold her tight and sing songs of rain.

Gods show love in torrents,

Torrents of tears,

Happy, they quench the thirst,

For thirsty plants,

Thirsty cow,

Thirsty dog

Thirsty cat

Thirsty bird . . .

Thirsty spirits.

She hummed the song, letting tears accompany the flow of the rain.

She remembered how the song had made her forget her fear of thunder, as her mother would sing louder when it rumbled the whole night.

The man who claimed to be her brother sat on a couch opposite her, staring at her. His eyes never left her face until the rain stopped. Then he excused himself and promised to be back in a while. He scribbled a number on a piece of paper torn from his pocket pad.

"Call me if you need me," he said as he handed her the paper.

And then he left.

Previous Day – Sunday – PEACEFUL SLEEP

Elima had not woken up when Najma left for church. Najma went to her room and watched her breathe for a minute. She had not stirred. She just breathed softly like a baby. The room smelled fresh, meaning she had not woken up in the night to create a jumble.

Sometimes, Elima's illness would strike in the middle of the night. On such nights, she would muddle up her bedroom, unpack everything from the cabinets, splash lotion on the windows, soak all the beddings in water, and create a wild mess. When she was younger, Najma would lock herself in her own room and cry. Sometimes, neighbors would send their house help to clean the mess and gather gossip about the situation.

Other times, the mess would stay, until her mother got well and cleaned it herself.

Once in a while, a woman would show up from the blues and clean the house, saying she had been sent by an anonymous benefactor. Mother never objected.

When Najma turned ten, she'd learnt to take care of the messes her mother created. She stopped asking for help. Sometimes it would take her days of being late for school, but somehow she managed. The strange women stopped coming, and only one would often come—Nana. Najma instantaneously took to her from the very beginning, the first time they met.

This Sunday, and some months before, her mother had been peaceful. She slept most of the time, even during the day. Najma would wake her up to shower and eat, after which she would go back to bed, saying she was too tired to sit. Sometimes, she would ask Najma to read a book for her. Najma loved reading stories from the Valley Digest magazines. She would laugh at some and just stare at others.

Najma was happy. Her mother was getting better. The medicine she had been given seemed to work.

This Sunday, she was going to thank God for her mother's recovery. It had been quite a long journey.

As she stood there watching her, she remembered the first time she'd realized her mother was sick.

They were at the market square. Her mother was sitting in front of a stall. Najma was running up and down the street. She was four years old at the time.

Her Mother was picking up things, stuffing them into her dress. Najma did the same, thinking it was a game. Her mother laughed loudly and Najma laughed too.

The woman who owned the stall stood by and watched them. She watched the pair for a while and then began to cry, cursing Najma's mother, throwing things at her.

Najma's mother stopped "playing". She took a piece of dirty paper and gave it to the whimpering woman. The woman gave her a look that made Najma shudder.

At that point, she knew something was wrong. No one had ever treated her mother spitefully in her presence. Her mother insisted and made an attempt of wiping the woman's face with the dirty piece of tissue paper. The woman pushed her away with so much force that she fell off the steps in front of the stall.

"Get off me, you madwoman!" the woman exclaimed. "The Gods can't even give me a real baby with an important person, but they gave you one . . . you, a lunatic!"

"Madwoman," Najma's mother said, laughing as she struggled to stand up.

She continued laughing and dancing, saying "madwoman" continually.

Najma followed her mother.

Najma was scared. She started crying. Her mother picked a piece of paper from the pieces she had collected in her dress and started wiping her tears. She kept on saying "madwoman" as she wiped her face. Najma started saying "madwoman" too.

They walked home. Her mother said "madwoman" till she fell asleep.

Najma remembered the nights they would sleep on the streets because mother refused to go home. She remembered shivering all night.

Nana brought them food every time Najma's mother was sick. She sometimes came to take Najma from the street when her mother refused to go home. They would sleep together in their house, and Nana would leave when Najma's mother came home.

Najma remembered her mother smiling every time Nana came around. Her mother would be happy when Nana was around. She ate everything the woman cooked. She also felt better a few days after Nana came home. Every time Nana wanted to go back to her home, mother and child would be overwhelmed with sadness.

As she watched her mother sleep peacefully that Sunday morning, she wanted to thank God for the kind people who had always watched over them when she was not old enough to take care of her mother. There was always food, and their house was always clean, even when her mother created messes every now and then. Nana would wash her and change her clothes, then disappear into the night.

Najma always remembered Nana's merry laughter. She was a voluptuous woman, with every bit of her body in excess. She gave the warmest hugs and embraces. Every time she came around, Najma would run to her and snuggle into her bosom. Nana's face was always ablaze with a bright smile, and her tiny eyes radiated like pearls.

Nana's hair was very long, and sometimes she would let Najma play with it. Nana would feed Najma, and before the cup of porridge was empty, Najma would be asleep.

Sometimes when Najma's mother became too ill, Nana would watch over them for days. Nana would wash all their clothes, air them and fold them nicely. She would then buy groceries and milk and fill the fridge. Nana showed Najma how to make her own breakfast when she was only three years old. By the end of the week, the house would be a mess again, and Nana would be there early on Saturday morning to tidy it.

Najma watched episodes of her life with her mother go by. Some involved her worst mental state and others her very best moments. She wanted to cry, but she felt that her crying would annoy God. Had He not been so gracious as to give her mother some mental stability? Had He not been healing her steadily? She lowered herself, kissed her mother's cheek, touched her face and closed the bedroom door behind her. She took her bible and went to church.

When she came back home from church that midmorning, Elima was missing! Najma was sure that she'd locked the door, but her mother had her own key. Najma checked the bedroom and saw that everything was in order. Elima's drugs were intact. The bed was neat, though not spread. The toilet was clean. Her slippers were next to the bed. Najma's mind stopped for a while. Where could she be?

Her body suddenly froze. Her heart flapped faintly, and her breath almost deserted her. A swarm of questions buzzed in her skull. Where could she be? Had her mother gone back to the market? Had she fallen ill again?

No one came to the house, except the young man who brought them new crispy notes every Monday. Nana still came over to wash clothes, but she'd requested Najma to let her skip this one.

Something was not adding up. When she left in the morning, her mother had been perfectly okay. She could not have fallen sick. Who had let Mother out? She rarely went to the market square after returning from the hospital. It was three months since she had had her last attack. The doctor who came to see her in the house said she was getting better.

"Mom!" Najma called.

Silence.

"Mommy!" she called again, this time louder.

More silence.

She walked out of the house and looked around. Most of the neighbors were not at home. One house at the far end of the wing was open. She ran there and knocked. A man came out.

"Please, have you seen my mother?" she asked, her voice wrinkled in fear.

"The crazy woman?" the man fired back.

Najma shot a dirty look at him.

"Go take a look," he said. "I think you'll find her at the market square."

Without another word, he turned and walked back to the house.

Najma wanted to throw a stone at him. She ran down the pavement, using the private road to go to the market square. She ran past the dispensary, her school, the primary school, and all the way to the streets. Her eyes scanned the verandas on the left, then the right. Her mother was nowhere to be seen.

The childless woman's shop was closed. She pictured her mother falling down the steps and the woman calling her a madwoman. She panicked and ran to the steps.

But it was all in her mind. Her mother was not there.

She sat on the lowest step, fighting a sudden urge to cry.

Just before a tear dropped from her eye, she noticed something unusual. The shop was locked from the inside, not the outside. That meant that there were people inside.

She stood up and frantically knocked on the door. She listened. There were muffled voices, and then it was silent.

She knocked again and again and again, but no one opened the door. Najma walked away, defeated. She wanted to go to the police station, but she knew what she would be told. She gave the stall door one last look and thought she saw her mother fall off the steps again but brushed it off. The police would only make fun of her mother.

'That crazy woman could be anywhere.' That's what they'd say. 'Perhaps she's at the dumpsite. Go home and report back after twenty-four hours.'

Those imbeciles! she thought. They only know how to spring to action for people who can bribe them.

She chose to walk along the streets, praying that she would find her mother. She walked from one corner to the other, not noticing that she had repeatedly done that many times over. She asked anyone who cared to listen.

Corner was often deserted on Sundays, with very few stalls open. There would be no cars at the market square. Standing at one end of the street, one would easily see the farthest end.

Prayed Najma silently. Please, God, let her be fine. Don't let anything harmful befall her.

Where could she be?

A black Nissan X-trail hooted at her, and she jumped off the road as it sped by, missing her by a whisker.

"Idiot!" she muttered to herself. Then she noticed it was the car that came over on Mondays to bring her money.

That was strange. What was it doing at Corner Street on a Sunday? Why did it speed away? She wanted to run after it, but it had already peeled around a corner. She ran home, hoping to find her mother back.

At home, the door was wide open. She sped to her mother's room.

Elima was not in, but the medicine cabinet was open. All the drugs and hospital reviews were missing.

Her face felt numb, and suddenly it felt like there was no air in the room.

She went back to the living room and only then noticed the envelope with money inside and a pack of chicken and fries lying on the coffee table.

Did the man come when I was away? she thought. Why on a Sunday? Was he the one who drove past me? Why did he take the hospital documents?

The sun was setting, and yet there were no signs of Najma's mother. Most neighbors were back, but none had seen her leave the house that morning. No one had seen the black Nissan X-trail either.

There was a knock at the door. She ran to the door and opened. It was the man who usually brought their maintenance money. This time, he was not wearing sunshades. He wore a blue fitted shirt, a huge Rolex watch on his left wrist, and black shredded jeans. A clean masculine fragrance filled the living room.

Najma noticed for the first time in years that he had the darkest irises that she'd ever seen. It made the white that surrounded them sparkle. His face was so familiar. She thought she'd seen him somewhere before he began to bring them money.

"Have you found her?"

"Who?" She was caught off guard staring.

"Your mother," he replied.

His voice was a deep bass but had a tremor in it. Like he was panicking.

How did he know Mother was missing? she wondered. I'm not going to say anything to this man. I don't trust his eyes.

"Don't leave the house again," he said when she did not answer. "It isn't safe."

What? she thought. Who gives him the right to order me around? His money? He thinks just because he drops us notes and food, he has authority over me? Who is he?

She turned around, picked the food on the table, with the envelope of money and threw them at him.

"Take it!" she cried out. "I don't want it! I want my mother! Do you know where she is?"

"I don't know where she is," he replied, catching the flying packet of fries in time before it could mess up his neatly pressed shirt. "I am also looking for her. Please stay indoors, okay?"

"Why do you always bring us money?" Najma yelled. "Who are you?"

"I am just a messenger." he responded calmly. "I go where I am sent."

"Who sends you?" she asked.

"I can't tell you," he replied. "At least not now."

"Get out," Najma shouted.

"Najma, I am here to help," he pleaded.

"I don't need your help," she responded.

But she knew it was a lie. She needed him. What would a sixteen-year-old do on her own? Her mother had just disappeared. The young man walked out and locked the door behind him.

Najma noticed too late that he had gone with the key. She couldn't leave the house.

She wanted to scream. Angry tears burned her face. She hated how her neighbors ignored the situation and lived their lives as if nothing unusual had happened. Did they even care that her mother was missing? To them she was just a nutcase of no value.

All along, the neighbors had behaved like mental illness was contagious. They never talked to her mother—nor her. Every time Najma and her mother sat outside, on the porch, the neighbors would quickly pick up their babies and dash into their houses. Curtains would be drawn and small cracks left for peeping. All playing children would disappear into their houses as well.

Najma would never forget one particular incident when she was seven-years-old. Her mother had asked her to go and buy milk at the market. Children were playing outside, and when she opened the door, one kicked the ball in her direction either knowingly or out of panic. She instinctively kicked the ball back to the children. They all scampered in different directions, screaming.

Najma was livid with anger mixed with shame. The ball lay where it had landed for days. Nobody would dare touch it. Najma picked it up one day on her way from school and put it under her bed, where it remained for many years.

Were it not for Nana, her childhood would have been miserable. When everyone rushed past their house like there was plague surrounding it, Nana would play on the lawn with her. When her mother fell ill and created a mess, Nana would be there to help her clean it up while the neighbors peeped through their windows.

Nana made her paper dolls and box cars, and sometimes brought her sets of Barbie dolls from the supermarket. Nana baked her birthday cakes and sang for her.

She would decorate the house and help her blow out the candles. Together, they would make one wish: for her mother to get well. Some of the neighbor's children were her age mates, and they went to school together, but she has never said anything to them. She rudely snubbed those who tried reaching out, giving them an overflowing cup of insane, to remind them that nothing had changed.

Her helplessness around her mother's disappearance crippled her, and her heart was flooded with sadness. She wailed softly, gasped and whimpered like a hurt puppy. She had never felt so much pain. She cried herself to sleep that night.

The sound of a key turning in the keyhole woke Najma up. It was morning already. She had slept on the couch, and her neck felt stiff. The events of the previous night replayed in her mind.

"Mother!" she whispered. "Please let it be mother."

It was not her mother. The man had returned alone.

"I brought you breakfast," he said, letting himself in and closing the door behind him.

Fool! she thought. What made him think I want to eat? Now the neighbors will think he is my boyfriend. I'm sure they are behind their curtains, peeping.

"Is it okay if I sit?" he asked.

It was not okay. She did not want him in her mother's house, yet she desperately needed him.

"Did you find her?" she asked, "I mean my mother. Did you find her?"

"Eat. You need breakfast," he replied as he sat down. "And then I will take you to her."

She noticed that he avoided her eyes, and his dark mouth quivered when he spoke. There was an eruption of sweat on his forehead too. Something was wrong. His fingers were knotted in hard fists so that his hands looked like clubs. Her eyes shifted between his pulsating temples.

"Where is she?" Najma asked. "Is she okay?"

Her voice rose and fell simultaneously. Her face rippled in concern. She did not have to look at his face to sense the intense desperation that was written all over it. She ran out before he could stop her and bumped head first into the news he was trying to conceal.

This time round, nobody was peeping behind curtains. The neighbors were gathering in small circles. She did not notice them staring at her when she ran out. She was not even aware that the man had followed her.

"What's going on?" she shouted, addressing no one in particular.

"Is that her daughter?" someone asked.

"Yes," another whispered.

An innumerable amount of whispered remarks flew in her direction…

"Good heavens!"

"What will she do?"

"Poor soul."

"Hope she doesn't run mad like her mother."

"This is a lot for a young girl like her."

"If it runs in the blood, stress might trigger it."

"She looks wild already."

"And who is the man?"

"Maybe a relative."

"That man drops by almost weekly."

"I think I have seen him before."

Najma could not believe that they were gossiping in her presence. No one answered her.

She ran to the market square, examining the childless woman's shop first. The door was shut and sealed with a metallic cross bar.

Was this cross bar there yesterday? she wondered. Where did the barren woman go? This shop never closes. Not even on Sundays . . .

The door was locked from the inside, and she thought she heard people talking inside. Then, there was a stiff silence.

The steps stared at her. She scanned the door, then the steps once again, and suddenly it hit her. Beneath the steps, near the pedestrian's pavement, lay her mother's body, frozen, taut, and naked. Her eyes were wide open, her mouth gaping. Some of her teeth were missing. She looked like a split log tossed into a thick pool of blood. She lay a few meters away from the spot where she'd fallen when the barren woman pushed her a few years ago.

Suddenly, it felt like déjà vu.

ZAIRE

After locking the door behind him, the young man gathered her in his arms and held her tightly. Her body was stiff for a few seconds. She didn't know what to do. She had no strength to pull away. No man had ever held her that intimately, and she didn't know how to react. Her body gradually loosened against his. She felt her heart beat against his. She felt his arms grow tight around her back and a soft deep cry of helplessness escaped from his hard chest. The cry was so sad that she let herself cry as well. She shook violently in sorrow. She gasped for air.

The young man held her tighter and growled like a wounded animal. For a while, all was quiet. Then he pulled himself away from her, held her face in his palms, lowered his forehead to touch hers, and together they cried some more. Their teardrops formed shiny diamonds on the grey carpet that layered the floor of her living room. When they finished crying, they let out a sigh together, took a step back, and stared each other in the eyes. Both of them had unspoken questions. Both of them felt the depth of their connection.

Najma knew at once that heaven had sent a guardian angel. He helped her sit down and gave her a glass of water.

"I am so sorry about your mother, Najma," he finally said after a dense silence.

Najma drank the water and placed the empty glass on the table. She said nothing but slowly sucked in air through her mouth and released it through her nose. Her eyes were red and puffy from excessive crying. She knew she looked terrible.

"Are you my brother?" She asked after a thoughtful while.

The man was taken aback.

She looked him in the eyes and noticed that they were still wet.

Why was he crying with me? she wondered. Did he know my mother before he began to deliver the money? Is he really my brother? What if he is my brother? Where does he live?"

"I am Zaire," he said.

Zaire? she mused. It sounds like a medieval musical instrument. Who even calls their child that?

She looked at him, her eyes urging him to go on.

"I'm not sure about being your brother," he replied, "but you can sure use one, now that you'll be alone."

He feigned a smile.

He's right, she thought. If not a brother, I definitely need a shoulder to lean on.

"I have watched you grow, Najma. I know a lot about you now. You are a strong girl. I saw you struggle with your mother, still managing to do well in school. I want to help you. Please let me?" Zaire pleaded with her.

"You are right," she replied. "I always knew she would die someday, but I never expected it to be this soon and so brutal. I wish I knew who did this to her . . ."

Her voice trailed off.

"Even if you knew, what would you do?" said Zaire. "This must've been planned. Someone definitely kidnapped her from this house. That means that you are not safe here on your own."

Najma didn't know how she would be able to handle the police and stay alone in the house afterwards without her mother. She wondered if Nana would keep coming now that her mother was no more.

She was certain that the house was her mother's. Therefore, there was no need for another home.

For the first time, she thanked God for the anonymous person who took care of their bills and for settling her mother and her on the elite side of Corner Street. She shuddered at the thought of what would have happened to her if she had been left alone in one of the apartments on the other side of Corner.

She subconsciously thanked God for Zaire as well . . .

Honorable Ploutus and his wife raised Zaire in their mansion, together with their daughter Nysa. Zaire's arrival in the mansion had been greeted with pomp and camera flashes, silky smiles, and velvet stares. He recalled with a trace of bile in his mouth, how Nysa had just stared at him and said nothing for a whole week.

Mrs. Ploutus, on the other hand, had been all smiley and touchy. Her silky-soft, always pale and powdered, face was plastered with a smile. Mother and daughter sandwiched Zaire at the back seat of the state-owned Mercedes-Benz Pullman.

Honorable. Ploutus sat alone on the opposite seat. The Statesman blankly stared at the new member of his family and threw weird smiles unexpectedly.

Meanwhile, the ladies would lean forward, whisper things in his face, lean back, and giggle.

Zaire did not know what to make of his new family . . .

If anything, he felt lucky. The whole state knew his name. He had just been adopted into the royal family. He felt fortunate that the Statesman had noticed his hard work and decided to take him in as his own son.

Zaire was proud of himself. Had he not worked so hard to do well on the final exams? Had he not been the best student across the four States, recording a mark that had never been seen before? Had he not been created to have dominion over everything on Earth as the priest always preached to them on Sundays?

Honorable Ploutus was going to take him to the secondary school of his choice, fully pay his fee, and be his father. He was finally leaving the orphanage.

Zaire was in all the daily news headlines, along with the best pictures of himself and his new family. He was on TV too.

He loved the fame, but most importantly, the fact that he was going to have a complete family. A sister was a bonus, even though Nysa had not even shaken his hand, let alone said anything to him. Being only a year older than her, Zaire had hoped that they would get along after some time.

With time, he got used to Nysa's temperamental outbursts that would cloud her beautiful teenage face.

He would sometimes stare at her velvety rounded cheeks and wonder why someone would paint a layer of sadness onto such a beautiful face. Her eyes would have shone like her mother's pearls if only she tried to smile a little. Her head sat with an air of opulence on her long, spirally neck, which was speared into an ever-raised full chest.

The arc of her back was so deep that sometimes Zaire would let his eyes linger on it and roam on the perfectly rounded mound, which bounced with a tight springy lilt beneath it, each time she glided through the corridors of their castle.

He wished he could get to know her, but Nysa had a wall of ice around her, and the winter words that she emitted kept that wall permanently frozen.

His new home was spectacular at first. Later, he got bored with the stiff affluence that forced a monotonous routine.

He began to miss the jagged carelessness of the orphanage. He missed skipping showers, eating when he wanted to, the shyness in the nuns' eyes, and the exaggerated harshness of priests.

At Ploutus's Castle, he had a whole wing to himself. There was a dining area, a guest lounge, and two bedrooms that he had no idea what to do with initially.

He had a personal cleaning lady and a chauffeur. He got rid of the chauffeur when he turned eighteen and got his driving license.

He couldn't get over the magnificence of the castle. He found the neo-gothic architecture, contrasted by highly modern final touches in the front and a touch of Renaissance in the back, ever-amazing. Whenever he changed his perspective, it looked like an entirely different castle.

Honorable Ploutus took time in explaining the excessively expensive building and how he had to hire a Russian architect to design the masterpiece.

Zaire would sometimes drive up the West Hills, solely to view of the castle, jealously guarded by a thick forest of monkey puzzle trees and Monterey cypress, complimented by the neat, lush lawns mounted by bushes of red, white, and purple rhododendrons.

Rhododendron Cynthia . . . Zaire's favorite.

Away from everyone and the tightness of order and rules inside, he would enjoy the panorama of his new home on his own. The Ploutus Castle was a sight to behold.

At the orphanage, a boy's only facility, he had enjoyed the comfort of a bed, friends, and food.

Some of the boys were worse off than him—total orphans—or their mothers had dropped them in a pit latrine and left them to die. Some came to the orphanage without names. Such boys were baptized immediately and given the names of saints.

The nuns and priests who took care of them were strict on discipline and prayers. He learned to worship God and say the rosary.

Before Honorable Ploutus adopted him, he had aspired to become a priest like Father Crus, his mentor. Most boys in the orphanage had wanted to join the seminary. Father Crus had been like a spiritual father to Zaire after his mother dropped him at the orphanage. Father Crus had found him crying outside the gates of the orphanage. The old man, with feathery white tufts of hair on his face and head, had stretched a wrinkled hand towards the crying boy, starting a relationship that would last a decade.

"You have a royal future, my son. I can see it in your eyes," he had said in a clear voice that sounded far younger than himself.

"Our spirits never get old. They are renewed every day."

And the lessons of self-awareness, ability, the soul, desires, vanity, the love Of God, destiny, and death had begun.

Five years later, the priest had blatantly informed Zaire that he could not be a priest. Zaire was mad at him.

On his deathbed, Father Crus told Zaire that the world would need him more in a suit than in a cassock. Zaire perceived the old man as a pot of wisdom handing him teachings that would help him execute the hardest tasks for Honorable Ploutus—and himself as well. The same teachings would guide him. It wasn't so different from following the Kung Fu master's advice not to take the path of vengeance when one learns the truth about one's roots.

Mrs. Ploutus was the rainbow in the emotionally cold and cloudy castle. Tall and graceful, curvy, slightly thick, and saucy. Her signature style of fashion was silk and chiffon—stylish garments that looked like they were caressing her milky-white skin. Her voice would melt in subtle orders directed at the house servants, who would slide into action when she spoke. No one had ever seen her lose her cool. Her smile was always present, and Zaire would soon be watching with glee as other statesmen drooled over her in the presence of the squirming Honorable Ploutus.

Her smiles brightened everything. They were brighter than the golden chandeliers that hung on the ceilings of the cosmic lounge in the castle. Her skin was softer than the creamy finish on the mansion's walls. Her hands were magical—long fingers dipped in silver rings and glowing nail polish. They were like the set of silver

Egyptian diamonds with dashes of Jeremejevite figurines, a souvenir that Honorable Ploutus showcased and talked about endlessly.

The ornament had been awarded to him by a prime minister of a respected nation upon a military achievement, and he prided himself in it. Just like Mrs. Ploutus, the figurines had a twenty-four-hour body guard and a GPS tracking system. Zaire would later learn that the figurines and Mrs. Ploutus were the only things that the Statesman was afraid of losing.

Both had a striking semblance of extraordinary beauty.

The morning Zaire fully comprehended who he truly was to Ploutus, it felt like his gall bladder had been punctured. His stomach churned, and the contents rose to his throat, filling his mouth with a bitter taste.

A close friend of Honorable Ploutus's, Wasp as he commonly known, was visiting, and all the bodyguards were afraid of letting the Statesman know that he had a guest. The guest was also getting impatient and running off his mouth, washing away the ambience of the morning sun in the castle.

Zaire the Honorable's favorite, had to be the bait. He was requested by the butler to go and get the Statesman from his sleeping chambers. No one else would have dared to do that, except Zaire.

The dialogue he collided into when he went to summon Honorable Ploutus changed his life. The dialogue had burrowed into his heart and planted seeds of vengeance. It had watered and pruned them while Zaire waited for the bounty harvest.

He had stood there, frozen, every part of his body taut, muscles twitching, fists clenched. He could taste his own blood as he bit deeper into his lower lip that was threatening to fall with his jaw. A searing pain had tarnished his heart, coated his ribs, and risen to his throat, making it hard for him to swallow his own saliva.

"He is your son, Ploutus." Her voice seeped through the small opening that had been left in the almost-closed bedroom door.

"That's the point, woman." His words stampeded out through the same crack.

"Then stop using him to do your dirty work." Her cajoles smoothly slipped out again, accompanied by the coco butter scent of her lotion.

"You won't tell me what to do with that bastard!"

His bellows clumsily fell on top of each other as they bundled together in an effort to all reach Zaire's ears at the same time . . .

"Come on, you don't have to be rude." She tried reaching his senses amid carefully submitted shuffles. "And please realize . . . this plan of yours might plunge him into danger . . ."

"I see," he retorted, "You want him for yourself, don't you? Did you think I don't see how you drool over his abs and firm ass?" he firmly yelled. trying not to shout."

"He's just a kid," she said dismissively, waving off his ridiculous interjection.

"Just like the bodyguard I killed last year?" he accused. "They are never kids! Not in your eyes. I will make him disappear if you persist talking about him this way."

"This is your own flesh and blood, for heaven's sake!" she exclaimed. "Why don't you try to be . . ."

A loud gasp escaped Zaire's mouth as the door flew open. A mixture of coco butter and Balade Sauvage poured forth. Husband and wife stood in the doorway, eyes wide—one pair clear, white, and sparkly and the other a tormented red and sagging with distress.

"How long have you been here?" Honorable Ploutus asked.

"I just came by to call you," replied Zaire, feigning ignorance. "The Wasp is waiting for you in the lounge."

He turned to leave, hiding the hot tears that were brimming in his eyes. Anger burned down his throat, making it feel like he was swallowing a flame. It burned his entire chest and blazed in his stomach. He wanted to leave the castle immediately and never come back.

WEEPING FOR MOMMY

After the police van took away Najma's mother, the sky wept. The entire Corner Street was floating on torrents rainwater. Thick sheets of rain assaulted the roofs, then flowed down the ridges angrily, washing down anything that dared to stand on its way.

Najma watched from her bedroom window as the pregnant grey sky broke loose and let down liquid lightning bolts. Her mother would be buried in a public cemetery at West Valley Capital—Valley View. She was angry with the rain. It was washing away all memories of her mother—everything that could've served as evidence to find her murderer. It had not rained for days, and now it poured like it had just been waiting for her mother to be murdered so that it could clean up after the killers.

Her mother's burial was sparsely attended. Najma's mother had no relatives to mourn her, except Najma herself. Zaire had not left her side. Nana was there too. No neighbors showed up. There was no memorial service. Zaire had bought a casket and a white lacy dress for her mother's body. He drove Najma and Nana to the homicide morgue near Valley View police station to pick up the body, then took them to the cemetery.

It was quiet. No one said anything to anyone. Not even the police spoke a word. That morning, when Zaire came to pick her up, she hoped one of the neighbors would at least ask about the ceremony, even if there was none. Najma had hoped they would feign concern.

She noticed that the doors and windows remained shut, but the curtains were pulled apart, very slightly. They were peeping at her, Zaire, and Nana.

Zaire had kept her company throughout. Presently, his car was parked close to her house. In the past, he would park at a safe distance to avoid speculation.

His dealings have been shady, she thought. He never even said hello to us. Why he is he suddenly so attached? Can I trust him?

Najma wanted to ask him why he suddenly clung to her, not at all concerned about the neighbors, but she decided to save it for later. She knew he wasn't going anywhere after the burial.

The red earth—wet, drippy and murky after the rains—greedily gobbled up the expensive casket that contained her mother. There was no priest to perform official duties at the burial. No tear was shed. Just a little cough by Zaire.

Najma noticed that his forehead was heavily veined. His eyes were lit with something that she perceived as anger.

Why is he so angry? she wondered. He barely even knew Mommy. Am I missing something?

Nana stared on and swallowed hard. The undertakers were very efficient at throwing the soil in the grave, like they didn't want the red earth to mess up the neatly trimmed lawns of the cemetery. She watched the mound rise.

It was then flattened and a concrete slab was laid on top. A layer of tiles was neatly arranged on the slab, and a headrest for the epitaph was erected. Before Najma could say anything, Zaire pulled out a neatly engraved golden plaque from his car. It contained the words **Loved one sleeping. Remember my stories, Mommy. Always loved.**

It was perfect. She hadn't thought of many things about the burial. She was thankful that Zaire had handled them all.

For the umpteenth time in the past two days, Najma thanked God for Zaire. She wanted to fly into his arms and be comforted. As she stood there, accepting the death of her mother and slowly admitting that she would never see her again, the memories of the relationship they shared came flashing before her sad eyes.

*****

She watches herself, as a little girl, barely three years old, trotting behind her mother, picking up papers with her, and stuffing them in her own little dress.

She sees her mother washing her face in the rain puddle by the road and joins her, scooping up murky water and splashing it on her face.

Her mother reaches for the hemline of her dress, turns it up and wipes her little muddy face.

Together they laugh and run down the streets.

Najma sees her mother sleeping calmly in her bed; she climbs in by her side and together they cuddle.

She is five years old, aware that her mother might be different. The incident of the stall woman pushing her mother down the stairs stings her heart. She remembers how it dawned on her then that both of them, her mother and herself, were different.

The memory of other children scurrying off when she joined them in their games makes her heart throb in pain. She hears the mothers warning their children never to go near her house. They warn them against playing with her. They tell their children to run or scream when she comes near them.

She remembers the pain of playing alone with her dolls, Mona and Mina. Her mother joins in her games sometimes, and together they rock the dolls to sleep. They make beds for them at the verandah of their house or at the market square. Together, they make mud cakes and biscuits for Mona and Mina.

She is eight years old. Her mother's illness is worsening. She has to stay at home sometimes when mother wakes up crying and saying 'Ploutus.'

She thinks Ploutus is a place or an animal. Mother cries each morning for days on end, calling that name.

Mother refuses to eat anything. She refuses to talk to her. Nana comes in on such days and escorts her to school when she's late. Teachers understand her predicament and don't punish her.

Najma doesn't stop thinking about Ploutus. She wonders why the name makes her mother sad.

One day, on her way home, she sees a newspaper on a vendor's stand. There is a portrait of a fat man on it. On his left is a petite woman with wavy hair; on his right is a small girl in front of a taller boy.

She reads the headline: Honorable Ploutus Adopts Abandoned Boy from Dominion Orphanage.

Najma digs in her school uniform pockets for change and buys **The West Daily**. She rushes home with it and shows it to Nana, pointing to Ploutus's photo.

Suddenly, Nana's face is ashen. Her eyes are wide with horror, and her mouth is gaping. She looks worried. Then she grabs the newspaper and hides it behind the kitchen sink, panting.

"Your mother must never see this," Nana says.

"Why?" Najma asks.

"You can't understand now," replies Nana. "Just never show it to her."

There is a tone of finality in Nana's cautioning voice.

Najma's memory stopped at age ten. She had never shown her mother the newspaper cutting she had made two years before.

Sometimes, she took it out at night and wondered why her mother cried so much about Ploutus.

Other times, she slept holding the cutting and staring at the pictures of the royal family. The girl in the picture does not smile. The woman with wavy long hair smiles radiantly. They really look alike—their eyes, noses, the waves in their hair, their thin lips, the color of their skin. The girl is a smaller version of her mother.

Thinking of the photo, Najma compared the boy to the girl in her mind. As far as she can remember, there is no likeness between the two. The boy is tall with a long, chiseled face. He looks about fourteen years old in the photo—a reflection of glittering pride in his eyes.

A sudden thought struck her: the boy looks very familiar. It's like she's known him all along.

*****

Nana put her chubby arms around Najma and motioned her toward Zaire's car.

"No, Nana. No." She found her tongue tied as the trance of recognition spilled over her face.

"What?" Nana wanted to know, perplexed.

"The boy in the magazine cutting," replied Najma

"What are you talking about, Najma?" Nana asked, now clearly concerned, her face grey with worry.

Now she thinks I'm losing it, Thought Najma. I know that boy. I have to get home now.

"Let's get going," said Zaire, heading to the car. It looks like it's going to rain heavily again."

Najma's eyes slowly rose to his face. She slowly walked toward him, her eyes fixed on his face. Without blinking, she reached for his face and touched it, looking at it attentively, with scrutiny.

"You are the boy on the magazine cutting." She said, matter-of-factly.

Najma emitted every word slowly, and firmly.

"Najma," he replied. "You are stressed. Let's go home." He took her hand and led her to the car.

Najma was totally quiet during the trip home. She didn't notice when they stopped to pick up some takeaway food and drinks at the hotel. She didn't notice when the car pulled up to her front door. When Zaire accompanied her into the house, she didn't even pay attention to where she was.

He is the boy from the cutting, she kept thinking. He is the boy whom Ploutus adopted just before the elections. He is the boy whose academic record I have been dreaming of beating all my life. He knows Ploutus . . .

She walked to her bedroom, entered and locked the door behind her. She lifted her mattress and took a long look at the newspaper cutting hidden in one of her drawing books.

There was no doubt whatsoever. The boy on the newspaper was Zaire.

THE BACKPACK

Growing up, Najma's desire had always been to be a model. However, she decided to become a psychiatrist on the morning when her mother—"the market lunatic"—was butchered and her body dumped at the market square in Corner Street.

It had been two weeks since her mother was buried; Najma was on her way back to school. She had never felt at ease anywhere, and **Golden Rise Academy** was no exception.

She was in the third year of secondary school, and the following year she would be graduating.

She had her aim securely set on the target. However, her dream to win a state scholarship via college were tainted. Doubt kept washing over her thoughts, distorting her dream with an impenetrable grey cloud of insecurity. The Statesman that she had known a month before when she set her target was not the honorable person she had thought he was. She wanted to drop the Zaire discovery as he had instructed her to do, but it kept showing up in her mind.

*****

It had been a long a journey—three years of studying while her mother was in and out of hospital.

Her mother's illness had interrupted her education to the effect that she doubted whether she would be able to make it to the list of the top five academic achievers in the state of West Valley. She remembered the first time when she walked through the gates of Golden Rise Academy. Her mother and Nana had brought her in to be admitted.

Najma was beside herself with joy. Her mother had been carrying her backpack and, and Nana had their packed lunch. Najma had been in the middle, flanked by the two ladies, carrying nothing. Her mother had been exceptionally calm that morning, and Najma prayed that her fits of distress wouldn't occur during the admission process.

As they approached the queue, a teacher had called to the trio, asking Najma's mother to hand the bag to Najma. "You will spoil that kid," the teacher said. "Let her carry her own bag!"

Her mother had ignored the woman and had tightened the grip on the backpack when Najma tried to take it. Najma had read concern in the cold eyes of the cumbersome lady, who turned out to be Miss Coco, her chemistry teacher. They would later have a very close relationship. Miss Coco would ensure that Najma got through her studies at Golden Rise Academy with the best of grades, even when she'd chronically missed classes.

Hours later, Najma's mother was still refusing to hand the backpack over to Najma. Najma remembered Nana softly coaxing her mother to let go of the bag. Her mother had vigorously shaken her head in disagreement. She would not let go of the bag.

In her mother's eyes, Najma saw a fear that she could not interpret. Was her mother afraid of letting her go to school? She had seen her go through primary school without any issue. Sometimes, she would sit outside the school gate waiting for Najma to come out. Together, they would then race down the road, scaring kids along the way. Why would she be afraid of letting Najma start secondary school? What had changed?

At the time, Najma did not understand why her mother had refused to let her go. Now that she thought about the scenario, however, she understood. She remembered that a few months into her first year in secondary school, her mother's health had deteriorated. She'd suffer one seizure after another, until someone had her admitted into hospital.

One day, when returning home from school, Najma had found the house in disarray. Broken glass was lying everywhere. She didn't notice the neighbors who stood outside their houses in pairs or trios whispering and pointing at her. She'd learned to ignore them with time. Her heart had stopped for a second when she walked into her mother's bedroom and found nobody there. The bed was neatly made as if no one had slept in it.

Najma looked around the room, scanning every corner as if she would be hiding in one of them. Dropping her school bag, she ran out of the house, heading for the market square.

Her mother was at the square, picking up papers and sweeping the street with twigs.

"Mom, let's go home," Najma begged.

Her mother had stared at her with a blank expression on her face and kept on sweeping. When Najma tried to move closer, her mother had waved the twigs at her and had nearly injured her eyes.

Najma had never before seen her mother throw a violent fit. She was always calm, picking up papers and putting them in her dress, running from one corner of the street to the other while singing to an imaginary baby. She'd never been violent before.

Nobody was afraid of Najma's mother at the market square. Many stall owners let her sit on the porches of their stalls. She was always cleaning and straightening things here and there, laughing at herself, biting her nails, and sometimes pulling at her own hair. She'd never harmed anyone.

This day, her mother was strange. Her eyes were red with fury, and she didn't let anybody approach her. For a moment, Najma didn't recognize her mother. She'd never left the house without shoes, but this day, she had no shoes on. Najma would discover years later that that was the same day that her grandfather, her mother's father who was a renowned chief in the villages, had passed on.

She tried pleading with her mother. "Mommy, don't! It's me, Najma!"

Her mother kept snarling at her, and she began to throw stones.

A crowd formed.

Women tried to calm her mother down, but she slipped into distress and began to wrestle anyone who'd approached her.

Suddenly, pandemonium broke loose. The street was in an uproar.

Najma had never been that scared. She'd begged the crowd not to touch her mother, and with the help of a few women who knew her well, the crowd was calmed.

Everyone dispersed when a siren was heard from a distance. It was an ambulance. A few days later, Najma realized that someone had asked for help on her behalf, and her mother was confined in hospital, courtesy of the same person who took care of their bills. That was also the first time that she'd seen Zaire. He had been in the ambulance. He'd asked the nurses to allow Najma into the ambulance and had helped her book her mother into Ward Nine.

"This girl is still in school uniform," a nurse had remarked, looking at Zaire. "How will she be able to take care of her mother tonight?"

"Someone is coming in, before 8:00 p.m.," Zaire had responded.

That was the first time she'd heard his voice as well. And just like he'd mysteriously appeared, he'd vanished into the darkness of the outer alley.

True to his word, Nana had come at eight. Najma's mother was sleeping.

Nana had begged Najma to go home and rest.

"You have to go to school tomorrow," Nana had said. "I will take care of your mother. This is my job and I have been paid to do it."

Reading the finality in Nana's voice, Najma had walked home that night, letting go of her fear of the dark; unaware of the tears that were flowing from her eyes; not realizing how angry she was. She'd let the anger that was gnawing at her heart take precedence. For the first time, she'd hated the world—the people at the market square especially. Were they really going to lynch a sick woman?

She'd hated her neighbors for doing nothing when her mother began to break things; hated them for always gossiping and watching her from a distance like she and her mother were lepers; hated them for not being kind to her and her mother.

That was all they'd ever needed: kindness—nothing more.

She'd reached home.

Amid her angry flow of thoughts and tears, she'd failed to notice that the house had already been cleaned, the broken items replaced with new ones.

She'd locked the door behind her, dived into her bed and cried herself to sleep.

*****

As she settled in her desk after her mother's burial, aware of the eyes of her classmates that were staring at her back, she knew that she would never be a model. Her passion for fashion would remain but a dream.

She folded up each component of her dream—ballroom gowns, swimwear, office designs, casual streetwear, the closet she'd always wanted, her own fashion line across the globe—made a neat pile, and locked away the thoughts in a small corner of her brain.

She picked up her chemistry book and straightened it, then fished out her biology textbook and asked her desk mate for her physics book back.

She would one day, years later, reopen that corner of her brain—her treasures moth-eaten but mendable—as she worked towards living her dream away from psychiatry. Elima's Fashion House would, one day, trend globally. But for now, it would have to be psychiatry.

"But . . . a few weeks ago, you said that you wouldn't be majoring sciences?" Her deskmate feigned concern. "What has changed?"

"I need my books back," Najma said, this time a crackling stiffness loading in her throat.

"Give the 'loony' her books," the girl sitting behind them mocked.

Najma got up and turned around.

"Easy, Najma," said the girl, her self-confidence having left her. "Don't lose it on me. I never thought it runs in the blood . . ."

The words had barely left the girls mouth when Najma landed a slap on her face. The class was torn between shock and the laughter that the girl's words were supposed to elicit. Then there was a sudden commotion as everyone was uttering responses to the incident at the same time.

The girl's face was grey with horror.

Najma's finger marks were rising fast on her soft left cheek.

"You shouldn't have said that to her here," said one girl.

"But it's true!" retorted another."

"She just lost her mother, for Pete's sake!" came a final response.

"Shut up! All of you." That had to be a teacher.

Everyone sunk back into their seats as suddenly as they had jumped out of them when Miss Coco walked in, her voice bellowing above the commotion.

A sudden silence filled the air . . .

"Najma," Miss Coco said, "what is going on?"

Najma could only cry.

The class prefect explained the situation to the teacher. Angry, she sentenced the entire class to mowing all the school's lawns, Scrubbing the ablution blocks, and picking up all the litter on the compound.

Najma was excused. Instead, she had to attend guidance and counselling sessions the whole day. When evening came, she ran all the way home, hoping that Nana would still be around.

"How was school?" Zaire asked, receiving her at the doorstep.

"What are you doing here?" she responded angrily.

"I see," he said calmly, ignoring her tantrum. "Your day was horrible."

"Why do you care?" she whispered as she opened the door, walked in and closed it in his face., locking it in the process.

"Everyone calls me a lunatic!" she yelled. "I'm not a lunatic! My mother was not a lunatic! Why can't they just leave me alone?"

The words poured out incoherently. She was convulsing in anger.

Zaire had his own key. He let himself in. He walked to her and pulled her in his arms. She tried to resist but he was stronger. This time he just held her and brushed her hair with his palm. He allowed her to cry her heart out. When she was done, he led her to a chair and made her sit down.

"I want to be alone, please," she said, sucking in a huge wave of air to calm down. "I'm sorry about my outburst. I'm so overwhelmed Zaire."

"I will leave in a minute," he replied. But before I go, I need to talk to you."

He lowered himself into the nearest chair after pouring them each a glass of juice.

Najma kept her eyes on him, getting angry about how easily he operated in her house. She wanted to throw him out, especially since he had refused to explain his relationship with Ploutus. He had just torn the cutting into pieces and grabbed her, held her till her sobbing subsided. He had then walked out without a word, leaving her and Nana behind. Nana stayed for the night.

"Najma, look," he began. "It's not within my power to decide whether I can be your brother or not. I also have no idea why I am so connected and attached to you. I have always wanted to have a small sister, but my stepsister, Nysa, has refused to give me the chance. She hates me."

He took a huge gulp from his juice.

"I just want to be there for you," he declared.

"Zaire," she replied. "I can't let you be there for me if I don't know who you are," she said.

Her voice was calm and collected. There were no traces of anger. However, her shoulders shot up beneath her neck like bat wings. She was evidently struggling to pull her flaring temper together, and he knew better than to press on.

"Najma," he said, "you know who I am. I have always been here with you. I have watched you play, cry, grow up, and become the young lady that you are today. Maybe you don't know this, but Nana does."

Nana? she thought. How would Nana know? Was she part of the Ploutus mystery? I feel so cheated.

She did not voice her thoughts. Instead, she urged him on to continue. This was getting very interesting.

"Honorable Ploutus adopted me," he explained. "He is my father, but he cannot expose the truth because of politics. And I know there is a reason your mother always said his name. I can help you figure it all out. I just want to be your brother. Please let me . . .?"

His voice broke off in a tremor. He was on the edge of crying. Najma wanted to run to him and throw her arms around him but chose not to. She watched him finish his juice, get up, and straighten his jeans. He gave her a look of assurance, dropped his own key on the table and disappeared into the twilight outside.

"How is she?" Ploutus croaked in the darkness.

Zaire was taken aback. Ploutus was still awake at this time? He wondered if he was waiting for him, Zaire, or whether there was something wrong.

"Who?" Zaire faked ignorance to give him an opportunity to think about what to say.

"Your sister." Replied Ploutus. "How is she?"

"I haven't spoken to Nysa in a while dad." He replied.

He was lying. He knew Ploutus was referring to Najma, but he chose to play with his mind. In Zaire's opinion, Ploutus had no right to talk about Najma. He had done more harm as a father than good. Although he had been taking care of Najma financially since she was still very young and had ensured that there were women to watch over her when her mother fell ill, Zaire knew that there was more than what met the eye. His guts told him that Ploutus was hiding something. The man never did anything good for anyone unless there was a secret that needed to be guarded or he was benefiting from the act.

Ploutus had adopted him just before the Statesmen election so that he would win over the voters emotionally. It was a move that led to him being re-elected, with a huge number of voters perceived kindness.

Years later, Ploutus began to use him as his dirty hand, to intentionally put him in harm's way so that he could die with the secrets. Zaire was his own and only son, yet Ploutus couldn't care less about him. Ploutus had shown off Zaire to his friends like a trophy, using his intelligence to twist minds and brainwash supporters.

Disgusted, Zaire remembered being so proud to have won the royal affection. He felt lucky then. It was wonderful working hard to win his adoptive father's approval and gain favor in his eyes just like Father Cruz had advised him.

For years, Zaire's life revolved around moving mountains for Ploutus. Ploutus even promised to make him an heir to one of his vast estates if he remained loyal. Being a young man, he had envisioned himself taking over the entire empire. Was he not the only known son, even if not by blood? Had God not revealed to Father Cruz that he had a Royal Destiny? Would God lie?

His sister Nysa was between hot and frozen. She openly despised him, time and again reminding him that he would never be a Ploutus because he didn't have royal blood in him. Nysa would often tell him to go back to the gutter where he came from. Zaire learned to shut her out of his mind and, later, out of his life.

"Who knows what kind of tramp your mother was?" Nysa had retorted one evening during an argument.

"My mother was a decent woman, Nysa." he had said in his mother's defense. "She was a nurse."

Zaire did not like his mother. She had abandoned him and driven off with another man. However, he was not going to allow Nysa to say horrible things about her. He was also not going to let Nysa break him down into pieces of misery with venomous words that dripped from her serpentine tongue.

"A nurse who abandoned her own child in an orphanage?" Nysa scoffed. "No decent woman could do such a thing."

"Don't judge her too harshly," Zaire replied. "Besides, I would never have been your brother if she didn't abandon me."

He said that calmly, struggling not to fight with her and get into trouble.

"You will never be my brother, bastard," she said, walking out.

Zaire now laughed at this memory. If only Nysa knew the truth! She would choke on her venomous tongue . . .

"Zaire," said Ploutus, shaking Zaire out of his daydream. "You know that I'm not talking about Nysa. You wouldn't know anything about her."

Ploutus sounded impatient.

He was right and wrong.

Zaire knew a lot about Nysa. More than what her own parents knew . . . but he dared not say anything.

It was also true that Zaire knew Ploutus was not talking about Nysa when he asked about his sister. He merely wanted to play with Ploutus's mind.

Ploutus lifted his heavy body, balancing it precariously on his twiggy legs that shot from a wide pair of corduroy shorts. Zaire could see that he was intoxicated. He staggered towards the drink cabinet and poured himself a glass of whisky. He retrieved a bottle of tonic water from the buzzing refrigerator, turning his back on Zaire for a few seconds. Zaire's eyes lingered on his thick neck that disappeared into the collar of his striped black and brown t-shirt. His eyes ran down Ploutus's wide back and overweight hindquarters, dropping to the black flip flops on his feet.

Ploutus turned to face Zaire suddenly as if afraid of something. He motioned Zaire towards a seat.

Zaire ignored him.

Instead, he walked to the mini bar and carefully selected a bottle of the finest cognac. He retrieved three ice cubes from the freezer and a glass from the mahogany cabinet. He placed the ice cubes in the glass and selected a couch away from Ploutus but directly opposite him. He sat down and placed the glass on the neatly curved, polished walnut stool, then poured some of the cognac into the glass.

The golden liquid sparkled beneath the massive crystal chandelier that majestically hung from the marble ceiling of the bar.

Father and son sat face to face, like wrestlers in an arena waiting for the best opportunity to launch the first attack and pounce on each other. Zaire was not looking at his father. His eyes were on the sparkles in his glass.

Zaire could feel Ploutus's eyes on him. He knew his father was boiling in anger and his eyes were blazing fire, waiting to lash out. He had intentionally picked one of his most expensive drinks and was withholding the most sensitive information that he knew Ploutus desperately wanted.

"The notes were accepted at Mainland Bank without any issue," said Zaire. "They were washed clean and watermarked perfectly this time. Wasp was there to ensure I would have no trouble depositing." He swirled the drink in his mouth and swallowed with relish.

"I already got the call from the bank, young man," replied Ploutus, his words laced with rage. "Now, please tell me. How was your sister?" Zaire enjoyed seeing him angry and anguished. He would've loved to press more buttons to make him angrier but chose not to. He didn't want to risk him knowing how much he hated him already. He wanted Ploutus to believe that he was still on his side. He couldn't afford to lose his support—especially with the elaborate plan of vengeance that was in the works. It was also the only way that he could keep Najma safe.

"Najma is devastated and sad," Zaire said after a short pause.

"That's not what I mean!" exclaimed Ploutus. "Of course she's sad! Poor thing just lost her mother, for heaven's sake! What I mean is: is she well taken care of?" His voice was torn between shouting and a choked whisper.

"Yes, Father," replied Zaire. "Her fees have been settled, she is back in school, she has enough pocket money, and she has stopped asking about you."

Zaire's voice was crimson with sarcasm. He began to stand up but decided to remain sitting when Ploutus told him not to call him father.

"And," he added, "she might figure out one of these days, that I am her brother," he said very fast, took a huge gulp of the remaining drink in his glass, stood up suddenly, and walked away.

Zaire knew that Ploutus was shocked by this information. Zaire knew that he had questions. He also knew that if he revealed more, Ploutus would ask him to silence Najma. So, that night, Zaire did not give him a chance to say anything. He could feel Ploutus's angry stare on his back. He happily let Ploutus wallow in the miasma of doubt for the time being. Zaire wanted him to lose sleep.

Zaire walked into his room, locked the door behind him, dropped his jacket on the floor, hopped out of his pants and gently lowered himself onto his bed. He ran his palms across his wide, heavily muscled chest with contentment. He did not bother to cover himself because he knew no one would walk into his room.

His mind shifted from Ploutus and settled on Najma. She was truly his sister. She had Ploutus's temper and urgency. However, she looked nothing like him. He wondered what the story behind Najma's mother's affair with Ploutus was.

There was his own mother. There was Nana. And there was the woman at the stall, at Corner Street, where Najma's mother died. He made a mental note of talking to Nana first thing the following day. He also decided to take Najma out for a cup of coffee after school. He planned on talking her into going to boarding school away from Corner Street for her final year of secondary school. This would keep her safe for a while as he dug deeper in Ploutus's vast array of secrets.

WARD NINE – A Blank Stare

A mixture of human waste and vomit overpowered the faint smell of bleach. Najma felt sick. The entire hospital smelled like rot. She felt her stomach turn, and a huge wave of saliva filled her mouth.

She wanted to turn back but decided to walk on along the alley instead. She noticed that the passage was mostly deserted, save two nurses who were whispering in each other's ears, creating a ghostly effect in the already chilling passage.

A doctor looked out into the passage and called one of them. They disengaged fast, like Siamese twins who had been ripped apart. One of them disappeared through the door from which the doctor had called. The other was swallowed by the cavernous far end of the passage.

This was two years before, when Najma's mother had been admitted to Ward Nine at the Valley Hospital. Ward Nine was the mental health wing of the hospital. Najma remembered it like it was just the other day. She turned in her bed to ease the pressure that was mounting on her left side due to oversleeping.

"Baby, you need to get out of that room already," Nana called from the living room. "Come and have some breakfast."

Najma had not left the house or her room after the incident with Zaire the previous night. She was still immersed in thoughts, remembering how her mother had struggled to get better. It angered her that just when her mother was almost there, she was brutally murdered. She thought about the key that Zaire had dropped on the table and wondered if she would ever see him again. Najma regretted being rude to him, but still her thoughts went back to her mother in Ward Nine.

*****

Najma isn't sure she remembers where her mother's ward is. She tries to locate the enquiry desk. The far end of the alley expels a fat woman carrying a metallic bucket and a huge mop. Her face is crisscrossed with thick creases of disgust. She drags her gumboot feet on the corridor floor, making the brownish tiles squeak irritatingly.

Najma tries to engage the woman with her eyes, but she ignores Najma and squeaks past her, leaving behind a disgusting gust of human waste.

"Najma!" somebody calls. She turns to see who it is.

"Nana!" she cries, relieved.

"What are you doing here?" Nana wants to know. "You should be in school."

"I just want to see my mother," replies Najma.

Nana swiftly glides towards her, carrying a basin and a towel. Her face is lit with a smile. Her face reminds Najma of the ambience of the church altar. Her eyes are like church candles, never burning out. Her mouth, a thick spread of gloss, curved in a smile even in sorrow. Her smooth cheeks are like copper chalices. Her voice is smooth and collected.

"How is my mother, Nana? Can I see her?" Najma forces her eyes off Nana's face and looks beyond her.

"She's okay," replies Nana. "She just woke up. Come, follow me. She was moved to Ward Nine from the normal female wards."

Najma follows Nana like a helpless toddler.

It is clear that her mother has been moved to a different wing of the hospital. She doesn't ask why she was moved. Nana leads her to a secluded room at the far end of the wing. Najma notices that there are other tiny doors along the wing engraved on the brick walled wing.

In her mother's room is a medium sized bed, covered in sky blue bed linen. Her mother's form, limp and weary, looks like a lost thing between the sheets. She looks like she had been wrapped up and then unwrapped halfway. Her left hand hangs by the side of the bed. Najma notices that it is fastened on the bed using blue rubber cuffs. The right one rests beside her on the bed, like a separate piece of her, palm bandaged. She stares back blankly. Her eyes are two tiny white saucers of milk with a shiny black bean floating in the middle of each one.

"Mother," Najma whispers.

Her mother tilts her head slowly and looks at Najma. There is no expression on her face. She just looks at her blankly. Najma wants to cry. She pushes back the tears that are welling in her eyes and swallows a lump of sorrow that is gathering in her throat. She sucks back the mucus into her nose with a loud slurping sound.

"She will be fine," says a male voice.

Najma looks up. A young intern doctor has walked into the room.

"I am Jotham," he says, stretching his veiny dark hand towards Najma. "I'm a psychiatry intern here at the hospital. How is Elima doing today?"

"I am Najma. Her daughter," she manages in a whisper as she takes his extremely tender hand in her own. It feels like cream in her palm.

How can a man be so tender? she wonders.

"I know," he replies. "Your mommy will be okay."

Najma is surprised that the intern knows her.

"Your brother is a good friend of mine," Jotham goes on. "We come all the way from the orphanage. I would never have managed without him."

Nana coughs loudly to interrupt what he is saying. Najma does not say anything. Instead, she registers the fact that Jotham talks about a brother. She has no idea which brother the intern is referring to. However, she doesn't enquire about what Jotham has just said.

She also notices that Nana is quick to change the subject.

She just looks at her mother and silently prays for her to get better. Her mother has not even blinked since she walked in.

"Why does she look so dazed?" Najma asks, ignoring the remarks about her brother.

"The drugs we are giving her are meant to calm her down and reduce her fits," he replies. "She is on very strong sedatives because of her aggression. She can harm herself or the people around her, so she had to be sedated at some point. She has not been responding well, but the doctor suggested that we should change the drugs starting tomorrow. She should be out of here in a month or so . . ."

"What?" exclaims Najma. "Why a month?"

"She needs close attention and monitoring to get better," the intern says.

Najma watches him as he goes about his duties, admiring his accuracy and deep knowledge of her mother's condition.

*****

Her mother was admitted for six months. She did not stop going to school because Nana made sure that her mother was okay at Ward Nine. She had moved into Elima's house so she could take care of both, keeping them comfortable.

"Najma, please!" said nana at Najma's bedroom door. "Do you want to give your Nana high blood pressure?"

Nana's voice slipped through the keyhole on Najma's locked bedroom door, cutting her reminiscence short. Najma was still scared of having a conversation about Zaire, but she knew that she had better get out of the bedroom now.

She knew Nana was going to blame her for everything that had transpired. Zaire was just trying to be kind, yet she had persisted on questioning who he was.

She dragged herself out of the bed, unlocked the door, and walked into the aroma of cinnamon and rosemary tea, vanilla pancakes, and Nana's lemon and rosewater perfume.

"Your brother will be back," said Nana. "He loves you too much. Don't sweat it," Nana said, reading her mind.

"Do you always know everything, Nana?" she asked playfully, smiling and planting a kiss on Nana's face.

PLOUTUS – Gods and Goddesses

"You sent for me, sir," Zaire said to Ploutus. He walked into the dining room with large strides, his shiny Cobra-skin sharp shooter shoes making soft sounds against the maroon velvet on the floor.

"Have you packed all the packages properly?" Ploutus asked, scanning Zaire from head to toe. Zaire was in black and white as usual, his signature *Ploutus Errands* attire. A silky black tie wound perfectly beneath the hard collar of a well-fitted, blindingly white shirt. The tie rode on his mound of chest and disappeared in the flat of his belly, covered in an almost tightly fitting black jacket. Black, slim-fit trousers, still shiny from the heat of the iron box, fitted tightly around the crotch and gingerly caressed his athletic thighs and legs all the way down, stopping slightly below the ankles. He stood legs slightly apart, shoulders spread, head held high, arm crossed in front of him, and deep brown eyes fixed on Ploutus.

"Yes, sir," he responded. He had resolved to call him sir, especially in public. Neither of them wanted anyone to know that they were father and son yet.

Ploutus had asked him to receive a package from Town Square at Corner and pack it. It was in a tamper-proof sealed envelope, and he could not peep without messing up the packaging. He cased it as usual in preparation for shipping, as instructed.

"Perfect," said Ploutus, sounding pleased. I don't want anything to go wrong. Osanyin will be arriving today. He should be bringing the necessary items for the elections next year. Have his suitcase packed and laced as well. We don't want him having trouble at the airport when he returns," Ploutus went on, slicing deeper into the roast steak, forking a huge cube of the pinkish meat and stuffing it in his mouth. Zaire watched him chew heartily.

He had not joined Ploutus at the table.

"What will the foreman do about the wasps in the dairy shed?" asked Ploutus. This was a coded way of asking if Zaire had supervised the money laundering with Wasp.

With the bodyguards always around the Statesman, this kind of talk was inevitable. Zaire found it illogical though, since all the bodyguards had been terrorized and sworn to secrecy. The butlers and maids knew a lot of things going on in Ploutus Castle, but they would not dare mention anything to anyone. Not even amongst themselves. They knew the consequences of snitching, and no one wanted to lose a finger or be shipped to another state without their family.

When Zaire was new in the castle, Ploutus had forced him to witness one of the bodyguards being tortured into confessing that he had leaked classified information to the opponent. It had been bloody and ugly. Zaire, however, had kept his cool, swallowed the bitter liquid in his throat, and observed the whole scene without flinching. Ploutus had been shocked and impressed.

Zaire was fifteen at that time.

"Everything is set, sir," Zaire responded, going to his usual chair on the table.

He could not hide his disgust anymore. He despised everything about this man that he once adored. Two years ago, he would kiss the very ground Ploutus walked on. He was his mentor. He had enjoyed the secret deals and mastered every move within three years.

By the time he had graduated from secondary school, Zaire was a seasoned underground dealer for Ploutus—like a baby latching onto a nipple. He would fake documents and smuggle anything breathing or dead across the four States. He would bank millions of unmarked currency in banks across the states and beyond.

He prided himself in Ploutus bragging about his expertise to his friends. He had loved the rewards of women, money, and sport cars. He wished he was his blood son. When the reality of their blood relation dawned, Zaire realized that there was actually no line between hate and love. He found himself on the extreme parts of both feelings with Ploutus leaning more toward hate than love.

Zaire was now Ploutus's nose, eyes, and mouth, and no deal could be made without him. Zaire knew the empire would easily fall without him, but he had to be very careful in planning his vengeance. He could not just exist without risking his own life, especially since Ploutus looked like he didn't care about him much. He needed a well-scripted plan.

"You're not eating," Ploutus said while chewing his food and slurping from a mug of black coffee. He emptied it in three huge gulps, then reached out for the watermelons and pineapples and threw huge chunks of each in his mouth.

"I'm not really hungry," Zaire said.

"Honey, looks like you have Zaire's appetite. Bring it down so that he can eat."

The sarcasm in Ploutus's voice did not offend Zaire. The fact that Ploutus was still insinuating that he might be having an affair with Mrs. Ploutus was what sunk a blade in Zaire's already wounded heart. He was used to his father's rants about other things, but this particular accusation hurt Zaire. Who did Ploutus think he was, bullying people around? Zaire was tired of worshiping him. He wanted to throw his untouched bacon in Ploutus's face.

As he had mastered with time, he buried his anger in the depths of his tough chest and smiled at Ploutus instead. He was about to say that he had a hangover and would eat later, but 'The Queen' had a better approach. She came out of the elevator with blocks of words tied to her tongue, ready to smash Ploutus's senseless.

"Here I am," she said sweetly. "You know he needs his sweet momma."

She walked toward the table slowly, dropping every word with malice. Zaire raised a glass of juice to his mouth, his eyes quickly surveying the approaching goddess of the castle covertly.

Her lilac fragrance filled the room at once. She was wearing nothing over her tight, blue denim hotpants and feathery pink camisole. Zaire noticed Ploutus's angry eyes feast on her bare yellow skin lustfully. Her thighs and arms were entirely uncovered. The shorts covered her tight butt cheeks and nothing else. The camisole was a see-through garment, and her nipples were hard behind the silk.

"Go cover up, woman," Ploutus hissed, spraying hot jets of fruit juice and saliva at everyone within reach.

Zaire noticed how the bodyguards struggled to keep their eyes off Ekesa's firm behind. The waitresses held their breaths in anticipation of what the Statesman would do to his wife for showing up indecent in public. It wasn't the first time either. The goddess had recently developed a taste for showing up half-naked, especially when Ploutus did something to annoy her. She looked like she enjoyed getting beneath his skin.

"Take it easy darling," she replied. "A woman has to breathe. Besides, this is how an appetite is grown . . . right, Zaire?" she cooed, toying with a glass of juice before pulling out a chair, seductively bending in front of the unblinking bodyguard and slowly lowering herself into the chair. The room was blanketed in conspicuous silence.

"Also, if all these men have had their way with me as you always claim, then there is nothing to hide anymore, right darling?" Ekesa went on unmoved.

There was a mean smile playing on her lips, and her eyes danced with an unknown fury. Zaire didn't know exactly where she was going with the act, but he enjoyed it, nevertheless.

Zaire shot one look at his father, and for the first time, he saw defeat in Ploutus's blazing eyes. Zaire knifed his bacon quietly, forked a sizable piece, and stuffed it in his mouth. He raised a glass of fresh passion fruit juice to his lips again and filled his cheeks. Just before he lowered the glass to the table, his eyes met Ekesa's. There was a second of connection, and a pact was made there and then. Zaire did not need a voiced assurance of an accomplice in future. He had a teammate on his mission to steal fire from the god of the castle.

"Meet me in my chamber now, Zaire," Ploutus raged, pulling his chair back clumsily, spilling juice and other beverages all over the table. The waitresses pounced on the mess like robots, wipes in hands.

"But his appetite just arrived, Your Honor . . ." Mrs. Ploutus seemed to be enjoying this moment. Zaire knew she was playing with embers. He would hate it if she got burned before the right time. She was attracted to this dangerous mischief like a moth was attracted to fire.

Zaire doubted if Ekesa was aware of how dangerous Ploutus could get . . . or perhaps she still thought that she was indispensable?

With Ploutus, as Zaire had come to realize, no one was an exception. Zaire ignored her remarks, rose to his feet, and quickly followed the Statesman to his chambers as commanded.

The room was freshly cleaned, books neatly arranged on the mahogany shelves, trophies glittering in their cases, and his royal chair neatly tucked under the huge grey glass and ivory desk. There was a mild fragrance of cheap perfume lingering in the air—a cleaning lady had just left the room.

Ploutus was standing by the window looking out. Zaire cleared his throat to get Ploutus's attention, but he was ignored for a moment.

"I am here, sir," he said, forcing confidence into his voice.

Ploutus still did not turn to face Zaire. There was an awkward silence in the room for another minute before he eventually turned to face Zaire, deliberately slowly swinging on his heels. Ploutus's face was a mask of wrath. The pulse beat beneath his Adam's apple was fast.

He looked at Zaire without blinking. For a moment Zaire was scared. He had seen him livid before but not this angry.

"Open that box," said Ploutus calmly, pointing at a golden box on his desk.

Zaire now noticed the golden box for the first time. He picked it up and clicked it open.

His eyes widened in shock and horror. There were four penises lying limp, preserved in formalin. Stuck on each penis was a golden plate with a name engraved on it.

Zaire was not sure what nauseated him more: the smell of formalin . . . or the sight of the slightly turgid male organs. He gasped for air and swallowed hard.

"Know this," warned Ploutus, yelling. "If you ever again just look at my wife like you did today and have fun as she disrespects me, let alone touch her, your miserable organ will be joining those."

Ploutus turned toward the window, breathing hard.

Zaire moved his gaze from the special collection and focused on the window that was now covered in warm mist from Ploutus's nostrils.

"Dad . . ." the word escaped his mouth before he could catch it.

"I am not your father, bastard!" yelled Ploutus. When it comes to my woman, I will forget every tiny drop of blood that forced our genes to match in the blink of an eye, young man." He turned, and walked towards Zaire in huge strides, grabbed his collar and pulled him to his feet. Ploutus stared hard at Zaire, panting, shaking him violently in anger.

Zaire had to think fast. He summoned hot tears from the pit of his stomach and let them flow, his eyes fixed on Ploutus's face. Ploutus softened his grip and allowed his own tears to flow as well. There was anger and pain, then misery. He let go of Zaire, walked back to the window, rolled up his shirt sleeves to his elbows, held on to the window, and wept.

"I am so sorry, son," he managed after what seemed like an eternity.

"It's just that this woman has robbed me of a chance to be with the love of my life. I can't stand it, seeing her sleeping around with bodyguards. She is the First Lady, for Pete's sake. How do I convince the world that I can rule over people when I cannot control my own wife? And now I am responsible for my love's death, and my daughter is all alone in the streets when she should be here with me. I am raising a body guard's daughter in my castle . . ." his voice trailed off. He sunk into one of the couches and cried even more. Zaire poured him a glass of whisky and sat beside him in silence.

"I loved Elima so much, Zaire. And I've just spilled her guts on the market square. And this . . . prostitute . . . has the guts to disrespect me in my house, in front of my servants. Is this the price I have to pay?"

He waited for Zaire's response.

Zaire said nothing. He just looked at him. Every piece of information he was dealt was tearing him into pieces. He was making painful discoveries. So, it was true that Ploutus had killed

Najma's mother. But how had he done it without him? Was he cutting him off from some of his deals? What else didn't he know? He did not mind it when Ploutus called him a bastard; he had refused to publicly honor him as a son for political reasons. He did not care about how he became his son. But it pained him that Ploutus was the one behind the death of Najma's mother, Elima. It was even darker that she was the love of his life. What was he planning to do about Najma?

"I know you think I've shut you out," said Ploutus. "But I couldn't let you have a hand in the murder of your aunt. She was your mother's sister."

Ploutus blew into a tissue and threw it into a dustbin in the corner.

"And poor Najma would never have forgiven you," he continued. "I am sure she loves you now. My poor little girl."

*****

Zaire had heard enough for the day . . .

He was appalled.

It was clear that he knew nothing about his father.

The information he'd prided himself in having collected for years was mere hogwash—garbage. He could use none of it to destroy this god that was suddenly confessing deeper truths that not only emotionally tormented Zaire himself, but also linked him more closely to this tyrant. Ploutus, his father, blood of his blood, flesh of his flesh . . .

What he thought he knew was nothing compared to what Ploutus was confiding to him now.

He did not want to hear it

It confused him.

The answers he had pursued for years were now right before him, staring him in the eyes . . . and he hated those answers.

How could his mother be Elima's sister?

What dark secret lay behind that revelation?

What about Nana? What lay behind her loyalty to Ploutus? Or was she being blackmailed?

What had really happened between his own mother and Ploutus? Was she but a loose end in Ploutus's dealings that had to be tied before it caused a major tripping?

Suddenly Zaire panicked.

He wondered if he had unwittingly participated in his own mother's disappearance.

All of these unexpectedly revealed answers to his questions now weighed heavily on his mind—his conscience . . .

However, he had to put on a brave face. After all, Ploutus's blood ran rampant in him. He was a god in his own capacity . . .

. . . and gods don't panic.

*****

"I will talk Najma into going to a boarding school at Mountain Crest," said Zaire, standing up. Ploutus knew Zaire was changing the subject. Ploutus also knew that Zaire had taken over Najma's financial matters and was not requesting permission.

"I am sure Etembi will not deny you the favor," Declared Zaire.

"Yes, that will be better," Acknowledged Ploutus despondently. Your sister will be safer there, and Etembi owes me. He will take in my girl."

Ploutus stared through the window dejectedly.

Zaire gloated within himself. He liked it when Ploutus got beaten. It meant he would let Zaire do things his way.

He did not want Ploutus to see his shock about Elima being his mother's sister. He'd get the answer to that question shortly. He knew Nana would have the answers . . .

She always did.

"Osanyin is at the airport, sir," declared Zaire. I'd better go pick him up. Collect yourself. Cameras will be rolling in two hours' time to announce his arrival in the state."

With that said, Zaire rose to his feet, patted his father on the back, and started out of the chambers after giving the penises in the case one last look.

"I love you, Zaire," Said Ploutus, still dejected. "I don't know what I would be without you."

The words caught Zaire before he walked through the door . . .

It was the first time ever that Ploutus had said he loved him since he was brought to the Castle.

BOARDING SCHOOL

"Have you ever been to Mountain Crest?" Zaire asked after they had settled in a corner at Essence Coffee Shop.

The place was quite scenic. Ivory lampshades hung above the heads of patrons. They fascinated her. She was amazed by how they were stuck on the ceiling, pouring glamorous beams of orange, red, and pink all over the place. The inside of Essence Coffee Shop looked like a million sunsets. The ambience and class bedazzled her.

Scanning the large pavilion with captured eyes. Najma noticed that most customers were ordering lattes and healthy bites. They looked like people who would be adamant about how polished the buttons on their shirts and dresses were. An aura of affluence surrounded them, and their children sat quietly at their tables, sipping milkshakes and drinking yogurt through colorful straws.

Adults conversed in calm voices, pouring out eloquent syllables while silently nibbling on their cookies. There was no crunching of bones from those chewing on chicken wings.

The ginger biscuits resembled wafers, and the manner in which women bit and sipped without messing up their lipstick amazed Najma.

Men were extra attentive to their ladies, pulling out the leather armchairs for them, hanging their fur coats over the backs of their chairs, listening to them with a close keenness that Najma had never witnessed before.

The humans in the café behaved in a synchronized manner, looked like automated machines. They were all similar, yet so different. She was astonished. She had read about the place, and had made cuttings of models posing in the café for her collection but had never been to the place before.

Zaire interrupted her daydream. "I asked you a question, young lady."

She obviously didn't want to answer that question. She had never been out of West Valley State before. To be honest, she'd never been beyond Corner Street. She was used to the silence and privacy of her house. She hated conversations and sharing her opinions. She enjoyed the discussions in her mind. Having been raised by a mentally unstable mother, molded her into who she was; a quiet, but eruptive young lady.

She was an active volcano . . .

Najma moved her attention to the smooth exotic wooden table, deliberately ignoring Zaire. She stared at the beautifully woven tribal mats. They must have been purchased from the native women living in the bamboo forest of West.

The artistic detail of the mats amazed her. She was always keen on well-made pieces, and she could bet she had never come across such finesse in art. The darkened bits in the fiber was so even and accurate, it smoothly flowed into the naturally preserved areas, making tiny differences in shades of brown and yellow. The mats looked like a leafy cup of latte.

"I want to go where they make these mats," she said, finally breaking her silence. "I want to learn how to make them."

The words spilled from her subconsciously, and when she realized that she said them, she covered her mouth in shame . . . but her excitement shot through her long fingers and brightened her eyes. She was ablaze with exhilaration. Zaire saw a little adventurous girl in her eyes. He wanted to get mad at her absentmindedness but chose not to. She looked so innocent and sweet. He also noticed that Najma did not know arguments. She would either shut out the speaker or shut herself out in conversations that she wanted to ignore.

"Why do you want to go to Bamboo?" he asked patiently but hesitantly.

"I love the patterns on the mats," she replied. "They are so artsy and beautiful. Imagine a model in a similar fabric. She will be out of this world!

The mats are like pieces of well-rhyming poetry with a neat selection of hard and smooth expressions. I love the mats, so I will love the women there . . ."

She was lost in her fantasy. Zaire could not understand why she was suddenly engrossed in the mats. He had been at the cafe before, many times but had never actually noticed the mats. Was she doing this to lock him out or was she genuinely thrilled?

Her eyes were sparkling. He loved how her face was a bright shade of brown, almost beige. The yellow lampshade above her made her skin glow. She looked beautiful and happy—so different from the sullen girl he had picked up from school that afternoon.

Zaire wondered if it was the sweet aroma of freshly roasted coffee beans or the sound of soft jazz music filling the air that had this effect on her.

"I will take you there," he said, "after you finish your final exams. We can take a tour to the Lakeside villages or at the Bamboo villages."

"Really, Zaire?" She almost jumped out of her seat. He had never seen this bubbly version of Najma. Not even during his visits in the distant past, when he would park his car a mile away from her home and watch her play alone. He sometimes followed her to the market square when her mother dragged her there, to watch over them. He felt like he had known her so well, though he knew very little about her.

"Yes. Really," he replied. "On one condition."

"If there are conditions, then you don't have to," she retorted and went back to sulking.

He liked her intelligence. He felt like she knew how to mellow him. No one had ever mellowed him. He never let anything get beneath his thick skin. Nothing excited him either. But looking at her happy face had formed a funny bubble in his stomach.

The barista was a tall young man with a smooth face and the smile of a girl. Zaire knew him well. Actually, he knew him from beyond the Essence Coffee shop. He was Zaire's favorite among the baristas in the café, and he seemed to enjoy this privilege.

He sauntered towards the pair in calculated steps, his face radiant.

"What will it be, sir?" he asked, his eyes more on Najma than on Zaire.

"Today I will take a café latte," replied Zaire, his eyes on the barista's face. "More espresso, less milk. I'll do my own sweetening. Just bring a scoop of syrup. No mint, please. Perhaps rosemary or bay. I will take ginger bites with the latte," Zaire said,

The barista listened with a keener interest in Najma than on what he was scribbling on his notepad.

"What about the lady?" he asked, his voice laced with what sounded like envy in Najma's ears.

"I will take a cappuccino," she said. "Cinnamon flavored. More cream. No pastries, please. I'm dieting."

She directed the last bit to Zaire who was dropping his jaw at her exotic version and expertise of choices. He was somehow shocked at how composed she was in making her orders. He thought she would falter or not know what to take.

He decided right there and then that he knew nothing about Najma and that watching her grow from a distance was no guarantee that he actually knew anything about her.

"How many times have you been on coffee dates, young lady?" It was supposed to be a thought, but it tumbled out loud.

"I have never been on one, old man," she responded, pressing harder on the irony of the statement.

"But . . ." he said, unable to find any words to complete the sentence.

"But what?" she retorted "Just because I don't live in a castle doesn't mean that I don't know different types of espresso, Zaire."

She was suddenly serious. The sparkle in her eye was gone.

Her extreme variation in moods and emotions confused Zaire. He made a mental note to ask Jotham, his psychiatric friend, to put her in therapy. Being alone with her mother most of the time might have affected Najma's ability to relate with people. This really saddened Zaire.

"Will you bring the orders, Jerry?" He growled at the barista, who scampered off. "What are you listening to?"

Najma wanted to laugh.

"He is gay," Zaire said flatly.

"I can see that. It's just that he is into you, and he thinks that I'm your date. You'd better tell your boyfriend I'm your sister before he poisons my cappuccino."

Zaire was taken aback by her ability to turn and twist conversations in her favor. Yes, indeed! She truly was his sister . . .

He smiled at her, even though he knew she wanted him to be offended by her scathing remarks.

"I will introduce you to your sister-in-law soon," he said. "Hope she likes your sarcasm."

"Only if you get one willing to deal with your tightness," she cuts back. "I'm a woman, we are related, and I don't even like you . . ."

"Let's just say you are blind," he countered. "You can't see what is seated right in front of you."

He watched Jerry placing Najma's coffee on her placemat. Cappuccino in a white china cup on a glossy saucer. The coffee was decorated with thick white cream and brown cinnamon dusted into the shape of a heart. A wisp of cinnamon aroma filled the air.

"Good choice of decoration, Jerry," teased Zaire, addressing Najma more than Jerry, "but for the wrong mouth. This lady has no idea how much her brother loves her. And her mouth could double for her gallbladder. So full of bile!"

"You have a sister?" Jerry squeaked, trying as much as he could to sound like a girl. Najma felt like she would burst with laughter.

"Yup!" replied Najma, nodding. "Hope you didn't poison my coffee . . ."

"Nuh," Jerry interrupted, placing a long frosted glass of café latte in front of Zaire. "He isn't my type. I like his sexy abs and cutely savage face, but he's too tight for me . . ."

The glass was frosty, and fresh rosemary leaves were floating on the milk. Jerry also set a saucer of four ginger biscuits beside the glass and avoided Zaire's flaming eyes.

"I told you, bro," teased Najma. "You'd better climb the mountains and join the Monks of the West . . . or die a lonely sad old man who can only be loved by his sister."

"Mmm," he retorted. "And that's why I'm taking you to boarding school at Mountain Crest."

"What!" she exclaimed, exasperated.

"Yea," Zaire confirmed. "It will be for your own good."

"Okay, wait a minute," she began, but he interrupted.

"Finally, I have your attention!" he retorted. "You can leave now, Jerry . . ."

"Idiot!" mumbled Jerry as he slowly turned away from the two. "Just when it's getting interesting . . ."

Jerry walked away, swaying his stiff behind expressively. Najma laughed out loud this time. Zaire wasn't sure if she was having fun with Jerry or laughing at his idea. He had just dropped a bomb and was waiting for the explosion.

"Finally, we can talk," he started. "I want you to go to boarding school in Mountain Crest. It will be safer there . . . for both of us."

"Who do you think you are?" she fumed, dropping every word with a measured tone and intensity. I mean, making decisions for me like that?"

"Najma," he replied gently, trying to explain. "I'm sorry. I know it's sudden, but I need to keep you safe. I don't know how your mother died yet. I cannot risk leaving you alone at Corner Street."

Najma stared at him blankly. He couldn't read her at all. She didn't even blink.

"It will be too risky to let you stay," he tried again. "That neighborhood is too hostile for you. Besides. I hate what I might do to those girls and boys in your school who keep picking on you. I can't take it anymore." He sipped on his latte for what seemed like an entire minute, then swallowed thirstily.

"Don't patronize me!" she spat, looking at him furiously. "Just answer my question!"

He was taken aback for a moment, confirming in his mind that Najma needed to see Jotham for therapy. She had no clue what the conversations were about. He needed her to at least be flexible. He also needed to make her see that there was life beyond the songs, stories, and silence that she was used to.

"I am your elder brother, and it is my responsibility to keep you safe," he continued. Just think about it. You won't be going tomorrow. Just consider it. You can tell me what you've decided when I pick you up from school tomorrow evening." His voice was calm. "I do intend to spend more time with you. It's not like I'm gonna throw you into a boarding school right after getting to finally sit and talk to you."

"How will whisking me away from my home keep me safe?" she wanted to know. "I don't know anyone in Mountain Crest. It's miles away from here. What if you merely want to dump me there? Take my house? How can I trust you?"

The questions seared past him like hot jets.

Sadness took hold of Zaire, knowing that Najma did not trust him. It kind of annoyed him. His hopes of being accepted and loved without question were being annulled once more.

He couldn't blame her though. Who was, he after all, but a distant observer who merely carried out orders to check on her? Assuming there were no such orders and Ploutus had not put him in charge of Elima's and Najma's safety and welfare, would he have been there at that time acting big brother?

"Najma, I am your brother," He said. "The only sibling you have. Your mother was my mother's sister. We share a father. That should tell you that our blood is the thickest on the planet. I don't know the rest of the story yet, but I intend to piece all the fragments together and lay them before you one day, each piece of the puzzle in the right place. I think that going to boarding school will keep you safe for the moment. It will only be for a year, then you will be off to college."

He tried again, reaching for her hand, but she jerked it away.

"Really now, Najma?" he begged. I worry about you every minute that you are out of my sight. If I knew you are safe in school and away from everything, it would give me time to figure out who killed your mom. Help me to help you, dear sister?"

"It's not as easy as you think," she said. "I have lived all my life making my own decisions. No one has ever forced me to do anything. It's so confusing. Mom's death, you, Ploutus . . . I feel like everyone is hiding something from me. Even Nana."

Zaire listened to her keenly without interrupting her. Finally, bit by bit, he was cracking open the wall she had built around herself. He understood her concerns.

"I promise that you will be safe at Hill Crest," he pleaded again. I also promise to tell you everything I know as soon as I get all the necessary information. Just give me time, okay?"

At last, Najma nodded in agreement.

"So, boarding it is?" he asked relieved, smiling.

"Yes. But," she began but he interrupted.

"No buts," he said. "Finish your Coffee. I have more errands to run. I should be taking you back to school. Your teacher said I can only take you for an hour. We have thirty minutes left. You should be back in class before the next lesson begins. Okay?"

Again, Najma nodded in agreement. There was no emotion on her face. Her resignation pained him so deeply. He wished he could explain more. He wanted to hug her and tell her all was going to be fine.

I am nothing, she thought. Even if I disappeared in Mountain Crest, nobody would be worried. Nobody would even know. My mom is dead. I don't know my dad. My brother is shady, and I don't even know how he is my brother. I have nothing to lose. If the universe doesn't need me anymore, then I will just join Mom. People always determine my fate. No one cares about what I want as long as they can do me favors.

Zaire saw tears shining in her eyes. She hadn't touched her cappuccino. She just stared into it and watched the heart shape spread into the cream.

I have waited for years to find out what a Cappuccino tastes like, she thought. Just when I was about to have a moment of my life, Zaire dropped a fart in my face . . .

She kept her poise.

"Let's go," he said, tossing a crisp bill on the table. Jerry jumped on the note and smiled. It was a huge tip.

"I'm sorry," said Najma. "I wasted the treat."

"Don't say anything," he said softly but firmly and rushed to open the car door for her.

Just before she got into the car, he grabbed her hand, pulled her in his arms and held her for a moment. He was not good with affection, but there was something about Najma that assaulted his compassionate side. She dug deeper into his soul and brought out a person he had no idea existed within him. He suddenly felt the urge to protect her and always make her happy.

"If you don't trust me, Najma, at least listen to my heart," he said. "I am doing this for our good. You are the only one I have in this life, and I will never let anything happen to you. I love you more than anything that has breath now. Trust me. Please."

His voice was trailing off from a firm timbre to a shaky fearful tenor.

She cried when he let her go. She cried all the way to school. She cried into the afternoon classes. She cried more while waiting for a cab to bring her home from school. She cried more when Nana opened the door for her at home.

She couldn't explain what she felt. She felt so vulnerable; yet all her life, she had wished to belong. Now she had a brother and a possible father, but it felt so different. It was not exhilarating as she had expected. Someone had taken it upon himself to watch over her, yet it still pained her.

"What's wrong, my girl?" Nana asked. "Is it Zaire?"

Najma walked past her and she closed the door behind her.

"My girl," said Nana. "Go to boarding school. Zaire means well, you can trust him."

"You know too?" Najma wanted to know. she was befuddled by the fact that everyone knew something about her, except herself.

"Najma," replied Nana. "This place is no longer safe for you."

"When were you going to tell me this?" exclaimed Najma. "I thought you were closer to me than him!" She stormed to her room.

"God, you have your grandfather's temper!" Nana said softly, but loud enough for Najma to hear her.

Najma walked to her bed, ignoring Nana's remarks because she knew it was a trap to get her talking more. She had no energy left. She sunk into her bed, covered her head, and cried till sleep carried her off to a peaceful place.

Osanyin waved at the security guards who had been sent from West Valley to pick him up. They were standing in a neat queue at the reception area of the airport. All of them were in black suits, white shirts, and black evenly tied ties. They stood with their legs slightly apart, hands folded and resting at their groins. They all faced the airplane. When Osanyin waved, they nodded uniformly without raising an arm. Some had earpieces in their ears and were listening keenly to the security details being spelled out to them by their counterparts. There were Guards all over the place, dressed like the delegates and officials of the state. One couldn't tell them apart.

Osanyin thrived on this kind of attention, and Zaire, on behalf of Ploutus, had made sure that he got it in surplus. He was clad in traditional royal regalia—his signature arrival outfit.

Women in neat rows, colorful sisal skirts around their waists, were twirling gently in anticipation; sashes of colorful pieces of cloth were tied around their chests to keep their rebellious bouncy breasts at bay. Tribal patterns were drawn on their faces with red soil and black coal.

Soft music, created by traditional drums, shakers, jingles, and string instruments, lingered in the air.

The women's feet were bare, painted red to the ankles; a sign of beauty and devotion. They stood ready, waiting for a signal to ululate when the Statesman's feet touched the ground.

The young men were in animal hides. Majestic leopard and cheetah skins were draped on their black suits, a sign of heroism and bravery. They all stood at attention, necks stiff, black ties dangling and disappearing underneath the animal hides. In the group of men in black suits and skin drapes, there were bodyguards—security officers from both West Valley and Mountain Crest. Some were strategically positioned on the roofs of unspecified buildings at the airport. Others were among the passengers, pretending to be part of the crowd.

Activities ceased for a moment at The Valley View Airport when Osanyin's plane touched the ground. Everyone waited eagerly for him to alight. When he did, his head was in Colobus Monkey headgear, fastened by a cowry shells and a leather strap that rudely disturbed the peace of the bush on his face.

He was in royal robes, blue with golden strips. The robes exaggerated his regal demeanor. His belly bulged, making the golden strips look like alien tendrils. He had a titanic smile plastered on his face. His eyes were on the women, who suddenly ululated and broke into a frenzied dance. They gyrated their hips, turned in unison, slightly bent their backs, and showed off the flow of oil around their waists. This was a traditional dance of wooing that brides performed for the groom, whetting his appetite on the eve of a wedding. Women also used this dance to provoke various statesmen into signing good business deals for West Valley. West Valley was known for its beautiful curvy women with strong, agile waists.

Osanyin was drooling openly. He pointed at one woman in particular and sent a bodyguard over to her with a wad of notes. This was supposed to fuel the women so that they would perform a more vigorous, hind-jerking dance, uniformly bouncing their behinds, their flying sisal skirts creating a mirage of beautiful colors.

The chosen woman was supposed to be sneaked into Osanyin's Royal Convoy. She would be the one to service the Statesman during his one-week stay in West Valley.

The two Statesmen were to meet at the Capital before proceeding to Ploutus's Castle. It was a business visit, so business had to be taken care of first. A fleet of vehicles carrying delegates and officers of high ranks accompanied him. The martial truck went ahead of the fleet, followed by an Internal Security convoy. Behind them, Zaire and Ploutus followed in the State Mercedes Pullman limousine. Behind the state car followed a winding string of guzzlers carrying the delegates and officials. Finally, another convoy of internal security cars completed the entourage.

"How did she take the boarding news?" Ploutus wanted to know. They were driving to the capital to meet with Osanyin and make a few deals before embarking on the private business that had brought Osanyin from Mountain Crest to West Valley.

Zaire wondered why Ploutus was thinking about Najma during a business event. He didn't want to talk about Najma. He also hated Ploutus's sudden interest in Najma. He had never shown any concern when her mother was alive. All Ploutus ever did was send money. To him, money was all that one ever needed.

Zaire wanted to accuse Ploutus of pretense and feigning concern because he was guilty of Elima's death, and he struggled to restrain himself.

"She's okay with it," he lied, then changed the subject.

"I believe the women and youth have done a great job at the airport., he said. "Let's check the news."

Ploutus seemed to understand Zaire's need for not talking about Najma, quickly switching the subject to what they should be talking about.

They sat in silence, listening to the live broadcast of Osanyin's warm reception at the airport on Valley T.V. The reporter threw in a few praises for Hon. Ploutus proceeded to state that the Statesman was on his way to Capital Base to receive Hon. Osanyin for business talks.

There was a quick slide of the Capital State Chambers—The CSC—well secured by men and women in uniform and the suited intelligence personnel.

"Sometimes, I wonder how my life will be once my second term has ended," said Ploutus thoughtfully, not addressing Zaire in particular. "I enjoy being in the limelight. It's the only good thing about my miserable life."

His bodyguard sat motionless like a statue, not expected to say anything. He was supposed to play absent.

"You are a rich man, sir," replied Zaire. You can retire from politics and continue running your empire quietly."

"I am growing old . . ." lamented Ploutus.

"No," teased Zaire. "Ploutus never gets old."

Ploutus smiled widely, feeling good about his lingering youthful look. Zaire knew which buttons to push.

He was not in his royal regalia. He was in a tuxedo, wearing gold rings on all his left fingers and a golden watch on his right wrist. His shirt was cuffed in gold as well. They were on State Headquarters' premises already, and the vehicles were pulling up and parking in their respective parking bays.

The CSC purple carpet was being rolled out for the Honorable Men's cars. Ploutus was just on the scheduled time, waiting for the lead intelligence officer to give a go-ahead for him to alight and receive Osanyin at the CSC. Osanyin's convoy was parked in the arena, waiting to be directed by the IO as well.

Zaire felt irritated by all the protocols. He hated joining the long talks in the chambers. The clicks of the cameras gave him a headache.

He had to wait for Ploutus to get out of the limo, ensure it was properly parked, change the drivers, and wire the new one for the ride to the castle. He had to assign a number of officers to guard the Pullman, then catch up with the IO on the security details as reported from the castle. He was also expected to meet the lead journalist for directives on the photographs and details of the meeting that should go to print and air on T.V.

Zaire detested his life. He wished he could quit, move away from West Valley and disappear for good . . .

GOD AND GODDESES – Young Blood

It was the third day of Osanyin's visit, and the pomp and frenzy were declining. The journalists had left the castle grounds, and there were new trends on the media already.

The gods, Ploutus and Osanyin, sat pensively in the castle chambers. Zaire was fixing scotch for them. He was also trying hard to read between the lines of their conversation. He had not been able to figure out what was in the packages and what Osanyin was to do with them. It made him nervous.

"How is Afula?" Ploutus asked Osanyin.

There were dense traces of distrust in Ploutus's tone.

Something wasn't right, and Zaire was sitting on the edge of his seat with fear. He had never seen Ploutus worried or worked up about anything. Was it the coming elections? Was it Najma? It was hard to figure out, especially since Osanyin was around. They couldn't chat about anything.

"You know Afula now," replied Osanyin. "She is a nasty headache."

Osanyin sounded distressed too. It felt like there was something they were withholding from Zaire. Afula had never been a headache. Zaire knew all state headaches, and Afula was not one of them. If anything, Zaire knew her to be the most devoted of the women Osanyin had ever been with in West Valley. It's just that, after her, there had never been another. He had yet to figure out what she really did to wrap Osanyin around her little finger.

"You should put her on reigns!" retorted Ploutus, feigning pride. "A woman could never control me!"

Ploutus and Osanyin laughed out loud. They both knew Ploutus that was lying.

Zaire did not join in the laughter. He had learned to be silent around these senior men, unless he was addressed or had major reason to voice his opinion. He had assumed his silent place of a youth dining with elders.

Zaire made sure to never become intoxicated when he was with them. In the past, it was because he needed to watch out for Ploutus, but recently, it was mainly for information. The two men got loose tongues when whisky ran deeper into their veins. He could unravel many mysteries about the gods and goddesses of the States by merely sitting and observing.

"Where are Barvo and Lorantu?" asked Zaire. "They should've been here by now."

He tried to make the gods talk about more sensible things that would be of benefit to him. He hated discussing women, especially with Ploutus and his ilk of friends. They talked about women in the most disrespectful manner.

"I wonder too," replied Ploutus, looking at Zaire like he was seeing him in the room for the first time. Those two are always late. Lorantu was supposed to welcome Barvo yesterday, and they should've been here by now. Osanyin and I have some private business to take care of at Lakeside soon. They're using Lorantu's private jet."

"We have sealed off the media so it will be a personal meeting, not regarding state issues," Ploutus continued, looking at Zaire. "I really hate those media puppets. They are like vermin."

It was clearly an attempt of changing the subject. Zaire could see Ploutus panicking when he looked at him.

Osanyin had a displeased expression on his face. It was obvious that what Ploutus had just said was not meant for Zaire's ears. Zaire was not supposed to know about Lakeside.

"What is at Lakeside?" Zaire feigned surprise.

"None of your business, boy!" Osanyin retorted.

"Don't talk to my son like that, Osanyin!" Ploutus exclaimed angrily. "And I hope your Nasty Headache isn't coming along!"

"What's wrong with Afula coming?" asked Osanyin, ignoring the first bit of Ploutus's sentiment. It *is* her idea, remember?"

"Can I come?" asked Zaire, meaning to push deeper into the raw subject.

"No!" Yelled Ploutus and Osanyin at the same time.

"You'd better put your boy in check, Ploutus," said Osanyin, avoiding Zaire's blazing eyes.

"And you'd better ensure that Afula is tamed, this time." Ploutus retorted. "I'm not in the mood for her outbursts,"

To many, Afula was the woman with the stall on Corner Street. To a few, she was the permanent and only mistress of Hon Osanyin in West Valley. He always picked her during the women's performances, and it had been known all over the small circle of gods that she belonged to him. She'd never been married, and she was barren. The stall on Corner Street was a cover-up for her chain of businesses across the four states. She owned land in the Bamboo Forest Village and other private facilities that carried out private dealings for statesmen.

*****

To Zaire, it was now clear that Afula was a key player in the secret mission at Lakeside, planned by the gods. Zaire was on the verge of piecing together the relationship between Afula and Elima. He wondered why Elima always spent her time on her stall's doorstep. He was also aware that, on the eve of Elima's death, Afula had closed down the stall and rented it out to somebody else a few days later. When Zaire asked the new occupant about the stall, the man claimed that he was given the stall by the Market

Square Committee. According to him, he had no idea who Elima or Afula was. Something was fishy, and Zaire didn't like the smell of it.

*****

There was a knock at the door. Barvo and Lorantu had arrived. Zaire went to answer the door immediately. It was a bodyguard who informed him that Lorantu's private jet had landed on Ploutus's heliport. Zaire excused himself from the chambers and went out to receive the guests. The Wasp was on his way up.

Zaire noticed that the Wasp was carrying two bags of money. Ploutus had not asked Zaire to get him cash. Why was he asking the Wasp now?

For a moment, he sensed danger. The mission at lakeside had to be special enough for Ploutus to keep him out.

Barvo saw Zaire first. He rose to his feet from the reception lounge, excitedly reaching his hand out to him.

"Young man! He said loudly, pulling Zaire into his arms for an intimate hug. "You are growing more handsome by the day!"

Zaire nearly choked in an attempt to ignore the smell of Barvo's cologne. The entire waiting lounge was filled with the nose-attacking scent. Zaire could feel it burning all the way down his throat.

"Welcome to the palace, sir." Zaire welcomed Barvo, trying not to suffocate. "The Statesman awaits you in his chambers."

Lorantu must have been in the washrooms. He walked into the room and joined the duo. He firmly shook Zaire's hand, scrutinizing his face.

"Your face grows younger every time I see you, but your body is bulging out of your skin, young man. You must have a throng of women on your heels!" Lorantu joked.

The three men roared in laughter as they waited for the elevator to get ready. Each one of them was to ride in their own elevator, accompanied by a bodyguard. Lorantu went first, followed by Zaire, then Barvo.

*****

Zaire thought about the deals that he still had to execute and seal. It was getting harder every day, especially with the approaching elections. He was supposed to print enough money for the campaign, check on the exports for more goods from Ploutus's empire before the ports were closed for the election period, and ensure that the media towed the line and the people were singing Ploutus's tunes. He was also expected to detect and neutralize any form of scandalous information that could possibly be released by Ploutus's political arch enemies during the campaigns.

And now, there was a secret mission on the plate of the gods that he knew nothing about.

Wasp, Barvo, and Lorantu were Ploutus and Osanyin's closest allies.

Wasp dealt with the banks and ensured that the fake money they printed was circulating. He also handled financial issues for Ploutus and Osanyin.

Barvo and Lorantu were business associates and delegates for their assigned villages. Barvo worked on the fake gold for Riverside village, and Lorantu dealt with humans for sale, hire, and ownership.

*****

Each elevator arrived within seconds of the one before it. Zaire led the men into the chambers.

There was a sickening excitement in the room, and Zaire felt like fleeing. He sat at the farthest end of the couches to avoid Barvo and his cyclone of cologne. Zaire hated how Barvo kept stealing glances at his chest and face.

Zaire called in a serving lady, who served them cold drinks. He instructed her to inform the butler of the two extra guests who would be joining the rest of the household for dinner. He also asked the girl to inform Ekesa, who probably had no idea that there were guests in the palace.

"It will be boring having only one lady at the table," said Lorantu. "We all know that Afula is a man. Osanyin, don't take offense."

The room was overpowered by the rumbling laughter of males, Barvo's cologne, the smell of Cognac, whisky and lime, masculine sweat, and a distant cheap perfume radiating from the maid's and butler's underarms.

"We need some young blood besides Zaire here," Lorantu went on. "Won't you ask Nysa to join us this evening? What do you think, Zaire?"

Zaire smiled and asked the maid to leave.

The men went on making ill jokes about everything and laughing out loud. Zaire started noticing that, in no time, every tongue was loose and mouths were spilling deep secrets.

"How is the Lake, Barvo?" asked Ploutus.

"The peasants want water for irrigation, your honor," replied Barvo with a lilt in his voice. "I need them stopped. They all hate me. I don't care, as long as they break their backs to dig up the imaginary gold I keep manufacturing for export. I hear they are getting sick and their women are having miscarriages because of the chemicals in the water. But I don't care about women. I don't care about their unborn pieces of flesh either. The money is good."

"Just keep them in check. I made them a promise during the last elections, remember? Release some water. I don't want to lose the next election you know," Ploutus said matter-of-factly. And those women you don't care about are Lorantus's capital, so be easy on them, will you?"

"I cannot afford releasing even one liter," Barvo protested. "You know the production needs a lot of water. This is science, and it has to be perfect. Besides, they keep complaining that the water we release is contaminated. Nothing can grow on the chemicals, you know . . ."

"I don't want anything affecting their loyalty," retorted Ploutus. "Your chemicals are none of my business. I need the gold on the market and the votes too. Figure it out."

Ploutus's voice was higher and firmer than usual. He was clearly angry.

The conversation about the manufactured gold went on for a long time. Zaire made mental notes of how it was to be moved from one state to the other. He also paid special attention to the how the gold got past the standards offices, without it being traced back to Barvo.

There were calls made here and there, especially to big jewelry firms. Barvo kept throwing glances at Zaire, which made Zaire uncomfortable.

"Would you take your eyes off my boy Barvo," yelled Ploutus, banging the table and giving them all a fright.

Zaire was not used to his father publicly calling him his boy. This new public display of affection suddenly unsettled him. Just a few days ago Ploutus had threatened to chop off Zaire's male organs, and now he was flooding the chambers with emotion. Something had to be wrong. Seriously wrong . . .

"What do you mean?" Asked Lorantu. "We didn't know you are . . ."

"What do *you* mean?" interrupted Ploutus. I love women. I just don't want Barvo looking at my son like he's a piece of meat. Besides, Zaire has held this state in his palm in the darkest way all of you can ever imagine, so stop treating him like vermin."

Ploutus gulped down more whiskey. His eyes were fiery red.

Zaire was openly shocked. He coughed hard after sipping on his scotch for the first time since the meeting started. He rarely touched his drink during such meetings because he also had to be alert, just in case someone dropped something in Ploutus's drink. No one trusted the other in such dealings since everyone had leverage against the other. But then, drinks were taking their toll, and the gods were talking carelessly. Zaire had a feeling that dinner was going to be a mess.

"I need more pieces of meat for my business, Lorantu," Osanyin said.

"I am still shocked at what Ploutus is doing," said Lorantu. Are we missing something?"

"Can you drop it?" said Osanyin. "The man is drunk. He doesn't know what he is saying anymore."

"Who cares if he is the son?" spat Barvo. "He is loyal."

"I was with Jerry, yesterday," Zaire said in an attempt to sway the gang from talking about what Ploutus just said.

They all fell silent to listen. Jerry was Barvo's weakness. They all knew Barvo was in love with Jerry but couldn't be with him because of the public and his partnership with Ploutus. It could cause chaos. They were also shocked that Zaire knew about it as well.

"So Barvo can finally stop drooling over my boy?" said Ploutus, deliberately thwarting Zaire's efforts.

This was beyond what was expected. Barvo wanted to retaliate, but Zaire quickly pointed at the CCTV, urging them to restrain their voices and fights.

"There is less young blood available Osanyin," said Lorantu. "Kids are scared. They don't care about the money anymore, especially with the many deaths that are being reported in the house. You know your people are animals. Perhaps you should talk to them.”

“You are the animal here!” yelled Barvo, displacing his anger on Lorantu.

“Will you shut up, gold ass!” Lorantu yelled back at him.

“Lorantu,” said Osanyin with vehemence, calling the room back to attention. “I have clients with huge appetites in my hotels. I need the meat supplied soon.”

All this time, Wasp was sitting in a corner, sipping on his drink quietly. His business was already done. Money had been printed clean, and the gentlemen had filled their briefcases as required. Wasp never participated in any of the talks. He was the silent mystery that Zaire sometimes admired.

Bodyguards were sent in to carry suitcases to respective cars and the jet.

Zaire wanted to sneak out of the castle to see Najma before dinner. He excused himself to accompany the bodyguards and slipped away to Corner Street, leaving the men to their talking and brawling.

WARD NINE – Jotham

When Elima got out of Ward Nine, she had gotten fairly well. She was calm and went about her business as usual. She had even talked about going back to school to finish her nursing degree. She experienced lapses here and there, but Najma had learned to take care of them. She had a constant supply of antidepressants and sleeping pills for when she got too anxious. She rarely called on Ploutus, and the nights that she did, Nana would come to sleep over.

Jotham had stopped paying regular home visits as well. He had visited to confirm that the drugs Najma's mother was taking were doing her good. He would come with new doses and a listening ear for Najma and Nana. He insisted that it was important for them to talk about what they felt. Jotham insisted that taking care of a mentally unstable patient was not easy and that it could take a toll on Najma and Nana if they didn't go through therapy themselves. There were days Najma broke down and cried and he would let her.

"How do you feel today?" Jotham would ask.

"I don't know any more. I feel so exhausted," Najma would respond.

"Why do you think you are exhausted?" he would go on.

"Because I can't sleep," Najma would say. "I keep thinking that my mother might get sick again. Then there is school . . ."

"You mother is on medication," Jotham would continue. "As long as she keeps taking her medicine, she won't fall sick. What's wrong with school?"

Najma had visualized a future where she would make her mother proud by doing well in school, winning the state scholarship for college and joining the modelling industry to earn them more income. Her mother had helped her draw some of her designs that she'd hoped to sell to fashion houses once she finished school. Everything was going to become normal.

Then, without warning, Elima was brutally murdered. Najma's world was slowly crumbling. New information was being heaped on top of her. She felt like she needed someone to talk to—someone who would let her cry like Jotham did.

Jotham had been more than a friend to her and Nana. Her mother had liked him. With Jotham around, the women laughed more, joking about everything, and Nana cooked her best. He would always ask for Najma to see him off. He sometimes held her hand when they walked out of the house. Najma suddenly missed him. The thought of going to boarding school made her heart cramp. She wasn't sure if she could trust Zaire. Nana had said it was okay, but still, Najma felt like she needed to talk to someone.

Najma felt like she was being whisked away to Mountain Crest, where she knew no one. She hadn't gotten over her mother's death, since she had no one to talk to about it. Nana was sadder, and every time Najma brought up the subject, Nana just cried and said nothing.

In her sadness and pain, Najma remembered Jotham. She wanted to see him again. Had he not promised to always listen? Had he not said she could tell him anything she felt like? It had been a while since she'd heard from him. This was the right time to visit him. She wondered if he still remembered her. She wondered if he was now a fully certified doctor. She also wanted to confide in him about her decision to pursue psychiatry in college. Most importantly, there was a part of her that longed for him—a part that she couldn't explain.

Najma remembered with nostalgia how he had been helpful when her mother was in Ward Nine. He had taken upon himself to ensure that Elima got the best treatment. Elima's room was always teaming with orderlies. Jotham had thought at that time that Zaire was her brother. Najma wondered if he knew the truth and did not want to tell her then.

She suddenly grew anxious. She wanted to go to Ward Nine to see Jotham urgently. There had to be something he knew back then. Why was he referring to Zaire as her brother? No one had ever mentioned that. What did he know?

A knock on the door interrupted her flow of thoughts. It had to be Zaire.

"Come in, son." It was Nana welcoming Zaire. That's what she called him of late.

"How did Najma sleep?" he asked before sitting down. "Is she okay?"

"I wanted to be here early, but you know Hon. Osanyin is in town, and I have to take care of things at the castle and the capital. Is she awake?" His voice was laced with anxiety.

"I am awake!" interjected Najma as she walked into the living room. I slept okay. I am going to boarding school, if that's what you are worried about. It's not like you leave me any choice . . ."

She knew she had to twist Zaire's arm for him to give her what she wanted. She wanted to see Jotham. She needed to go to Ward Nine.

"Hey, little missy!" Demanded Nana. "Give your brother a hug! "That is no way to greeting your elders. I have taught you better!"

"Okay mom!" Najma responded with a tight pout on her lips. She walked into Zaire's arms. He held her for a while. Then he released her, just looking at her.

"I need to go to Ward Nine," she said urgently. "Now. Then we can talk about boarding school."

"What?" Both Nana and Zaire asked in unison and in shock.

"It is the only thing I am asking of you," She said in her defense.

"What for?" Zaire asked. She noticed that there was a playful smile on his lips.

"What's funny?" Najma retorted. "It's the only place that holds the best memories about my mother."

"Or someone wants to see her crush before going to boarding," teased Zaire.

"You don't have to take me if you are going to be nasty about it." Najma feigned a sulk.

Zaire threw his arms around her and pulled her closer to him, laughing. He ruffled her hair and laughed even louder. Nothing made him happier than seeing his sister happy. It was pure bliss for him. For a moment he forgot about the castle and the malevolent political schemes. He forgot about forgery and fraud. He forgot about smuggling and human trafficking. The best side of him shot out.

"You know," he continued, pulling her leg, "Ham is my best friend. He has been asking about you lately. You'd better talk to me nicely . . ."

There was a twinkle in her eyes. She wanted to ask what Jotham asked about her, but decided against it. From the corner of her eyes, she noticed that Nana was not just pouring them glasses of juice. She was also observing her intensely.

The two emptied their glasses in no time, like kids anxious about jumping out to play. Nana was beside herself with joy just watching them. She watched them walk to the car. Zaire opened the door for Najma. Najma settled in the passenger's seat and they sped off.

"Take care of your sister, Zaire," she shouted after them.

On their way to Valley Hospital, which was a twenty-minute drive from Corner Street, Zaire had to stop at Essence Coffee Shop to give Jerry a message from Barvo. They then headed to the hospital after Zaire called Jotham to inform him that they were on their way.

"He will be happy to see you," he said to Najma teasingly.

"How sure are you? He doesn't even remember me," Najma said anxiously.

"He does. He always talks about you," Zaire said with a shrug. Najma couldn't believe they were talking about her crush so easily.

"What does he say about me? I'm sure he just pities me," Najma said sadly.

"No," replied Zaire, looking into her eyes briefly. "Not pity. He likes you. You are a brilliant girl. Only a fool would pity you."

She felt so nice about herself. No one had ever told her that. Not even her teachers. She wanted to hug Zaire, but he was driving. He reached out and touched her hand.

"Thank you, bro," she said softly. "I don't know what I would be without you."

There was a quiver in her voice.

"By the way," he said after a brief silence. "Can you keep a secret?"

Najma nodded.

"Ham is Nana's son," he said flatly. "Nobody knows it but me. And now you."

Najma was too shocked to notice that they were approaching the hospital already.

The watchman opened the gate. Ham was waiting for them in his car. He asked Zaire to park outside.

"You can go to his place." Zaire said, opening the door for Najma. I'm cool with it, and I trust him with you. I will pick you up later tonight. Behave yourself."

Najma regretted asking to see Jotham. She hated and loved Zaire at the same time for bringing her over. She wondered how she was going to behave around Jotham with the secret Zaire had just told her. Did Zaire do it on purpose to ruin her evening?"

"Let's go, Najma," Ham called for her. He was out of the car holding the door for her.

"What did you say when I was getting in the car?" she asked when he walked back after talking to Zaire and watching him drive off.

"I said you look lovely."

Najma's gaze dropped to her lap.

"I would like to see Ward Nine before we leave please," she whispered.

"No," he replied. "I have something better to show you."

With that, he drove off to his home.

GODS AND GODDESSES – The Clanging of Castle China

The Castle's dining lounge was decorated to impress the gods who would be attending the feast.

Dinner was themed black and white. Only a few drops of red here and there were scattered about to inconspicuously set off the black and white. Black, white, and red draperies of pure silk were loosely fastened to the mosaic walls by invisible clasps.

The chairs were covered in red and set off by large black satin bows. The tables were covered in shiny black, and crisp white napkins, folded in sharp triangles, were placed in each of the table corners, erect and attentive, like sentinels.

The shiny white china and polished silver cutlery were meticulously arranged

The main table was set on a dais at the front of the room. This table was reserved for the statesmen, their wives or dinner dates, and a few close allies. The table setting was similar to the rest of the tables in the room, except that the cutlery was of polished gold and the wine glasses were shiny silver chalices.

Soft jazz music played in the background. The State DJ knew his job, mixing exotic music with tribal beats from across the four states. The waiters and waitresses were dressed in yellow shirts and blouses and navy-blue trousers and short skirts, respectively. They had navy-blue bowties around their necks, silver trays balanced on their left palms, nametags on their chests, and frequently rehearsed smiles glued to their faces.

A purple carpet ran along a purposely created aisle.

Guests were not allowed in before the guests of honor were settled. Zaire would signal when to enter. The host and hostess would join the event last.

Zaire was in the waiting lounge, keeping some of the quests company, chit chatting and catching up on state events. They were formally invited delegates, party officials, and a few senior state officials. Businessmen and influential decision makers were also present. As were Barvo and Lorantu, chatting with elite businessmen who happened to be in the state's inner circle of friends.

*****

Upstairs, Ekesa, the lady of the house, was getting ready for dinner. Ploutus ogled her from the corner of his eyes as he slid into his royal robes. He was working on the golden waist band—a symbol of royalty—which encircled him like the ring of a huge planet.

"Will you put on a tux please?" remarked Ekesa. It's not a tribal function, for heaven's sake!"

Ploutus ignored her, so she came and stood before him, stark naked, repeating her sentiments.

Ploutus caressed her skin with his eyes, studying her perky breasts, hard pink nipples that defied her age, her flat tummy and the depression of her navel. He looked lower to her clean-shaven groin. It had been a while since he saw her naked, and she was sending his blood on a rampage.

"I want to make an impression," he growled, his words coming in breathless gasps. "This is my castle, and I should dress like a king!"

"You won't be one for much longer," she said, slightly parting her legs to distract him more. "You'll lose this election."

She looked like she was on a mission to provoke him. She wanted to get under his skin.

"I am getting back to the capital, woman," he growled, his eyes on her thighs.

To provoke him further, she shook her head in disagreement and sneered.

"Don't talk to me like that woman!" he said as he closed in on her.

"I have not said anything . . ." she said, a plea in her voice.

He grabbed her hand and pulled her to him roughly.

"I will be the Statesman, till I die," he said, breathing in her face.

Her eyes twinkled with lust. His hand ran down her back and her body erupted in goose bumps. His anger excited her.

"You are going down, Ploutus," she said. "And I will make sure that you do," she whispered in his ear, slightly biting on his lobes.

There was fire in his body. He pushed her onto the massive bed, so hard that she bounced when she fell. He tore off his royal robes like an enraged gorilla. He ripped open her legs, exposing her moistened pink labia. His hot tongue touched her cold hard nipple and he sucks on it so hard that she moaned in pain. He could taste her blood as he sucked. His fingers ravaged her. Suddenly, he savagely plunged into her, grabbing her by the neck and covering her mouth with his own, drool flowing into her gaping mouth.

"Ploutus . . ." Her voice was muffled.

"Yes, baby!" he grunted. "Now you know who is king!" His eyes were fiery red. He squeezed her neck harder.

"Ploutus . . ." she said again, this time urgently.

"You're right baby," he grunted again. "Say it one last time and I will make you pregnant tonight."

He enjoyed her misery. It drove him over the edge.

"Ploutus, you're hurting me!" she managed to exclaim, struggling to push his heavy body off her.

"No, I'm not," he said. "You like it savage. Don't you baby? When did it change? And you just ruined it by talking." His hands relaxed around her neck, but he turned her over, making her lie on her belly. He parted her butt cheeks and plunged into her once more, this time letting himself shoot inside her rear. He grunted like an animal. When he was done, he rolled off her, pushed her aside, and walked to the bathroom, leaving her on the bed, panting.

"I would have considered giving you my baby tonight," he said, "but your tongue will be your undoing. Come on, get ready. The male guests are waiting to lust for you."

He spat in the sink and disappeared into the bathroom.

"Son of a dog," she whispered. She tried to get up, but her whole body ached. She would need some time before she would be able to lower herself into a bathtub.

Her plan to get pregnant by him had failed again. It always did. She longed for the day that she would give him a son. An heir. Someone that could trample Zaire and get him out of the way. She was also aware that Ploutus knew that Nysa was not his daughter.

"Did you just call my father, Ploutus the god, a dog?" he yelled over the running water.

"Well, he is," she responded.

"You will pay for that dearly, my love," he promised, gargling water and words. "You have not seen hell yet!"

"I live in hell, Ploutus," she replied. "Nothing bothers me anymore."

She managed to stand up and walked to the bathroom.

*****

The security had been reinforced every state security agent and intelligence officer was alert. The IOs were settled in the CCTV room, and Zaire confirmed that all was okay. He'd sent the butlers for Osanyin and had instructed a waiter to inform the guests of honor that they should take their seats at the main table.

The guests of honor entered the dining lounge gracefully, talking in low tones, arms hooked at the elbows. Most ladies were in red gowns, displaying various shades of red—some glossy, others matt; some backs bare. Others were displaying excess cleavage—some gowns long, others short. All women carried classy clutch bags and balanced precariously on exotic stilettos of various silver, golden, and black designs.

The gentlemen were in black tuxedos and white shirts, wearing black shoes and red bowties. Barvo's red cobra-skin moccasins contrasted sharply, his cologne trailing him all the way down the purple aisle.

Once all the guests of honor were seated, the rest of the guests were invited in.

*****

Ekesa pulled out a wine-red gown from her glamorous collection and admired it before sliding into it.

"Help me fasten the zipper, Ploutus," she said, standing in front of him with her back toward him.

He was struggling with his bowtie. He had, after all, opted for the tux as she had suggested.

"Thank you," she said when he had done, then turned around to help him fix his bowtie.

"You really look handsome, darling," she said sincerely.

The fight they'd just had was buried and forgotten. It would be dug up after dinner . . . or days later...

"And you look beautiful, Love," he replied. "You are the most dangerously beautiful creature that the gods ever created."

He picked up her arm and slipped it through his, so that they stood arm-in-arm. They walked to the mirror and admired themselves for a while. Then they turned toward the door.

"Let's go win this second term together, my love," he said pleadingly.

He pulled the door open and walked into the corridor where the bodyguards were waiting. They walked down the corridor to the elevator.

Ekesa left first with her bodyguard, and Ploutus followed immediately after. A minute later, they were at the door of the dining lounge. Nysa was there already, waiting for them, wearing a short red frock showing off her shapely legs, and black high heels with stockings. Her accessories were petite, shiny diamonds in silver setting.

She stood beside Zaire, who was a healthier and more handsome replica of Ploutus. Like the guests of honor, he was wearing a black tuxedo, white shirt, black shoes, and red bowtie. He held Nysa's stiff hand loosely in his. Together, the two pairs walked down the purple aisle, the ladies rhythmically swaying their hips and the men smiling and waving at the guests, who rose to give the royal family a standing ovation.

The family settled into their seats at the main table, each face plastered with a smile. Zaire chose to sit away from Nysa after pulling out her chair.

Ploutus sat beside his wife, their hands intertwined for the camera.

The jazz music was still playing, now softer, as the guests talked amongst themselves. The sparkles in the white wine glasses reflected the light of the massive chandeliers, casting rainbows on the faces of the guests, creating an ambiance of festivity in the room.

The waiters and waitresses were doing a faultless job. Dinner trays were already exchanging hands.

Steak in peanut butter sauce, the local delicacy, transformed into an exotic dish by the state chefs, who added imported spices and herbs to make it special, was welcomed. A variety of well-prepared spuds accompanied the steak, caressing the palates of the guests.

Various poultry dishes swiftly glided down throats, accompanied by an assortment of fruits and vegetables—wild, organic, or modified for different palate preferences.

Wine was flowing freely to wash down the state chefs' efforts.

At the far corner, a boar was roasting on a grill. Lovers of game lined up for a sizzling slice.

People were walking around, talking and exchanging of contacts details and ideas before the room was called to order.

As always, Zaire was taking it easy on the wine. Nysa, on the other hand, had already had too much and was openly flirting with Lorantu. She laughed out loudly and tapped on his thigh.

Barvo was lost in conversation with a new official that Zaire was not familiar with.

Ekesa was pensively sitting beside her husband, looking pink and horrible. Her makeup was smudged and in need of retouching. She knew she was supposed to go to the restroom to do that, but she sat tight.

The State Spokesman rose from his chair hitting a gong to call silence the crowd.

"Good evening!" he said. Welcome to all you important men and women, gods and goddesses of West Valley State and beyond—the State that is highly favored by the gods who have given it their own colleagues to rule and guide us with wisdom and understanding from the clouds. They bring the sun and moon at the right time; the two never collide."

There was a loud cheer and thunderous applause.

"With us, however, is the Statesman of Mountain Crest, another favored state. The gods of the hills and mountains sit still in readiness for anyone who dares to mess with the mountains so that they can pour hot lava on their faces."

There was another wild drunken uproar.

"Let us welcome our statesman who will allow his counterpart to make his remarks before introducing his royal family to his loyal servants."

Another loud applause.

Osanyin gets up and makes very brief remarks as instructed by Ploutus. He receives shouts and cheers as he sits after giving over to Ploutus.

"By my side," Ploutus began, "is the most beautiful woman on the planet: my wife, Ekesa, the mother of generations."

Ekesa smiled awkwardly and waved absent mindedly.

Ploutus turned to face Zaire.

"My son," he said, "the glory of my loins, Zaire. Stand up. I want the world to see you."

He turned back to face the audience.

"Contrary to what you have all been led to believe," he continued, "Zaire is not adopted. He is my flesh and blood." He drummed on his chest in pride, not noticing when Zaire signaled that he should stop.

He didn't notice Nysa dropping her glass in shock.

Neither did he notice his wife squirming in her seat like an animal attacked by hostile flies.

He continued talking about Zaire's intelligence and how he would be proud to announce him to be his heir in a few years' time.

The room fell silent.

Zaire was shocked beyond comparison. His hands flew to his head, desperate whispers escaping his lips. He muttered beneath his breath, cursing every second of that dinner. He knew all along that something was not right with Ploutus. He had a feeling that Ploutus was playing a dirty game to win elections, but he couldn't figure out what the moves were.

"What are you doing, sir?" Zaire asked, trying via the wireless security devices they both wore on such occasions to get Ploutus to stop.

Ploutus ignored him. He went on ranting about his son.

Before Ploutus could move on to introducing Nysa, Ekesa stood up and began to talk. Every eye turned to her.

Zaire jumped to her side and tried to pull her back down, but she resisted and yelled even more.

"And this is Nysa," she pointed at the startled girl who looked like she'd just been awakened from a nightmare. Lorantu was holding on to her tightly, but she tried her best to break loose.

"Please, Mom, sit down," said Zaire. "Don't embarrass yourself."

"I am not your mother, you bastard!" she yelled at Zaire, who retreated.

Zaire wanted to slip out and get away from the chaos that was on the edge of a cliff, leaving it to roll off. Instead, he requested the IO through his earpiece to send in more security and call for backup, since things were looking ugly.

"This is my daughter," continued Ekesa, "the girl hated by your Statesman because I had to buy seed from a bodyguard to get pregnant . . ."

Zaire was shocked by her words. He knew a lot of secrets about the Ploutus family, but this one had escaped his scrutiny.

Nysa broke out of Lorantu's arms. She went to her mother, giving her one look of disgust, and then dropped a slap on her sticky face.

The room gasped . . .

Suddenly, there was uproar among the guests.

Ploutus remained standing beside his wife, seeming to enjoy what was going on. He rubbed his hands together, watching, without making any attempt to separate them, as Nysa and Ekesa took turns abusing each other.

"It's a lie!" Nysa exclaimed. "You are lying! I am Nysa Ploutus! Ploutus is my father! Don't use me as a scapegoat for your fights, Mom!"

Almost crying, her voice was filled with tremors of rage.

"So, you think I'm lying?" replied Ekesa, looking at her daughter, then turning to face the crowd.

"You all think I'm crazy, right!" She yelled, addressing everyone. "Right? Well let me tell you the truth! You have no idea what kind of a devil sits in the Capital Chambers on your behalf, making decisions about all of you. You don't know who he is!"

"Should I have her locked up, sir?" Zaire asked Ploutus in a whisper.

"No," replied Ploutus. "Let her talk"

He said that loud enough for Ekesa to hear him.

Zaire wondered what the game plan was. He felt hazardously locked out and alarmed by the sudden publicity initiated by Ploutus. He looked forward to an explanation.

"See?" yelled Eklesa. "He is planning to have me killed by his son! I need security! I need protection!" She hysterically screamed out the last two sentences.

"I need protection! She yelled again, now frantic. "Guards! Guards!" she kept yelling frantically.

No one moved. The cameras were flashing and recorders were rolling. Tapes were being exchanged too.

"That boy is planning to kill you, Ploutus!" she carried on. "He will be the end of you! One day, you will remember this . . ."

She staggered back, took ahold of the table cloth on the main table, and walked away, dragging it with her, carrying her shoes in her hands. Behind her, she left a spectacular trail of breaking china, falling cutlery, clanging glasses, and diners darting out of the way in order to save their clothes from being soiled by food and drinks.

"You can take me to Ward Nine!" she said loudly, facing Ploutus.

She finally turned and made for the exit.

"Have me killed at the market square like you did your lover," she yelled as she reached the exit. She stopped, turned toward the crowd for the last time, and gave an extravagant curtsey and stepped into the elevator . . .

When Jotham pulled into the driveway of his compound, Najma's heart sank to the pit of her belly. She could feel it slide deeper as he approached the main gate.

When the gate rolled open and a short, stout man in uniform saluted the car as he drove in, her heart sunk and she cringed in pain.

He must be married, she thought. 'Else, why does he have such a huge house? Naturally, there has to be a wife? And why does it hurt me so much? What did I expect? He is Nana's son, anyway. He could also be my brother, like Zaire. Perhaps he is, who knows?

"Welcome to my humble abode," Jotham announced.

She looked around her, taking in every detail of the splendid, neatly kept compound. There was an unfathomable cloud of tranquility, causing both warmth and a cold stare from behind the rose and hibiscus bushes. The lawn was neatly mowed, and the lime green grass glistened beneath bulbs that shone on it all over the place.

A serving lady stood by the door, in a short pink plaid skirt and a plain pink blouse. She walked to the car and picked up his briefcase and books from the back seat. She opened the boot and took out a grocery bag full of fruits and vegetables.

"Hello, Kuti!" he greeted, smiling at the giggling girl. "How was your day?"

She had a perfect set of white teeth with a gap between her lower incisors. Her face was clean, smooth, and shiny like a river stone. She smelled like rose water. Najma couldn't help staring at her.

Kuti? Najma thought. *They are on first name terms. It is a tribal name, though. She must be from Bamboo. God, she is beautiful!*

"I am fine, sir," replied Kuti. "The day was fine. Welcome home, sir. Hello, madam." She curtsied shyly without looking at Najma's face.

Najma felt pity for her—and admiration at the same time. She looked like she was only a year or two older than herself and therefore should be in school or starting college. Najma nodded in response, not knowing what to say or do with her.

"This is Najma," said Jotham. "She is my special friend. She will be joining us for dinner. Make something special, okay Kuti?" he ordered, dropping an arm around Najma's shoulders. Najma held her breath. She was surprised when she saw Kuti do something like a dance of excitement behind them.

"Yes, sir," she responded and disappeared through another door with the briefcase, books, and grocery bag, giggling all the way.

"Is she okay?" Najma asked immediately when Kuti was out of reach.

"I guess she likes you. I never bring girls home. It's just excitement," he stated flatly.

So, he isn't married, thought Najma, feeling her heart settle back in its place.

"Shouldn't she be in school or something?" she asked to keep the conversation going.

"Yea," he replied. She takes evening culinary classes. She wants to be a chef."

"That's really nice," She replied absent-mindedly. "I love cooking too, sometimes. It is therapeutically relaxing."

Najma looked around once more, noticing that the whole compound was lush green. The house was a huge Victorian with marble details. The walking paths were mosaics set into the neat lawns. There were flower gardens and lawn benches.

"You like gardens?" he asked enthusiastically. "Should we sit outside?"

"Maybe I should say hi to your house first?" she teased. "Wife?"

"Nah," he replied. "I'm not married."

"Why?" she asked. "Not like it's any of my business."

"I'm not in a hurry," he replied. "Or let's say, I haven't met anyone I like yet."

He led her to the house. It was simple and elegant: grey box couches in the living room, glass stools and a matching table; a fluffy zebra patterned wall to wall carpet; tribal wall paintings; a carving of a naked woman and a grand piano near the dining set. A guitar box rested near the piano stand.

"Do you play?" she asked, walking towards the piano. She felt at ease.

"Yes," he replied. "I love music. Playing keeps me sane."

He followed her. Najma was engrossed in the keys and the magnificent stand. The piano sat on its stand like a god on a throne. It was beautifully majestic. She caressed the keys and closed her eyes when they vibrated in response.

"Teach me?" she asked, fumbling with the keys and the music papers. Key noises filled the tranquil house.

Kuti walked in stealthily with a tray of glasses.

"Sir, warm juice or frozen?" she asked timidly.

"Ask the lady," Jotham teased.

He watched her mouth curve in a naughty smile. Her long lashes swept her cheeks gently.

"We will do warm glasses of passion and pineapple smoothies. Use mint garnish on mine, and stick a straw of cinnamon in his, my dear," Najma said, smiling at Kuti.

Kuti nodded.

"Madam is very beautiful, sir," she said and walked out quickly, giggling.

Najma's eyes dropped to the piano. She trembled under his stare. She was sure she'd made an impression. She wanted him to see her in a different light—neither as a school girl nor Zaire's sister. She wanted him to see the Najma that was keen on details. The Najma who knew something more than the rest. She had seen him chewing on cinnamon sticks a few times, so she knew it was his favorite flavor.

"She's right, you know," he said deeply, touching her fingers that were spread resting on the piano. "You are really beautiful."

Her fingers, long and slightly fleshy, were crowned with white fingernails that looked like candle flames.

There was a flood of warmth under her skin. Her heart was racing. Her eyes sparkled, and his eyes were ablaze. He lowered himself onto a stool next to her, facing her. Their eyes locked for a moment.

"Let's see if you can play," he said, turning to the piano.

He played her favorite classic piece, "Deeper than You Know." Her heart was steady. Her eyes closed to the smooth melody that filled the room. She wanted to stand up, but her body was weak. She was floating. She couldn't feel her heart. Her eyes welled up, and she let her tears flow.

"Do you know the song?" he asked softly.

"It is my favorite song, Ham," she whispered.

He turned to look at her, noticing for the first time that she was crying.

He stopped playing, turned her stool to face him, and took her face in his palms. She gasped and tried to open her eyes but couldn't.

He lowered his face till their foreheads touched. For a moment, their eyes were closed, each feeding off the other's pain and pleasure. It was a magical connection. When they parted, her tears were dry. Her heart beat softly in her chest. She could feel it.

He picked an envelope from the stand and gave it to her. Najma opened it slowly. It contained a picture of herself in school uniform at Ward Nine. She was seated on a bench, under a tree. She looked at herself, two years ago, young and exhausted. In the photograph, there was a sad shade in her eyes, like she'd been crying. It was a beautiful picture. She stared at it so hard that she didn't notice when he stood up.

He stood still, waiting for her to look up. She didn't. He lifted her chin with his fingers and looked into her eyes.

"You were only sixteen. It's okay," he said, his eyes burrowing deeply into hers.

It seemed like his eyes were saying something different than what came from his mouth. She wanted to understand it but was scared.

In a panic, she stood up and walked to the couch, sat at the edge, and rubbed her sweaty palms on her grey dress. She suddenly felt insecure. She felt uncomfortable around him. She thanked heavens when Kuti walked in with glasses of juice and a playful smile on her face. She needed a distraction.

Najma wasn't sure if she was happy or not. She didn't understand what she felt. A few hours ago, she longed to see Jotham. She wanted to talk to him. She wanted him to tell her it was okay to go to boarding school. She wanted an assurance that Zaire was being honest. She also wanted to bid him farewell, just in case she never saw him again. Now she just wanted to walk away and never come back.

The photo changed everything. She couldn't tell exactly what it was that had changed, and that made it more confusing.

Why does he have a picture of me? she wondered. What else does he have? What does he know? Something is not adding up. Why did Zaire not object to bringing me to him? What plans do they have? I need to get out of here . . .

She lifted her face to look at the chiming wall clock. It was just 7.00 p.m. There were still two more hours before Zaire was due to pick her up.

"I want to go home," she said flatly after a long silence. He said nothing. He just sat across her and stared at her. After a while, he spoke. "You can tell me." He said. "What is bothering you?"

His voice had a thick film of feelings around it. She couldn't explain his tone. Her feelings confused her.

"Please take me home," she begged, tears brimming in her eyes.

"Zaire will come for you," he replied, desperate and clueless. "What happened Najma? Did I do something wrong?"

"I'm just scared," she said. "That's all."

"Why?" he asked. He suddenly got up, walked to her and sat down beside her. He took a folder from beneath the table and handed it to her.

She opened it, her fingers trembling. She didn't know what to expect anymore.

The folder contained pictures of her and her mother—many of them.

In some photos, she was walking in the gardens of the hospital with her mother. In others, she was reading her mother a book. In others, she was sitting beside Elima's bed, watching her sleep peacefully. In others, Najma was giving Elima medicine.

It felt like her whole life from two years ago was replaying before her. She had all of it on her lap . . .

Najma was mystified by the photographs. It was the sweetest surprise. She didn't notice when Kuti set the table for dinner, stealing glances at them. She didn't notice when Jotham got a clean handkerchief and wiped her delicate face. She didn't know when she surrendered to him and let him hold her in his arms.

"Do you still want to visit Ward Nine?" His voice jolted her back.

"No," she said, smiling. "I think I'm hungry."

He didn't have to tell her that dinner was for the two of them. The beautiful table said it all. The flowers and candles made her teary eyes glitter. He took a picture of her again.

This time, she was aware and she struck a model's pose.

"Why?" she asked, sipping on a glass of juice. She was only eighteen and still a student. Wine was out of the question.

"Because I really like you, Najma," he declared. "More than you will ever know."

"I'm too young for you," she replied.

"I didn't mean it that way," he teased. "At least not for now," He quickly continued when he read hurt in her eyes.

"Will you wait for me?" she asked after a while.

"For how long?" he asked teasingly.

"Till I clear my psychology degree," she hinted.

"That's what you want to study?" He was taken aback.

"Does it make me less beautiful?" Her eyes widened with the question.

"No, of course not," he said. "On the contrary. It makes you more attractive."

Her eyes faltered in shyness. "Do you think I have what it takes?" she asked.

"You are the most intelligent and elegant girl I have ever met," he stated.

"Then psychology it is."

The gate rolled open while they were eating their dessert and discussing a book they had both read. Zaire was there to pick her up. He accepted Jotham's invitation to share a beer with him as Najma ate her ice-cream and listened to some music on Jotham's iPad.

An hour later, they left.

The cluttering dinner was something of the past.

Everyone knew that Osanyin had left West Valley.

Business was back to normal for Ploutus.

The two statesmen sat in silence, each occupied with their own thoughts. Neither of the two states knew the exact whereabouts of their King. Each was here secretly. They were in one of Osanyin's unidentified personal vehicles.

Keeping the journey private was important.

The chauffeur was sworn to secrecy. It wasn't like he wasn't aware of what happened to those who gave out secret information.

The bodyguards were also familiar with the 'tongueless' rule. There were only two of the most trusted bodyguards on this trip, one for each of the statesmen.

The whole team sat quietly. Each eye was fixed on something—a phone or a book.

Afula pensively sat beside the driver, her eyes fixed on the dark road.

*****

Osanyin thought about what was in store for him. He fully trusted the doctor they were visiting.

However, his friend Ploutus looked like he was developing some doubts. His hopes for having Ploutus re-elected was fully dependent on this visit. He desperately needed Ploutus to stay in power. Ploutus's outburst, especially about Zaire, had upset Osanyin. Ploutus looked like one who was staging a fit and was becoming senselessly edgy about everything.

Ploutus, on the other hand, was very skeptical about the visit and the doctor in general. On their first visit, the Cosmos doctor had demanded things that Ploutus found impossible to procure: a newt's eye, the hide of a black raccoon, and a root of the mimosa, among others. Osanyin ensured that all the items were available for the winning ritual.

The doctor had also said that Ploutus was to never ejaculate into a woman's private parts, especially his wife's, until his ruling period came to an end. He foretold trouble and a storm that would engulf his empire if he dared do otherwise. He said by disobeying, Ploutus would be smearing dirt on his luck.

The doctor also revealed that Ploutus's luck spirits dwelt in the depths of women, and he should treat those depths with respect by not smearing his seed all over them if he wanted to lead successfully.

At first, Ploutus had though it unrealistic. That night, he had met Ekesa with such a ferocious desire that he'd forgotten to follow the doctor's instructions.

The following morning, there was an inexplicable fire in his oil company and his penis was shriveled for weeks. After that, it had then suffered inexplicable blisters that his doctors had found impossible to cure.

Ploutus was forced to go back to Cosmos for a cleansing potion. This had been the beginning of his worry about what he was getting himself into. When he'd won the elections for the second time, even though his name was tainted with scandals, he had begun to partially believe in Cosmos's magic.

*****

Osanyin interrupted his thoughts. "Why are you doing this, Ploutus?"

"Do what?" Ploutus asked absent-mindedly.

"This isn't a joke," replied Osanyin. "We are deep into this. Going back won't be easy."

*****

For a moment, Ploutus was scared. Osanyin's tight, mature face reminded him of Cosmos on the first day they had visited. Ploutus had thought it was a joke. He had never been to a sorcerer before, and the moment was awkward.

"You think this is a joke, young man?" Cosmos had growled, his tiny eyes suddenly red, his unkempt beard twitching in anger. His face was the darkest shade of grey, wrinkled and tough. Though his body was that of a younger man, his face looked old. There was something about his face that had scared Ploutus to death.

Osanyin had insisted that the man was effective and his potions had never failed.

At that time, Ploutus was contesting for statesmanship for the second time. He had easily taken over for Ekesa's father who had groomed him like one would his own son.

Ekesa's brother, Umali, the hypothetical heir to the non-hereditary "throne" of West Valley state had openly declared his lack of interest in politics, thus falling meters away from his old man's withering hands for the final blessing.

The old man had died in his sleep a night after sending Ekesa's brother away on an errand beyond the four states. On his way back, news of the old man's death had made Umali call for a celebration. He had gotten into a drunken fight, ending up with a broken beer bottle in his skull.

On the day of his father's cremation, the only bodyguard who'd been brave enough to face anyone who cared about the boy, had brought Umali home.

Ploutus, who had just been engaged to the sister, Ekesa, had to take over the issue. The rest of the security team that had accompanied Ekesa's brother ran away, fearing for their lives. Ploutus had never bothered to trace them.

Ekesa had mourned her brother Umali for a week. The doctors had said that the piece of glass was lodged deep in the brain and that a surgery would have been fatal.

He was euthanized later, to save the family cost and more pain.

Ploutus felt lucky when his father-in-law and brother-in-law paved an easy way for his ascension to power. The family had been hit by tragedy, and the only way the state could show sympathy was to at least reward the immediate suitable family member with the ruling mantel. His way to the party nomination was a smooth sail. The old man had already recommended him to those who pledged allegiances. He was accepted quickly because, at that time, he was engaged to Ekesa and ran his own oil company, which supplied refined oil to all of the four states and beyond. His father-in-law had appointed him the patron of his property, and Ekesa and the children the beneficiaries.

Now, with much regret, Ploutus considered how power had changed him. He had wanted to live a private life away from the public eye. He remembered how Ekesa had begged him to take the position.

At the same time, the love of his life, Elima, was pregnant with his child and was dropping out of college for him. He had promised to marry Elima.

There was a web of messy events around him that he was unable to untangle himself from. Important people had seen to it that he ascended to power, to continue the allegiances and legacies that his father-in-law had begun.

On the day of his first inaugural ceremony, he was late by an hour. He had gone to see Elima. The news of his marriage to Ekesa and statesmanship had hit her in the face like a sledgehammer. She was devastated. She'd almost lost the baby.

He remembered her face turning blue in anger and pain when he told her he was going to contend for the statesmanship and was going to marry the former Statesman's daughter just before the Election Day. Elima had gasped for air and staggered. She'd rolled back her eyes and had collapsed in his arms.

Their daughter had been born prematurely. To save her, she had to be incubated for two months. He'd seen the tiny little thing struggle to survive in the incubator. That was the first and last time he'd ever seen his daughter.

With his lover bedridden and sick and his baby in a glass box surrounded by cables and purring machines, his heart had been broken into tiny pieces. He had walked away, tears soaking his then well-chiseled face.

He went straight to the Capital to tell the Statesman then that he wanted the wedding arranged as fast as possible, and it was done.

The elections ran smoothly, and he won by a large margin.

When he went to see Elima to tell her that he had won and was going to take her as his second wife because the state allowed it, she was nowhere to be found. The baby wasn't there either. There was no one to tell him where she'd gone to. It had wrecked his nerves. His heart was in a million pieces.

Ploutus sat on the royal chair in the capital chambers with glee. Having lost everything that mattered to him, his love and his daughter, he had focused on what he had gained in exchange: statesmanship. The aura of power had felt like a million orgasms. He knew he belonged there.

He started by altering the laws to favor his third re-election within the first two years of sitting. He had more positions created for his cronies in the business sector. He had his oil empire expanded and spread to the rest of the continent. He began to export gold and secretly print his own money. He made coalitions with the other three states—Lake Side, Mountain Crest, and Plateau

Plains, and made great business deals that benefitted not only his empire but the entire state of Valley View.

By the time that the first term was coming to an end, the entire media was painted with the greatness of Ploutus. There was a neat spiral of roads in the capital and beyond. Industries were running. There was clean water. Young people were getting employed. The farmers in the villages were reaping from their products. The miners got better equipment, and their gold was bought as soon as they got it from under the rocks. Schools were renovated, and basic education was made free.

Ploutus thought of the pride he'd exuded when he walked around, his subjects calling him a god. They'd literally worshipped him.

He enjoyed it when they'd lined up along the streets to wave at his motorcade. When he stepped out of the Pullman, they'd literally collapsed onto their knees with their faces mopping the roads. Women had cried in awe.

He'd hold a child in his arms once in a while to increase his public relations polls. On such days, he'd carpet the roads with new crisp bills, and his subjects would scramble to collect as much as they could, like hens scraping the ground for maize.

He was a lucky man. He'd even forgotten about Elima for a while, while she rotted away in the village and his daughter struggled with the mental condition that had come with the post-delivery stress and trauma.

It wasn't until Nana had come to the Capital, looking for him with the news about Elima that Ploutus had remembered.

The memory was like an itchy pimple that had grown into a painful cyst.

*****

"We're almost here, Ploutus," Osanyin said, switching him back to the trip. "I hope there is no mistake in the packaging. Did your boy ensure that the money is well printed? Papa Cosmos doesn't take mistakes kindly. He can help you remain in power forever, my friend—if you want to . . ."

*****

His thoughts wandered off again to Elima. He was no longer interested in what they were coming to do. He didn't want to be Statesman. He wanted to go and find his daughter, talk to her, embrace her, and tell her that he loved her. He might have lost Elima, but he wasn't willing to lose his daughter, Najma, as well.

*****

"Man, you need to come back!" demanded Osanyin. "What are you thinking about?"

"I don't want to go back to power," declared Ploutus. "I'm not running for the third term."

He didn't want to take the parts that were cut off Elima's body to the witchdoctor. He was not ready to see her breasts, tongue, teeth and private parts messed up in sorcery.

"Cosmos can go to hell!" he said. "I don't believe in this shit anymore. I'm tired, Osanyin."

"What's wrong with you?!" Osanyin almost jumped in his seat. "Are you coming down with something? First it was the public declaration at dinner about Zaire, and now this? What is going on?"

"I just want a quiet life, Osanyin!" declared Ploutus. "I'm tired of struggling; of killing; of losing the people I love. I just want to go to my daughter and bring her home. I want to give Ekesa the divorce she wants. I never loved her anyway."

Ploutus looked like he was in a trance.

"I am tired of using my son to clean the messes I create," he continued. "He's barely thirty, and he needs his own life."

Osanyin was lost for words. They had come too far to back down now. There was a stiff competition against him, and his dirty deals were threatening to spill all over each public sector. Ploutus's opponents had stepped on a sewer lid regarding Ploutus's life, and the smell was all over. Osanyin knew that if Ploutus went down, his own state would not spare him either. His rivals were working towards exposing his dealings in West Valley. It would be disastrous if Ploutus went down. Losing that election would render Ploutus open for investigations. Cosmos would save them the pain.

"My friend," Osanyin tried to reason, "Everyone desires power, but it comes at a cost. Losing family is one of those costs. It is too late to turn back."

"It is never too late," said Ploutus. "I have a plan. Remember what Cosmos said about my son?"

They both recalled . . .

*****

"You have a son from your heyday," declared Cosmos that night, addressing Ploutus. His voice thundered above the chirruping of the crickets and the croaking of the frogs in the bamboo swamp. The fireflies dimmed their lights at the declaration. His mouth curved into a mean smile when the cowry shells landed on the cobra skin that was spread the earth floor.

"He will be your rise and fall," he said. "You need him with you if you want to go back to the Capital Chambers. He will be the reason you will leave as well. He must be brought into the fold, and when you are done with him, kill him. The gods want him for a sacrifice. His blood will wash away your evils. His blood will silence the blood you will shed when sitting on the royal stool."

That day, Ploutus had walked out of the tiny room trembling. He knew the son Cosmos was talking about. He knew Zaire was in an orphanage then.

Zaire's mother had wanted to trap Ploutus with a one-night stand by falling pregnant. How could he leave Elima for her younger sister? He had to clean the scandal before it got out of hand. He had tried to force Zaire's mother to get rid of the pregnancy, but she refused. She wanted to use it as her economical leverage. When things did not work out as she had planned, she'd dropped Zaire at the orphanage and ran off to Lakeside with a rich man.

Ploutus had followed her trail and had her and the new husband killed before adopting Zaire from the orphanage. He didn't want anything to jump out of the closet to mess up his charity script that he was staging for the elections. When he declared that he was adopting Zaire, the polls rose like a thermometer on a feverish body. Every tongue sang his name. Every wave from the media came rolling with his kindness. Cosmos was right. Zaire was his way up . . . and down.

*****

Osanyin was panic-stricken

"Ploutus," he said. You have to get rid of the boy as instructed."

"I will not kill my son," Said Ploutus with finality. "I don't want to go back to the Capital. If you are scared of going down, you can sever our links tonight. I am going to give that Cosmos man a piece of mind tonight."

The body guards were visibly uncomfortable. The talk was escalating. They were about to hear what they weren't supposed to. There were only the two of them—one for each—and if anything happened, it would be bodyguard against bodyguard to save the master.

"You are not thinking straight, man!" exclaimed Osanyin.

"I know what I'm doing," said Ploutus calmly.

"We will all go to prison if our deals are made public," Osanyin said resignedly.

"Then we will be paying for our mistakes," declared Ploutus. "Our sins. But I'm not going to humiliate the love of my life in that shithole. That pervert doctor of yours can eat his own shit. I am done."

The rest of the ride was quiet. No one spoke. Afula sat still, having listened to the men talk all this time, and said nothing.

The car drove up a narrow bamboo-lined path that led to doctor Cosmos's home. He now had a mansion with a main gate. He had a decent room for his practice and a whole spare wing for his guests.

Some spent nights there with the spirits to get their problems solved.

Some had spirit babies in the process.

Some sacrificed their relatives.

All for riches, power, and influence . . .

As usual, the bodyguards got out of the car first. They surveyed the area and then signaled for the statesmen to get out.

Osanyin got out first, then Ploutus.

"Please don't ruin this," begged Osanyin.

Ploutus kept quiet. He walked towards Afula, who rode in the front chauffeur to help with directions.

"If you back down now," she warned in a mean, firm tone, "there will be consequences. This road we took has no turning back."

She was wearing a tight trouser suit with a bright yellow veil on her head. The veil made her head look like a bulb in the darkness. She had high heels on as usual, and when their eyes got used to the dim light, Ploutus noticed that she was wearing her makeup right. She also had a small bag with her.

"I will be spending the night here," she declared. "I need to be cleansed of Elima's spirit. She is haunting me. The doctor said her spirit will be bound with another dead man's spirit for her to leave me alone."

With that, she began to walk toward the servant who had been sent to receive them.

Zaire drove silently, on their way from Jotham's place. Najma kept stealing glances at her pensive brother. She had seen him serious before but this time there was something off about him.

Zaire had realized that he was not up to date with the events that were taking place in the castle. There was obviously a lot that he needed to find out. His plan was to start his mission of revenge at the beginning of the election month, but things were playing out differently. He needed to talk to Ploutus to find out what was cooking. Ploutus was behaving strangely, and the sudden outbursts from Ekesa were disquieting.

What were they playing at?

Could he still trust them around him?

Was it time to move out of the castle?

He wished his godfather was still alive. Father Cruz would have given him some insight. He had taught him to always listen to his instincts. But no matter how hard he tried, his instincts were mute on this matter. He felt something was really amiss, but couldn't lay a finger on it.

"How was your dinner event, by the way?" Najma asked when she noticed that her brother was abnormally contemplative." There was nothing on the news about it."

Zaire knew he had covered up all the media leakages on the dinner, and if Najma had not seen anything about it on open platforms, then he had done a perfect job.

He had called all the media houses earlier and warned them against broadcasting anything about the dinner, unless he reviewed the footages of what was to be uploaded. He also ensured that the videos leaked on open social platforms were pulled down as soon as they were posted, and were made invisible.

It was explained to the public that the videos were pulled down for security reasons.

Later, Zaire had asked the State Spokesperson to address the state early, to clear the air and the murmurs. He also had told him to include a small section on Ekesa's outbursts, insisting that they should be linked to her bipolar condition that she had suffered as a child.

"Dinner was okay," he replied, trying to maintain composure in his voice. He failed miserably.

"How was it really?" she asked, watching his face.

"Just a few mishaps," he replied, looking at her. "Things you will hear about . . . but don't pay any attention to it. The media is always nosy and publishes information that is untrue," he said.

Suddenly, a wild raccoon crossed the road from the bushes. Before he could step on the brake pedal, he had run over the poor thing.

Hitting a raccoon was either a good omen or a bad omen, depending on the color. It was dark, and they couldn't tell whether it was a grey one for good luck or a black one.

"I hope it was a grey raccoon," Zaire groaned. "I can't survive more bad luck tonight."

"Gosh, Zaire! You believe in that crap?" Najma exclaimed.

"In my world, both heavenly covering and ancestral gods are important. You can't afford to be on the wrong side with any." His voice trembled miserably.

"You are not okay, Zaire. Pull over, Najma ordered. "We need to talk."

Zaire had never seen this version of her. He pulled over like a child who has been ordered to do something by a strict mother.

Najma threw her arms around her brother and held him for a moment. She noticed his body move from being rigid with surprise to relaxing in surrender. She then let him go and started interrogating him.

"Now talk to me. What is going on?" Her voice was thin and straight. It cut through him. It bared his hidden worries, and he spilled every detail of what he felt was worth disclosing about the dinner, leaving out the part where Ploutus called him his blood son. Najma listened keenly, as if looking for loopholes in the story. She threw in questions here and there to ascertain what her brother was saying.

"Is she bipolar?" she asked when he finished spinning his yarn of tale.

"She was," he responded.

"How did you know?" she asked.

"I snooped around in her past," he said.

"I am going to need your boyfriend on her case," he added urgently.

Najma knew that he was trying to hit below the belt to divert her. She let his remarks pass.

"Is she aware that you have revealed her condition to the public?" she asked.

"No," he said flatly. She will be shocked. She attacked me publicly, and I had to defend myself."

"What if she decides to sue you?" she asked, her eyes wide with worry. "What about Hon, Ploutus? Will he be okay with you revealing that about the first lady?"

"I will brief him as soon as I get to see him. I am doing this for him." He started the car engine after saying this.

"Can we go now? I need to get back to the castle and see if everything is back in order," he declared.

"Okay," she agreed. "Just don't kill more raccoons because you are angry. They have no part in your fate. And, for the record, Ham is not my boyfriend."

He drove off with a smile on this face. His previously tensed body was relaxed, and his face looked less worried. His eyes were clearer, and the veins that had lined his forehead had disappeared.

"I want to study psychology in college. Ham thinks the best college for that is in Lakeside. Will you let me visit there with him when I come back from Mountain Crest?" she asked after a while.

"That is a whole year from now, darling," he said.

"Just answer me," She persisted. "I won't forget to remind you when the time comes."

"I will let you go with him. If you—"

"No conditions, Zaire," she said, cutting him short. "Either you do, or you don't."

"Okay, girl," he said as he pulled up at the front porch of Najma's house. "You can go to Lakeside with your boyfriend after you finish school."

The lights were on. That meant Nana was still awake. Najma remembered the secret about Ham. How was she ever going to look Nana in the eyes and tell her nothing? What if she'd been searching for him? What if she was suffering loss and guilt, thinking her son was dead? Najma wanted Nana to find out. But then, there were a few questions that she needed to ask Nana first. As Nana opened the door to let them in with warm hugs, Najma shot the question amid pleasantries.

"Nana, are you related to me by any means by blood?" Najma asked, shocking both Nana and Zaire.

"What do you mean, my girl? she asked, eyeing Zaire suspiciously. "What has your brother been telling you?"

"I guess I have had enough surprises for tonight, I am just going to let you two talk." With that, he pecked Nana on the cheeks and pulled Najma in his arms for a goodnight hug.

"We will be shopping tomorrow," he said to Najma. "Don't go to school. I've already cleared you there."

He didn't wait for Najma's response.

Najma and Nana walked out with him to see him off, and a few seconds later, he was gone.

He had done her a favor. She didn't want to go through the process of explaining to her teachers where she was going and why. She was also glad that she didn't have to see the mean boys and girls from her school again.

She thanked God for Zaire and his wisdom, then walked to the house, following Nana's heels closely.

Nana was clearly upset by her question, but she needed to hear her answer it. It was hard imagining life in future without Ham, just because they were related. She would rather deal with her loss now.

Najma sat down, looking at Nana in anticipation.

"Your mother was my sister," Nana said immediately as she took a seat across Najma. "Her parents took me in when my parents were killed in a tribal war long ago. We were not related in any way, but they took me in because of her father, who was a kind chief back then. We grew up together."

"So, there is no blood relation between us?" Najma asked, her eyes on Nana's face.

"None," she said flatly, her eyes fixed on the carpet. Najma saw the hurt in them. She saw how pained she was. Najma was sad that she had made Nana gloomy but elated that nothing was going to hinder a future relationship with Ham.

"Don't be sad, Nana, you will always be my mom. I promise."
She went to her and threw her arms around her. Nana embraced
her tenderly as she had always done since she was a child.

"I hate black raccoons," Nana said after letting Najma go.
"When I found one on the porch today, I knew you were coming
with some terrible things to tell me."

Najma remembered the raccoon that Zaire hit.

"Oh my God!" Najma whispered. "It was a black raccoon."

"What are you talking about, baby?" Nana almost screamed.

"Zaire ran over a raccoon on our way here," she mumbled.

"That is horrible!" said Nana. "That is so bad. That is a dark
omen!"

The two ladies sat pensively, saying nothing to each other
afterwards.

"That boy has a dark cloud around his head," said Nana. "I
hope it clears. Oh God, let it clear."

It was more of a plea than a statement.

THE SPIRITS – PART 1

When Ploutus started doing business with Osanyin's crew,
West Valley became a Super State. West Valley produced oil and
supplied to the other states.

West Valley undertook to supply geothermal power and
purchased Green energy from Plateau Plains State, supplying it to
the other four states.

Ploutus had his own empire going on besides running West
Valley Matters. He had the biggest and most exotic palace in the
four states and the most loyal servants on the globe. He hated the
thought of not being powerful.

When he pushed for a referendum to change the term limits
for statesmen, his popularity took a massive knock since this move

was significantly opposed by the opposition. As usual, though, he succeeded, forcing his way to endorsement of three terms instead of two. Polls at that time showed that his opponent was far ahead. The state was upset with him, and citizens wanted him out. He tried using the media to calm the incited masses down, but there was an attempted coup and he nearly got overthrown. At this point, Osanyin and Cosmos entered the arena, introducing the potion that Ploutus had paid dearly for.

Osanyin had taken Ploutus to Cosmos alone the first two visits, but from then onward, Afula had accompanied them each time they visited the sorcerer.

Ploutus had learned that it was Afula who'd introduced Osanyin to Cosmos and that they had made a pact of being spiritual soul mates. He'd also discovered that Afula had been given a potion for wealth in exchange for her womb, which was the reason why she could never bear children. Her spirit had been married off to Osanyin's and they were procreating in the spirit world, producing lots of spirit children to take care of their physical needs.

Each time that Osanyin had visited West Valley, he'd met with Afula, and together they'd connect spiritually to sire more spirit babies for the world of sorcery.

Osanyin, on the other hand, had to forfeit his ability to make his legal wife pregnant ever again, in order to gain renewed health to rule for as long as possible.

He had an unmarried daughter back in Mountain Crest. He wanted his daughter to have a son, who would take over the kingdom when he was gone, but it was taking time and his daughter was not in a hurry to settle down.

He gave his scrotum to the spirit world to procreate—not only for Afula but for any available spirit womb that Cosmos would demand. Osanyin had done it faithfully for years and he was now on his fourth term since the constitution in Mountain Crest allowed for a Statesman to rule all the way to his grave, as long as his subjects loved him.

Mountain Crest, unlike West Valley, Plain Plateau, and Lakeside, was stuck in its hereditary kind of ruling that allowed members of only one tribe to rule. The chosen royal tribe would stay in power until the gods decided otherwise.

Osanyin's tribe was favored with leadership and herbalist title roles across the whole state. They were curers of even the darkest infections. However, Osanyin had no son to take over the throne, and his cousins had threatened to grab the scepter from his house. He also had an infection in his stomach that was ailing him. No herbs back at home were working. Cosmos's potion only worked when he was with Afula. He was afraid that he would die before his daughter could bear a son.

*****

This night, each of the three had their personal reasons for visiting Cosmos in Bamboo Village.

Osanyin wanted his stomach cleansed to buy him time till his daughter bore a son. He wanted protection from death and any disease that would rob him of the scepter. He also wanted to renegotiate the terms under which Cosmos had put him. He needed a son for the future of his name.

After talking to Ploutus and reading his mood, he had developed another need . . . Protection from jail and exposure. That was a tall order, he knew, but he believed there was nothing the spirits could deny him; had he not serviced the spirit world with his own seed for years? Had he not let the hungry spirit women suck on him like vampires, draining all his energy and leaving none left for his own wife? What could the spirit world possibly deny him?

Ploutus, on the other hand, wanted his freedom back.

He wanted to be able to make love to his wife without torturing her.

He wanted to let his son live.

He wanted to introduce his real daughter to the world.

He wanted to be able to mourn his lost love and expose Afula for killing her.

He wanted to let go of the capital and the businesses that Cosmos had helped him capture for himself.

He felt like he had killed enough people to quench the thirsts of the spirit. They demanded the blood of his son, and now and it was not going to happen. Had he not quenched them with the blood of his only love, Elima? They had demanded that she be of pure heart, incapable of harming anyone—a mental weakness. They had said they needed her pained and anguished by love. Elima had been the perfect candidate. It was as if they had known exactly how to describe her.

*****

Cosmos had assigned Afula with the task of having Elima killed, both for herself and for Ploutus.

Afula had killed Elima gaily. She had enjoyed every slice on her flesh. When she had her kidnapped that Sunday, after Elima's daughter had left for church, it felt like a dream come true. Cosmos had told her that, to heal her womb and release it from the burden of spiritual pregnancies, she'd have to bring a fertile spirit to replace her. It had to be a royal one too.

Elima was a daughter of a Chief. She'd gotten pregnant by Ploutus. Ploutus was from a royal house. Therefore, Elima was the perfect subject.

Together with Ploutus, Afula, Osanyin, and Cosmos had plotted to have Elima killed.

Ploutus had sent Zaire, who watched over Elima and Najma, on an out-of-state errand that fateful Sunday, providing a chance to have Elima kidnapped. By the time he had returned, Elima was already missing and he could not do anything to rescue her.

For extra pleasure, Afula had Elima assaulted before having her murdered. She'd hated Elima in life.

Growing up in the village, Elima was the princess, while Afula was the witch's daughter.

Elima had three beautiful sisters, Nana included, while Afula was always on her own.

The sisters always had the finest of clothes and many admirers, and Afula hated them.

Her mother had tried to cast spells on them, but royal charms protected them.

It wasn't until the girls broke their father's heart that they were accessible. Losing their father's protective love had left them vulnerable.

Just before Afula's mother died, she granted Afula her wish of seeing the four girls suffer. She planted premature death by related hand on the youngest, Akusa, mental grief on Elima, guilt and loneliness on Arthenia, and toil without fruition on their adopted sister Nana. That is why Nana had attracted a peasant's son and why she'd eventually lost her love and spent her life toiling for others.

Every day that Elima sat on her shop's doorstep with her beautiful daughter had caused Afula excruciating emotional pain. The young child looked like the full moon to Afula. Afula always felt mocked by the madwoman and her child.

The day she had pushed Elima down the stairs had been a good day to Afula. No one said anything to reprimand her.

How she'd longed for the day she would have a daughter too. What right did a mad woman have over her? Why would the gods not favor her?

She'd ensured that Elima was thoroughly tormented before her miserable life was extinguished. She'd watched with satisfaction—every minute of it—thinking about her own excruciating pain that she had to go through every time Osanyin, or any other spirit man that Cosmos had sent to her, had to impregnate her spirit.

*****

Afula was not here this night to set herself free from the torture of spiritual conception. She'd gotten used to it. She had started to enjoy the nights when spirits filled her and planted dark slimy seeds in her. She had learned how to get over the pain.

The only thing that had bothered her, was the spirit of Elima. In her moment of ecstasy, watching her being tortured, she had missed Elima's spirit as it had left her body. Instead of it walking into the bottle that was supposed to hold it captive, it had left the room and floated away. She had been unable to catch it and present it for its work. It would be impossible to appease the rewarding gods if she could not capture Elima's spirit.

To rid herself from the constant attacks by Elima's spirit, Cosmos had arranged a mating spree for the spirits of the underworld and the roaming spirits. Osanyin and Afula both had to be present because their spirits would be participating in the spree. Theirs were the royal ones, and they needed to show the way. There was hope that the aroma of mating would attract Elima's spirit.

However, since it was a spirit scorned by love, Cosmos wasn't sure if it would comply. It could be repulsed by the call of mating and choose to run away from any sign of love from other spirits. That would mean that he would not be able to present the sacrifices to the gods.

Afula should not have tortured Elima. Cosmos had instructed her to ensure that Elima died peacefully and the necessary body parts be brought in without being tarnished. But Elima's private parts had been soiled by common seed and he had to cleanse them with the blood of the perpetrators. If Cosmos could not present the sacrifices to the gods, Afula would have to pay for torturing Elima to death with her own life. Afula could only escape death if Elima showed up tonight to be captured. This, Cosmos had not yet disclosed to Afula.

*****

There was a tense atmosphere in the spirit room when the trio walked in.

Covered in smoke, Cosmos was in his feather costume, burning incense and chanting incantations. His legs were apart and sunken in the ground, covered with a thick, slimy substance all the way to his knees. He was facing the wall of fire.

"Don't come any closer!" he shouted amid incantations.

The servant who'd received the trio handed them each an altar robe and a head covering. He waited for them to take off their clothes and shoes to and replace with what he'd given them. He took away the clothes and the trio dipped themselves in the black gowns and hooded their heads, then bowed in supplication as Cosmos continued to chant.

GODS AND GODDESSES – Artemis and Arthenia

"What are you going to do, sister girl?" Artemis asked Ekesa, her voice dropping lower because of the approaching footsteps on the corridor. "The media has been told about your childhood condition. And you never even told your closest friends about it?"

All media houses, visual and print, were discussing mental issues narrowing down to the first lady.

"I don't know, my friend," replied Ekesa. Perhaps I should just give up the fight. The psychiatrist is on my case already. They think I'm a lunatic. I will never win against Ploutus and his son. They are always a step ahead."

She rubbed her puffy eyes with a piece of cotton wool dipped in cucumber water and lemon. She had a honey mask on her cheeks and coffee grinds on her forehead to cure the wrinkles that her stress was causing. She looked extremely tired.

"Can I come in?" Nysa peeped through the door and squinted due to the luminous green light that washed across the castle's private parlor.

"Yea, come in, baby," her mother cooed. The other two ladies exchanged knowing looks and focused on the girl who had just cat walked into the parlor.

"What are you gossipers looking at?" Nysa wanted to know. She curled her lip and addressed Artemis before turning to Arthenia, who sat coiled on a couch away from Artemis and Ekesa, and nodded a greeting at her.

Arthenia had a fashion magazine on her lap, covering the bare thighs that her short, green velvet skirt had failed to cover. She was wearing a black crop top, exposing her pierced navel, which had two silver rings and a diamond. Next to her was an ivory-legged stool with a glass top, hosting a long glass of lemonade with cuttings of mint leaves floating on top.

"Girl, watch your mouth. We are like your mothers here!" Artemis threw her the words with an angry look hidden behind her long lashes and thick purple eye shadow. She craned her long neck to look at the shoes that Nysa was wearing.

"Nice shoes though. Can I borrow them for dinner tonight? I'm meeting up with Lorantu, ladies."

She smirked after saying that last bit, then eyed Nysa for a reaction but got none.

"No," replied Nysa. "They were a gift and I can't share them. Plus, you should be able to guess whom I got them from."

Nysa's words were laced with sarcasm. She bent near her mother to whisper in her ears. Nearly half of her behind was in Artemis's face.

"Girl, move your shit away from my face!" Artemis shouted, slapping Nysa's behind playfully.

"Sorry!" retorted Nysa as she stood upright. "I'm done anyway. You can go on gossiping now, hypocrites . . ." She quickly turned and walked toward the exit. When she reached the door, she posed like a model on a runway, turned to her mom and said: "Momma, these bitches aren't your friends."

She walked out, banging the door behind her.

Nysa's words echoed in the suddenly quiet room, leaving behind a wisp of strong rosewood, lavender, and traces of chocolate. Her bangles jingled and her stilettoes made a *ting tong* sound on the tiles as she walked down the hallway.

"Ekesa, you need to put some reigns on your daughter," said Artemis. "I heard she was all over my man during your nasty dinner."

She stood up to refill her glass of vodka and added some ice cubes from the freezer.

"And you need to reduce your intake, lady." Ekesa lashed back. "You will start peeing vodka soon!"

"Your girl is treading on murky ground, baby; and those bangles she wears will make her limbs lame one of these days!"

Artemis threw the words with her head tilted backwards, laughing at her own joke.

"Shall we talk about something better than balls and bangles please?" interjected Arthenia, rocking quietly on the mahogany rocking chair that swallowed most of her thin frame. "The jingle is too loud . . ."

The trio went on talking about Ekesa and her fate now that everyone knew she was mentally unstable. The public was already sending in encouraging messages to Ploutus and applauding him for keeping it a secret for years.

One or two bloggers wrote about bipolar disorder in detail and why it was impossible for Ekesa to get children. Subsequently, Ploutus was excused for having a son out of wedlock. There were questions about Nysa's parentage on some sites; others discussed Ekesa, surmising that she was only able to give birth to one child in her lifetime.

"Can you believe those idle online rumor mongers?" Ekesa spat out the words forcefully, almost falling off her seat. "They have the cheek to doubt my impeccable fertility? I am a normal woman, for heaven's sake!"

"I believe it was all Zaire's doing," Arthenia said with a fake sneer on her face. "That boy needs a dose of mama's medicine."

The three women laughed loudly. The other two ladies understood what Arthenia meant by "mama's medicine . . ."

Arthenia was a florist. An exotic florist for that matter. Her company supplied all sorts of flowers, including the poisonous lilies and pyrethrum, which contained extracts that didn't only kill household insects but also eliminated larger parasites that proved problematic. She silently assassinated people on behalf of statesmen and businessmen. She silenced their political and business threats respectively and cleared the way for her clients.

Ploutus was her frequent client, and she'd set up many of the castle and capital secret deaths. She was behind the deaths of bodyguards who'd leaked sensitive information, politicians who'd threatened Ploutus's name, and once in a while, women who'd claimed to reap from empires in which they did not sow—paternal privileges as a result of big men's sexual appetites and escapades. She was always welcome at the castle as one of Ekesa's best friends on the surface, but her dealings were more connected to Ploutus than Ekesa.

In their girly rants, Arthenia distanced herself and read her pesticide books and beauty magazines. She was a graduate from the West Valley College of Science and Research and had worked at the state as the lead pesticide researcher for a few years before starting her own private practice, thus forcing the closure of the State industry.

She had hired most of the men from the state pesticide industry; however, she'd also had to fire a good number to make way for her cronies and village mates. She'd thrived on her relationship with Ploutus and had been introduced to many men of power who'd used her knowledge of silencing motor mouths with jets of lethal silencing sprays. Most of her clients were in the topmost circle, and that had rocketed her status, socially as well as financially.

She had met Artemis during one of her meetings with Ploutus. The meeting was about supplying pesticides to farmers in the villages. Artemis was with Lorantu, and they looked like a couple to her. Arthenia was the only lady amongst men. In spite of that, they found that all of them were on the same wavelength; they got on with each other in one way or another.

To her, Artemis was a beautiful bimbo who used her looks to get promoted, at work, as well as in society. They became instant friends when Artemis told Arthenia that she liked her silver and diamond stilettoes, which a few days later she'd borrowed from Arthenia and never returned.

On the night of the meeting, she'd learned that Artemis ran a brothel together with Lorantu and that they'd shipped young men and women across the borders to other exotic brothels all over the world. The couple literally supplied people to the highest bidder.

Arthenia had been amazed by the glaring danger of their business. She had, however, found a market for her products; she'd begun to supply to the clever girls, who wished to teach mean buyers a lesson.

When she'd found out what the two did, it served as a confirmation that Artemis had naturally been destined to be her friend and partner.

*****

Ekesa had, by default, been introduced as the third wheel to complete the trio. She'd been the daughter of the former Statesman and the wife of the current one. She had no life beyond the pampering and affluence of the castle that had belonged to her father, and later to her husband.

She'd confided in house servants, who'd blackmailed her for money and set her up every time she'd attempted to do something new behind Ploutus's back.

On the night of the third state party, to celebrate Ploutus's election, the three had engaged in their first social three-way liaison. Ekesa had known that she could use Arthenia's pesticide to once and for all eradicate the vermin that had gnawed on her secrets and blackmailed her. There had been heart attacks here and there in exchange for fat wads of bills.

On the other hand, there had been a constant supply of orgasms and unending stamina from Artemis's chain of human shops. Ekesa had bought commodities and smuggled them into the castle. Sometimes, she'd sneaked out of the castle, under the guise of visiting her friends, to quench her thirst for love and care.

For her, it had not as much been the sex as it was the masculine care and attention that she'd craved and lacked in her marriage.

Pesticides had always been available to vanquish the emasculated vermin that dared spill the burnt beans.

*****

"Ekesa," Arthenia warned after listening to the senseless rants from Artemis about shoes and Lorantu, "you should play cool. Don't let your emotions control you ever again."

What was I supposed to do?!" Ekesa exclaimed angrily. "That son of a cow dared to disrespect me in my own home! How dare he introduce his bastard son to the public like that?"

"Maybe Arthenia should help you get rid of the bastard son," said Artemis, winking evilly.

Arthenia ignored Artemis's uncalled for interjection.

"He is his son, Ekesa," she said, infuriated. "Deal with it."

Arthenia was annoyed with where the conversation was heading. Neither of the two was aware that Zaire's mother, Akusa, was Arthenia's sister. Arthenia was also the one behind Akusa's death. Ekesa and Artemis had no right talking about Zaire like that.

The man with the weirdly perfect set of lips sat behind the principal's desk, his eyes fixed on a computer monitor that blocked most of his face.

My eyes are playing tricks on me, Najma thought. I know those lips.

She was completely spellbound—stuck at the door to the effect that Zaire had to push her into the office.

"What is wrong with you?" Zaire whispered to the frozen girl.

"He was at the market square when Mother was murdered," she whispered back.

The secretary had shown them to the waiting couches and pulled her big behind out of the office, dragging her big flat shoes over the tiles. She left behind a perfumed trail of strawberries mixed with daisies.

Najma was in her new school uniform—a short blue and red tartan skirt, a red blouse neatly tucked into her skirt and a blue tie tightly wound around her neck. She carried her new blazer on her arm. The blazer was blue and featured red ribbons around the wrists and collar.

Her hair was in a neat, tight bun at the center of her head. A glossy mint lip balm was applied on her pink girly lips.

"I know him." Replied Zaire. "We'll talk about him later." He sat next to her.

Zaire watched impatiently as the man focused on his computer, rather than addressing them. He hated school principals with their uptightness. He hated his over-pressed navy-blue pin-striped suit that made his shoulders shoot out like a bat's wings. His shirt was unnervingly white, and his tie, the same color as the suit, was tied with an exaggerated big knot around his neck, just beneath his bobbing Adam's apple.

There was a faint fragrance of a masculine cologne mixed with something that smelled like coco butter lotion.

Najma elbowed Zaire.

He knew it would be awkward whispering in the tight man's presence, so he cleared his throat, trying to call the man to attention to avoid hearing what Najma had to say.

"Just a minute, young man." The man said. "I will attend to you and your sister in due course."

Najma's eyes were still fixed on his lips. She watched how they moved when he spoke, not noticing the deep baritone in his voice and the rare sparkle of his teeth.

Then, suddenly, it occurred to her . . .

How did he know that Zaire was my brother? she thought. That day he had said I should go with the young man.

Why had they acted like they don't know each other?

Zaire easily got me into this school in the middle of the term without any trouble.

What was this man doing at the market square that day?

What am I missing . . .?

It was Zaire's turn to elbow her. Her eyes were fixed on the man, thoughts assaulting her temples.

"What?" she whispered.

He showed her something on his cell phone. Just before she could turn to see what it was, the man behind the desk cleared his throat and spoke.

"Young lady," he said. "Welcome to Mountain Crest School for Girls. This is a very popular school, known for its good performance and discipline among girls within the school and beyond," he said, his voice booming across the office.

Najma nodded. This time, she tried to focus on his clear eyes that were bushy with brows and lashes. He reminded her of someone, but she couldn't figure out who.

"I am Professor Etembi J. Senior. All girls call me Prof. Etembi."

Najma nodded again.

"Your brother has told me about your good conduct and your excellent grades. I also know that you've recently lost your mother and that you need a break from the harsh environment back at home."

She nodded.

"You will be left in peace here, provided that you keep your secrets to yourself. Girls are a fertile ground for grapevine, so you have to be very careful who you share your personal life stories with."

She nodded.

"I can see here that your school fees have been fully paid and that the enrollment process is complete. Could you kindly please step outside so that I can talk to your brother. Afterward the secretary will show you to your dormitory, where you will spend all the nights of your stay in Mountain Crest School for Girls."

She nodded, stood up, slightly curtsied, and left the office. She intentionally stood right at the closed door to try and eavesdrop but, no matter how hard she tried, she couldn't hear what the two were discussing.

They might have noticed that I know their secret, she thought.

What are they planning?

Who is this man? He really looks like someone I know.

The secretary handled some noisy papers. Najma smiled at her and looked over her to read the information that was on the notice boards in the reception area. There were names of girls on the list of honor, who had performed well each year of their stay at the school.

The phone rang loudly and the secretary answered it. After listening to what the caller had to say, she got up with a bit of effort and disappeared into the principal's office.

Zaire came out immediately and pulled her aside.

"I have to go now," he said in a hurry. "I will visit you at the end of each month. If I can't come myself, I will send someone whom you can trust."

"Send Nana," she replied urgently.

"No." he said. "She can't come here."

"Why not?" She wanted to know, feeling desperate.

"The principal might be your father-in-law soon," he replied. That is if Ham is serious about waiting for you."

With that said, he started walking away.

The secretary came out of the office and grabbed one of her suitcases.

"You have to bid your brother farewell, Ms. Najma." she said "It's time to settle into school."

She had a sweet, melodious voice. Najma knew immediately that they were going to be very close. It felt as if her mother had assigned kind, maternally inclined women to watch over her wherever she went. She felt her mother's presence each time she was afraid of something.

Najma walked to where Zaire was waiting. She threw her arms around him so that she could ask him a question. "Is he Jotham's father?"

He nodded.

"Nana's husband?" she continued.

He shook his head.

The hug was getting too lengthy, so Zaire pulled away. He gave her some pocket money, then rushed off to his car. She hoped he would look back, but he didn't. He opened the door, slipped into the driver's seat, rolled the windows down and drove off without turning to look back at the baffled Najma.

"Najma, you should join the rest of the girls before the next lesson begins," said the secretary. "Let's hurry." She picked up Najma's second suitcase. She had to pull Najma to get her to follow.

"I am so sorry about that," said Najma as they walked toward the hostels. "I hate it when he doesn't say goodbye to me properly."

"Where are your parents?" the secretary asked. "Why did your brother bring you?"

"They were busy," she lied. "Work things, you know."

"You seem very close to your brother," the secretary persisted.

The advice from the principal came booming back to her, so she kept quiet. She just nodded and walked on, following the secretary.

"Do you prefer a room for two . . . or four?" the secretary asked when they reached the hostel's main gate.

"Two will be fine, thank you," Najma replied. "Four is too crowded."

Two days had gone by, but Elima's spirit was still impossible to summon.

The fragrance of jasmine did not attract her to the spree. Other spirits were already releasing pheromones and mating. The invisible mirrors surrounded the room cluttered with the unseen motion. There was rattling in the air and the non-consuming flames of ecstasy leaped from all corners of the room.

Still, Elima's spirit was unavailable. Not even sandalwood incense attracted her. Sandalwood was supposed to attract any good spirit that was within reach.

Nothing happened.

Cosmos tried roast blood mixed with rosemary, a scent that no spirit, good or evil, could resist.

Still, nothing happened.

He tried mirror trapping, but the glass shattered in resistance, splinters sinking into his flesh and causing great harm to his inhabited body.

There were only two ways left to get Elima's spirit's attention: either Afula's spirit, or Ploutus's spirit.

He wouldn't dare mess with Ploutus, who was reserved by the gods and had the advantage of royalty. His death would cause a lot of unrest and havoc in the whole state. Cosmos's cover would be blown and the spirits would have to look for another host. That would mean no livelihood for him.

The only option was Afula. Sacrificing Afula would let her spirit loose in the atmosphere, and Elima's would seek revenge. All spirits were vengeful—even those from the kindest of bodies.

Cosmos was sure Elima would show up to pay Afula back for what she had done to her. It would be up to Afula to put up a fight, or else she was to meet the same fate, or worse, than Elima had. And that, Cosmos decided, was none of his business. What he cared about was, firstly, delivering Ploutus's third term, since the spirits were not done with him yet, and, secondly, to keep Osanyin in power for the sacrifices of young blood and siring more royal spiritlettes.

He also needed the money for creating his own empire, since being a sorcerer was not a lifetime duty. More sorcerers were rising, and there was a lot of competition in the hierarchy. His enemies were out to end him by ensuring that he would come tumbling down from the top. Should that happen, he would need a safe place to land.

"You look so tense today," Osanyin said, an evident tremor in his voice. They had been standing in the room for over thirty minutes, watching Cosmos trying to compel the spirit to accept the gifting of the body parts that they presented.

The room was tense and no one said anything.

"It is not easy when the one who is offering the sacrifices is not willing to let go of them," Cosmos replied angrily.

"What do you mean?" Osanyin asked.

"Ploutus!" exclaimed Cosmos. Care to explain what is going on with you? There is a lot of negative energy around your star. I can't break through the barrier." Cosmos shot the question to Ploutus who was absent-minded. He even had his hood lowered. He looked like he was not part of what the three were doing.

"I don't believe in this crap!" replied Ploutus "You are messing with us for our money, and today we are putting an end to it," Ploutus said fitfully, his eyes fixed on the sweaty face of Cosmos.

Suddenly, Cosmos let out a long, guttural laugh and turned back to the wall. His face was plastered with a smile. That was contrary to what the trio expected. Afula had held her breath in fear when Ploutus let out his tirade and Osanyin had almost collapsed.

"I got you Elima!" said Cosmos. "So, his voice is all we needed? Here we are!" Cosmos said triumphantly.

They could suddenly see a mirror on the wall, And Elima's image came floating in. Cosmos was captivated in trying to pull the spirit from the mirror and into the offering bottle. There were large columns of incense and a huge fire in the middle room, separating the trio from Cosmos.

Afula, Osanyin, and Ploutus had their jaws on the floor. They had done lots of things in Cosmos's ritual room, but this was beyond what they had ever seen. Ploutus was dumb-founded. He could not utter a single word. His eyes were on the struggling spirit. Elima's eyes were on him. He felt like they were drilling a pit in his soul. There was blazing anger in her red eyes. Ploutus felt a huge pang of regret for what he had done to this woman who had deeply loved him all her life. Even in death, only his voice could get her attention.

"What are you going to do to her?" he asked when he had his voice back.

"Decorate her with her body parts," Cosmos said with a sharp edge of sarcasm. "Soak her in fragrance and flowers and offer her as a goddess to the gods. I thought she wouldn't show up. Thank you, Ploutus. Your sacrifice will bring you lots of favor from the gods."

"Let us get to work," said Cosmos, now filled with renewed strength. "The gods cannot wait to meet their new bride . . ."

He tore open the wrappings on Elima's teeth, tongue, breasts, and private parts and started attaching them to their respective places on the mirror. Each part disappeared into the mirror while Cosmos chanted. Ploutus had never before experienced the kind of emotional pain he felt when he saw Elima's spirit screaming in pain.

"What are you doing to her, you fool?!" Ploutus shouted. He wanted to jump over the flames that separated them.

Osanyin held him. Cosmos kept attaching pieces, unflustered.

Afula watched keenly, her face covered in sweat. She looked as if she was half scared and half enjoying the whole thing.

Ploutus struggled free, picked up a stool from a corner, and smashed the mirror. Suddenly, the air was filled with howls, shrieks, sparks of fire, blinding light and, ultimately, complete darkness.

Afula collapsed. In the darkness, no one noticed the blood oozing from her mouth as spirits tore her flesh to pieces.

Osanyin screamed in horror.

"You fool!" yelled Cosmos as he turned to Ploutus and grabbed his throat. "Do you have any idea what you've done? Those were more than thirty spirits you let loose from that mirror!"

Cosmos continued choking the air out of Ploutus.

The guards smashed down the door and ran into the room when they heard Osanyin screaming. They opened fire, using heavy duty assault weapons, and Cosmos's brain splattered into the dying fire.

With his head separated from the body, Cosmos's hands were still wrapped tightly around Ploutus's throat, squeezing the life out of Ploutus, who was sprawled on the ground. The two bodyguards failed to peel the headless man's fingers off , but eventually Cosmos's entire body went limp and let go of Ploutus's neck by itself.

Ploutus was unconscious and Osanyin screamed orders that no one listened to.

The room was dark. There were sparks of the dying fire here and there. A pungent smell of roast brains and bones, and a distant fragrance of sandalwood and other incense still lingered. Someone rushed in with a bucket of water and threw it out on Ploutus and the embers of the fire.

The fire was something of the past. Ploutus coughed but didn't regain consciousness.

The two bodyguards struggled to carry the heavy Statesman to the car.

"What happened to Afula?" Osanyin asked, addressing no one in particular.

Ploutus's phone suddenly rung.

"Check who is calling," Osanyin directed one of the bodyguards." If it is Zaire, tell him his father in danger. He should organize to move him back to the capital immediately. He needs to see a doctor urgently."

The bodyguard nodded as he answered the phone.

"Tell Zaire what happened, he will know what to do," Osanyin barked.

Cosmos's two servants stood at a distance, watching the trio. They were immersed in a conversation too.

The rumbling of an approaching helicopter sent everyone in a hurry to look for shelter from the wind.

Zaire addressed the servants, who had huddled in a corner, shouting, to be heard over the helicopter, when it landed about twenty minutes later. "If I were you, I would take whatever I can and leave this place before dawn. Go as far as Plateau Plains. We don't know you, and you don't know us."

The man and woman rushed inside. No one saw them when they disappeared into the thicket of bamboo forest.

"Where is my dad?" Zaire wanted to know. It was more of a demand than a question.

"In the car," one of the bodyguards said.

"Get him safely into the helicopter," Zaire ordered. "Osanyin, accompany him. I will come with the car."

"Only his bodyguard will go with him into the helicopter," he said to Ploutus's bodyguard. You will remain behind with me."

Zaire spilled the words in jets.

The men sprang into action, everyone doing whatever they were directed to do.

"There was a woman," the bodyguard said after the helicopter noises disappeared in the darkness.

"Where?" Zaire asked, shocked.

"In the room. They went into the room together. She was lying on the floor when we moved honorable Ploutus out."

Following the bodyguard's directions, Zaire found the room.

Afula was lying on her back, her eyes wide open, mouth gaping, teeth and parts of her body missing; intestines strewn about her corpse.

A sharp pain shot through Zaire's chest, and he doubled up, his eyes clouded with tears. Memories of Elima, Najma's mother, came back to him. She had faced a similar death.

Zaire felt himself gasp, and then a wail escaped his throat. He could not comprehend the kind of sick business Ploutus was involved in.

"Siphon some gas from the car and set the place on fire," Zaire directed and struggled out of the room. The bodyguard did as instructed.

"Sir, what could've happened to the woman?" The bodyguard asked as the container filled with gas. "She had just collapsed when we left her."

"I have no idea," Zaire said desperately. "Let us burn the place and get out of here. I hope the servants have cleared the area."

Zaire watched his father's secret go up in flames. It was not the first time he was covering for Ploutus, but he was sure . . . this was the last. He had made up his mind about moving out of the castle. He knew the following day the media would be flooded by news of the property that burnt to ashes, and his moving out would not be speculated upon.

Zaire struggled with nausea all the way to Corner. He couldn't stand being in the castle anymore. He needed a breath of fresh air. Only Nana could offer him that at Najma's house.

Lorantu gave Nysa a visual examination over his glass of whisky and ice cubes.

Nysa was steadily sipping a Bloody Mary.

"Go slow on the drink, young lady," Lorantu sermonized. "I don't want you passing out on me. The media is all over."

"I don't care anymore, Lorantu," Nysa replied, her eyes floating in tears. "I just want to drink and sleep. I want to sleep and never wake up."

"Be careful what you ask for," he said. "You're only twenty-four years old! What is going on?"

He pushed a napkin at her, looking around uncomfortably.

"Stop crying," He said. "I don't want people thinking that I'm doing something horrible to you."

"People! People!" Nysa shouted, drawing attention to the table. "Everything is about people! Everyone worries about what people would say! When will people get over worrying about other people?!"

"Will you calm down!" he exclaimed, banging the table with his fist.

"I don't care about people anymore," she yelled. "They can go to hell! I just want to live my life without worrying about what people would think! People are none of my business!"

The argument went on and on, with Nysa losing her cool completely. The two were nearly kicked out of the bar at one point because of Nysa's outbursts, but Lorantu called in a few favors from the manager and bought them some time. He had to silence

Nysa but did not know how. A rumor erupting about him having an affair with a young lady like her would cost him his political dreams.

He wanted to run against Ploutus, but he was not sure about the promises of support he got from the investors. It was difficult trusting anyone and he had to be careful about his moves. He still had Ploutus in his circle of the most trusted people and was waiting for the most opportune time to spill the beans about his dealings. He wanted to put a chain around his fat neck when the time was right. Nysa would be a flea in the flesh, and she had to be dealt with.

He realized now that Artemis had been right all along. Nysa was an immature brat who needed a little spanking.

As the sun sunk deeper into the horizon and the capital shone brightly under street floodlights, Lorantu produced a plan. He was going to prove to Artemis that there was nothing between him and Nysa. They were going to have fun with her tonight and teach her a lesson about keeping off mature grass. They were going to rip away every ounce of self-respect she had for herself and throw her back into the castle to either commit suicide or end up in a sanitarium. He called for an unmarked taxi and sneaked out of the bar with Nysa.

Artemis was waiting for them at his house. There were dozens of young people by the pool, smoking pot, drinking, and waiting to be shipped out. Lorantu was clearing the stock for his commodities, and the remaining heads were waiting for passports to be sent overseas.

He wanted to pull away from Ploutus and Osanyin and have his own deal struck. He had discussed it with Artemis, and they had a plan of finishing off the remaining goods by sending them to Mountain Crest with Osanyin and closing up business. Lorantu had political ambitions too.

"I want to go home."

Nysa struggled to speak. The drugs Lorantu had used to spike her drink were already taking a toll on her.

"Please take me home or call my chauffeur," she pleaded.

"We are home, baby." Artemis received the wiggly girl in her arms and walked her upstairs. Lorantu cleared the taxi bill, including the extra fee to buy the diver's silence, then joined the duo after ensuring that the young people by the pool had not seen the two sneak Nysa upstairs.

The young people by the pool went on making out and smoking pot like they had not seen anything. And even if they had, no one would dare say anything to anyone.

The carpeted room upstairs had a single bed and several couches. On a stool were an ashtray, a stick of bhang, and a saucer of cocaine, as well as syringes and hypodermic needles.

"Do you like her?" Lorantu asked as he walked into the room, bolting the door behind him.

"Look at those breasts!" said Artemis. "I am going to suck the life and bounce out of them."

She stripped the last bits of fabric off the unconscious Nysa's body.

Lorantu watched the pair, his eyes burning with lust. He was already out of most of his clothing. He held a syringe loaded with dissolved cocaine.

*****

As the night progressed, Nysa slipped deeper and deeper into slumber, oblivious of the spanking, the drilling, and the chaining that the couple was inflicting on her. In her dreams, she saw a beautiful garden, with no people. She was by herself, surrounded by daisies, marigolds, and roses.

The air was loaded with the sweet scent of pollen and floral pheromones.

The sun was high, bright, and warm. The sky was blue, and there were no clouds. Birds were singing melodiously, and the butterflies were beautiful shades of yellow, orange, maroon, royal blue, and turquoise.

She wore a princess' gown and a tiara. Her hair was in long braids, flowing down her back and resting on her behind. It was all quiet and peaceful.

She was sitting on the soft grass of the extensive flower gardens.

Not a single soul to worry about.

No media, no make-up, no fashion trends . . .

No Zaire.

Her mom was not there with her gossiping cronies. She loved the freedom. She loved the beauty around her. She loved the serenity.

Then there was a bee from nowhere.

She remembered her fear of bees. She remembered how a bee had stung her once, when she was a kid. She remembered swelling up like a bear. She remembered how her mother had rushed her to hospital in a nightgown.

The media had made a fuss out of it. News had been full of her recovery. When she got better, she had decided that bees were not her friends.

And now there was bee in her beautiful garden. It was buzzing around her head. She noticed that she could not lift her hands to protect herself from the sting. Her legs were too heavy, and she could not move. She felt desperately helpless. She started calling out for people to help.

She suddenly wished there were people to save her from the bee. She needed someone to be there.

Then the bee stung her in the neck. She felt it begin to swell.

Her whole body was swelling.

Suddenly, she could not smell the flowers' sweet scent.

She could not hear the birds singing.

She could not breathe. She could not swallow her own saliva.

She was dying . . .

*****

"There is something wrong with her," Artemis yelled at Lorantu, who had dropped limp by her side, sweetly exhausted.

"There is nothing wrong with her," he replied, dismissing Artemis. "It's just the drugs. She will be delivered to the castle once I'm rested."

"No!" Artemis yelled louder, jumping out of bed. Lorantu! Look at her! She is swelling! Her body is swelling!"

"What?" Lorantu was shocked out of his reverie. He had not seen that coming. This was supposed to be his first move against destabilizing Ploutus's campaign. The girl was not supposed to get in any life-threating situation . . .

Nysa's body was swelling up. Her eyes were oozing tears, and her mouth was frothing.

"What is going on Lorantu?" Artemis shrieked. "Is she going to die?"

"I don't know," he said, clearly in a panic. "What are we going to do? She can't die!"

"This was your idea," Artemis said, walking to the dresser to get something to wear.

"What do you mean?" Lorantu shouted. "You are the one who wanted revenge on her for loving me! How was I supposed to know the bitch was allergic?"

"I am out of here," Artemis said.

Lorantu caught her by the hair and pulled her back onto the bed.

Artemis's eyes were wide with horror. Lorantu had never treated her violently before. She didn't recognize the man who was angrily breathing all over her face. For the first time in many years of her slaving for him, she feared him.

"If you step out of this room, woman," Lorantu bellowed at her, his hands balled tightly, "I will show you the other side of me—one that you've never met."

Nysa had stopped breathing. She was now a huge human balloon, lying on the bed, oozing liquids.

"Now, you listen to me," Lorantu said, trembling in fear and anger. "We are going to figure out what to do together. If I go down, I'm taking you with me."

Artemis nodded, too afraid to say anything else.

As usual, Nana was not asleep. The luminous yellowish lights that were struggling to break through the thick curtains gave Zaire some comfort.

It was late in the night, and he was not about to start disturbing Nana for attention. But he needed an ear badly. He wished Najma was around. He couldn't imagine that Najma's absence would affect him that much. He was missing her terribly.

The door swung open before he even stepped out of the car. Nana was standing at the door, her smile shining brightly in the darkness. Her presence by the door melted his tension. He turned off the engine and walked to the door. There had always been a motherly aura around Nana. She deserved to be a mother of many children; she always had enough room in her heart for everyone.

She spread her arms to receive him. He walked right into the arc, breathing in the lavender and lemon that emanated from her clothing and skin.

"Come in, my son," she said. "I had a feeling you would stop by tonight."

The woman never ceased to amaze him. She had a sixth sense about everything and everyone. It surprised him that she had never suspected that he knew who her son was.

Zaire felt a pang of guilt for never telling her the truth but brushed it aside, hoping that one day, he would muster the courage to tell her. It would have to be soon. Mr. Etembi had asked about her when he took Najma to school and he had promised to take her to him.

Zaire was concerned about Najma—that the issue would complicate her stay in school. He also wasn't not too sure about Nana's reaction—whether the move might hurt her.

He wished he could see beneath her thick layer of calm to see what lay hidden in her heart.

Zaire thought about Jotham for a moment. His best friend knew nothing about his parents. Jotham believed that when his mother died, his father had taken him to the orphanage because he would be unable to raise a child on his own.

*****

Zaire knew it was not true and wanted to reveal the truth to Jotham. They had talked about their families at the orphanage, and he was not ready to revisit the subject just yet. Zaire was still piecing together bits of how Etembi and Nana came to be.

In his daily uncovering and concealing of truth for Ploutus and the people around him, he'd learned that Jotham's family had been inhibited for political and social reasons. He had stumbled on a pact between Etembi, Ploutus, and other parties. When he had probed further, he'd discovered that the story that both Jotham and Nana believed was untrue.

To unearth the truth, he had made a point of visiting the villages of Riverside, bringing pictures of Nana and Elima after Elima's death. He'd wanted their relatives to know that Elima was no more and that perhaps they could perform a ritual for her spirit to find its way back home even though she was an outcast. He'd also wanted to use the moment to find more answers to his quest.

From what he'd gathered, Nana and Etembi fell in love in the Riverside village. Having been adopted and raised by the Chief, Elima's father, she was a princess by adoption. Back then, there had been rules related to the royal courtship and marriage.

Etembi was an ordinary son of a peasant who could never have been allowed to marry Nana. In the middle of hiding the affair from their parents, Nana had become pregnant.

When the girls had discovered that one of them was pregnant, Elima and Nana had run away from the village to seek refuge at the capital. Elima had been in college then, pursuing her nursing degree, and Nana had been planning to join a teacher training college in Bamboo.

Elima had been in love with Ploutus, who'd been a renowned businessman then.

At the time, Etembi had been in and out of the training college at Lake Side. Due to a lack of funds, his peasant father had been unable to pay the college fees, and his mother had been bedridden. Etembi had been forced to work shifts to pay his bills and send some money home for his siblings.

On behalf of her sister, Elima had asked Ploutus to offer Etembi a job in his company. Ploutus had agreed, offered Etembi a job, and took him as a close ally. He'd finished college and furthered his studies.

Nana had not been that fortunate, though. Hers had been a case of biting the hand that feeds. She had developed a complication during the birth of Jotham, and it had been attributed to the disobedience and the pain she caused the chief when the two girls had run away in rebellion. Many around her had been convinced that she had been cursed by the chief, since breach births had been very uncommon back then. At the time of Jotham's birth, which had been by means of a caesarean section, Nana had lost her ability to ever have children due to a complication during the operation.

Zaire had also talked to Etembi to hear his side of the story. Etembi's desperation to have Zaire help him win Nana back had driven him to reveal the deepest secrets of his life.

Zaire had discovered that Ploutus and Etembi had been very close at the time. Etembi had helped Ploutus cover up a number of his dirty tracks that had the potential of getting him in trouble with the capital.

To have power over Etembi, Ploutus had decided to brainwash Etembi and to separate him from his family. Etembi had bought into Ploutus's theory that having a family would adversely affect his ambitions.

Etembi's dream had been to be a professor.

The doctors had informed him that Nana would never be able to bear him more children and that their newborn baby had already been very unhealthy. He'd been aware that he'd have a bright future if he'd stick to Ploutus. Ploutus had promised him more wealth if he'd stay faithful to him.

Ploutus's help, Etembi had run off to further his studies and hopefully find a strong woman who could bear him children. Shortly after, he'd left the hospital without Nana.

When Nana had woken up from the operation, Ploutus had already arranged for the child to be sent to the orphanage and a lie to be fabricated. Nana had been told that she'd delivered a baby girl who died during the operation.

When two days passed without a visit, it dawned on her that Etembi had abandoned her.

When she'd recovered, she'd returned to the village and had begged her adoptive father to forgive her. The chief, Elima's father, had given her an ultimatum—that she'd bring Elima back home, in order to earn his forgiveness.

By the time that Elima had decided that she'd return home with Nana, the chief had already been very ill, too weak even to open his eyes. He had turned away from the message bearer when he received the news that the two girls had returned home, Elima mentally ill with a toddler on her back and Nana withered and thin after having lost her baby.

While on his deathbed, he'd never even taken a glance at either of the girls, right until he'd released his last breath.

Subsequently, Elima had lost her mind completely.

Ploutus had kept the child's survival a secret, not informing Etembi, for reasons that had been unclear to Zaire. He'd committed himself to uncover the whole truth for Nana and Jotham's sake.

Later, he'd found a signed pact that had bound Etembi to keep the operations of Ploutus's oil plant a secret. Upon finding the pact, Zaire had immediately suspected that, to have gotten Etembi to commit to leave West Valley for good, there must have been something that Ploutus had done that could've damaged his reputation. It had to be bigger than what the document and agreements said.

*****

Presently, as he walked into Nana's arms, he vowed to uncover the complete truth. Why would Ploutus have told Nana that her child was a girl? And why was the son allowed to live? Why separate Etembi and Nana?

"Come on in," said Nana, pulling him into the house. "The food is still hot. I can see you haven't eaten yet."

"Can I spend the night here?" he requested urgently. "It is almost morning already, and I haven't slept in days."

"Of course!" Replied Nana said. "You may sleep in your sister's room. It's empty."

"Afula is dead, Nana," said Zaire suddenly. "The woman with the stall at the Market Square."

He couldn't hold back the words. He didn't think that they would have the effect on Nana that they did.

Nana gave him a look that he had never seen on her face in all the years that he'd known her. She staggered and then heavily sunk into a couch.

"Nana, I'm sorry!" he exclaimed, quickly walking towards her. "Did you know her personally?"

"Yes," replied Nana. "She was not just any woman with a stall at the market. We grew up together. I have a feeling she had something to do with Elima's death. I just . . ."

She stopped talking and started sobbing.

For a moment, Zaire did not know what to do. He just held her and stroked her hair.

"You just what?" Zaire asked when the sobbing had subsided.

"I just hoped she would be alive long enough to face justice," she said, blowing her nose. I also hoped that, perhaps, she would mention the names of all of those who were behind the brutal death of my sister."

"For a moment I thought you may have known her better than that!" said Zaire, relieved.

Nana shook her head in protest. She knew nothing about Afula, save for the fact that they grew up together back in the village and that some thought that her mother was a witch. Every time that Elima went to her shop, Nana knew that one day, Afula would do something horrible to her. When she died at her doorstep, it was a shock to Nana, but she wasn't surprised that Elima's body was found on Afula's doorstep. Afula was definitely behind her death. Nana did not know how to prove it, and she hoped that, with time, Zaire would be able to.

"She was our only lead to justice for my sister," Nana said after a pensive moment.

"Promise me one thing, Zaire," she said, going down on her knees before him. Promise me . . ." This caught him by surprise. He didn't see it coming. Why would Nana go on her knees? What did she want?

"Yes, Nana?" he encouraged.

"Promise me," she replied, "That my sister will get the justice she deserves."

"Her spirit still roams in Corner Square. I can feel it all over. I even see her image in birds and dogs."

"All the people behind her death MUST be punished. Even if they are senior state officials."

"I trust you, Zaire. Promise me!"

She let the words spill out in torrents, not giving him a chance to say anything.

He wanted to tell her that he was aware that all the people who kidnapped Elima had died mysteriously. That he had seen the CCTV footages of the market and had scrutinized them before destroying them as Ploutus had instructed. That he had seen all the faces of the men who took part in her death and that none of them were still alive.

Two had died in a motorbike accident and one jumped off the bridge at Riverside. He also wanted to tell Nana that the way Afula had died was the exact way that Elima had died.

He wanted to assure her that the purported government officials involved in Elima's death were on their way towards the arms of justice already.

But he kept silent, and just listened to the weeping woman.

"I know he is your father and you cannot do anything to hurt him. I just want justice for my sister," she went on.

"I know where your son is," he whispered.

She'd caught the words, and when she looked at him, her face was ashen.

"What did you say?" she asked, confused.

Nothing escaped Nana. Not even a whisper. Zaire immediately regretted what he'd said. Why did he have to blurt it out like that?

"Jotham," said Zaire. "Please! You have to do your best."

"I can't do anything," replied Jotham. "I'm only a psychiatrist. He hit his head badly, and I'm told that his throat has collapsed. The Statesman might lose his entire memory."

He wanted to hang up but then remembered that he needed to ask Zaire about Najma…

"You need to fly him out for the recommended surgery," he said. There's hemorrhaging in his brain. The MRI shows that the bleeding is covering a huge mass. Between the two of us: it's urgent."

"Which hospital do you recommend?" Zaire asked anxiously.

"Mountain Crest,' replied Jotham. They have the best facilities and the neurosurgeon is great. He is a friend of mine. We'll link you up."

"Okay," replied Zaire. "Just call me when he's ready."

"I can accompany you when you fly him there Zaire," said Jotham. "I need to see Najma. Please."

Zaire heard his plea and gave his consent.

"Okay man," he said. "Just watch over the Statesman until I get there."

Smiling, Zaire hung up. He was thankful that his sister would be well looked after when she marries Jotham.

Jotham placed the phone on the table and exhaled sharply. He was exhausted. He'd been attending to the Statesman since he was secretly flown in. He had no idea what had happened and wondered why the media had been kept out of it. Something didn't add up.

Whatever the case may be, if Ploutus was dying, the citizens should at least be informed that their leader was not well. They deserved to know.

Jotham had been friends with Zaire for ages, and he knew about most of his dealings. In Jotham's opinion, this situation was out of hand. He would've alerted someone from the capital, but wasn't sure who to contact.

He walked out to breathe in some clean air.

He noticed that there were security officers all over the hospital. That was not good. The security officers could upset his patients.

He walked to the administrator's office to lodge a complaint.

A man sat behind a desk. He wore a plaid brown suit and came across as being absentminded. His nose looked as if it was overwhelmed by the weight of his oversized spectacles.

The room faintly smelled of disinfectant. He was the lead doctor and the decision maker when it came to major events in the hospital.

The Statesman was in an unidentified intensive care unit room.

Partly owned by the state, a large part of the hospital was privately run.

The psychiatry section belonged to Jotham and Zaire. Zaire had helped Jotham pay for it, but Jotham was in the process of settling his debt to Zaire so that he could be the sole owner. Zaire was not interested in owning a part of the hospital.

The maternity wing, cancer center, dialysis room, and mortuary belonged to the state. The emergency units and nursing homes belonged to one of the state politicians. The administrator, however, was a state employee whose job it was to ensure that the various departments within the facility were properly coordinated.

Jotham had a dream of owning the complete facility, taking over the rest of the facility from the government and the other private owners soon. He wanted to fully dedicate the hospital to psychiatry because it was strategically situated for that purpose.

When Najma confided in him that she'd wanted to study psychology in college, it had fueled his desire to own the place and convert it into psychiatric facility. Jotham and Najma could turn the place into a family legacy, should she agree.

He had plans of convincing the government to build a referral hospital away from the capital, and move it to a more central place that could be accessed by all the villages and towns in the state. He also had a plan of including a Heli-port for an air ambulance, should the government accept his proposal. With Zaire close to Ploutus, he knew this deal was possible and that it would catapult him toward financial success as well.

"Excuse me, sir," he said, approaching the indifferent man's desk. "Could I talk to you for a minute?"

The administrator was known for his cruelty and his hostility towards workers. Nurses would literally shiver in his office. He was a qualified chemotherapist, but most of patients died under his treatment. In order to keep him away from the wards and patients, the majority of the doctors at the facility had voted for him to be the hospital administrator. He was very nearly fired and his practicing license withdrawn when his flaws became known to the state. However, he was presently still in office due to political favors.

"If it is about the Statesman," said the administrator, "I am sorry. It is not in my jurisdiction anymore."

He slightly opened his thin lips for the words to force themselves out and went back to what he was doing when Jotham entered his office.

Jotham was infuriated but decided to continue. "Sir," he said firmly. "It is about the security officers. They are upsetting my patients."

"Sorry," replied the administrator. "To me, the Statesman's security is more important than the lunatics that you call patients."

Jotham boiled. He just stood there staring at the man.

"If you don't mind," the man said, pointing at the door. "I have things to do."

Jotham wanted to break his bobbing Adam's apple but decided against it. He wouldn't stoop to the administrator's level of heartlessness. Besides, he was baking an eviction cookie and didn't want to crumble it by means of petty temper issues.

"Okay, sir," he said. "Hope you don't find yourself in Ward Nine someday."

He turned around and walked out of the office, not caring to stop and listen to what the administrator was retorting behind his back.

Most of the morning went by restricting the security officers and calming down the panicking patients. Severe cases were sorted out by sedating the patients involved. Worst case scenario cases were handled by putting the particular patients into restriction beds.

Jotham was tremendously relieved when a helicopter landed to pick up the Statesman.

When Nysa's body was dropped at the castle's outer gate, Ploutus was in a coma at Mountain Crest Hospital.

The guards on duty disappeared when the truck that had dropped the body, sped away and disappeared.

The wall snipers shot at the truck but missed. They were too horrified to take any further action. One of them plunged himself down the wall, succumbing to head injuries, and the other one shot himself in the head. Neither wanted to expand on what had happened, and neither was ready to go through the agony of having to explain why they hadn't caught the truck in time. Had they known that the Statesman was in a coma, they might have taken their chances.

Dropping off the body and speeding away took only a few seconds. The CCTV cameras were unable to capture the registration number of the truck. The driver was wearing a mask. Obviously, this was a well-planned operation performed by professionals.

The gunshots caused instant pandemonium, inside the castle and out. The media was at the gate within minutes, and cameras flashed as interviews were conducted.

The Intelligence Team was on the body, taking prints and samples.

Servants thronged up and down the stairs, receiving and obeying orders from anyone they thought was superior in the castle.

Ekesa had not left her room yet. She was still struggling to get through to Artemis in vain. She tried several times to call Lorantu to find out where Artemis could be, but he wasn't available either. Ekesa's anger was overflowing.

Eventually, she called Arthenia.

Arthenia picked up her phone on the first ring.

"Hey, girl," said Ekesa. "Have you heard from Artemis? I am trying to reach her but to no avail."

"You got me, baby," said Arthenia quickly. "I'm so sorry for your loss. I'm coming over. On my way already."

"What are you talking about?" Ekesa felt her heart going into palpitations.

"What do you mean?" Arthenia asked, her voice laced with surprise. "Tell me, where are you at the moment?"

"I'm in my house," replied Ekesa. "I haven't left my bedroom yet."

There was a knock at the door.

"Hold on," she said. "Someone is knocking. Will talk to you later."

Ekesa hung up. She threw a night robe around her bare skin and strode to the door barefoot.

It was a house servant. Her face was a mask of horror.

"Madam, you must come down!" she said. "The police want to talk to you."

Ekesa was not sure what to say. Her mouth gaped, but her throat was too dry to get out any words.

"What about?" she managed a whisper.

"Nysa, madam," the servant said, trembling.

"What about Nysa?!" Ekesa shouted, ran back to the room, quickly donned a dress, and shot back out.

"What have the police got to do with my daughter? What has she done?"

She followed the servant, who was clearly running away from her questions.

An elevator was ready for her, and there were security officers inside.

"What is going on?!" Ekesa shouted.

No one said anything to her. No one was allowed to. They all stared at her blankly for the seconds that seemed like hours to her.

Intelligence officers and detectives flooded the castle's waiting lounge.

"She doesn't know." Arthenia broke the thick silence that hang in the lounge when Ekesa walked in. Please let me talk to her first."

Ekesa stared blankly as Arthenia walked toward her.

"Sweetie, you need to sit down. Arthenia said to Ekesa, trying to make her sit. "Something terrible has happened to Nysa."

Ekesa's body became rigid like a log. She didn't even move an eyelid. She looked like she was about to drop dead.

"What has happened to my girl?" she asked hoarsely, having trouble to speaking with a dry voice.

Someone handed her a glass of water.

"We don't know yet," replied Arthenia softly. "But a truck had dropped her body at the castle gate a while ago. The police are here to ask some questions."

Arthenia put her arm around the shoulders of the pale, mortified woman. Ekesa looked as if she was about to faint.

"Guys," Arthenia said to the police. I don't think she will be able to talk now. Please give her some time to process her shock."

She walked Ekesa back to the elevator, and together they went back to Ekesa's room.

"Barvo," Arthenia said when Barvo answered her call. "You need to drop the gold project at Riverside."

"Who is this?" Barvo asked, pushing Jerry off him. The two were at Lakeside for a weekend in a private resort.

"You know who this is." Arthenia replied calmly.

"I don't take orders from you." Barvo said arrogantly.

"Fine!" she responded icily. "Now listen. Either you drop the gold project and return my people's water to them, or your lover boy will be fertilizer in my poisonous garden soon."

She said each word with the velocity of a machine gun releasing bullets. She didn't wait for Barvo to respond. She hung up and walked to her study.

*****

Her father's land was lying desolate back in the village. According to researchers, not even her toxic gardens could grow in the soil. She had no brothers to defend her father's land. Two of her sisters were dead already. She was her father's only living relative who could fight for her people's right to a clean environment.

When she'd heard about Elima's death on the news, her heart was broken. Elima was the most reliable. Nana was also dependable, but there was a wedge between them at the moment. She really hoped that she would one day get Nana to work together with her on their father's land.

She'd wanted to find Ploutus in person to ask him why he had had Elima murdered. Arthenia had known that it was him, and her research on Elima's death had led her to Afula's doorstep.

The thought of Afula with her creepy mother had given her the shivers. However, she hadn't found an opportunity to sneak up on Ploutus and pin him down to choke the truth out of him.

Ploutus and Nana had been the only people who'd known the truth about her. Nana had never talked to her. Arthenia had tried in vain to get closer to her.

Nana had chosen to stay with Elima, even when she'd been mentally unstable. Arthenia had admired Nana for her kind nature. Nana had also been aware that when she'd returned from the village to seek help for Elima, Arthenia had turned her down.

Arthenia had been jealous of Elima, who'd remained their father's favorite even after she disappointed him. Arthenia had worked hard to get where she'd been at the time, but their father had only seen Elima's efforts.

When Elima had broken the chief's heart, Arthenia had tried her best to get his blessings, but it had all been in vain.

Arthenia had then severed all links she'd had with her family and chosen a life of solitude away from those who'd known her. Only Nana had known where she'd lived, but because of her own bitterness from the past, Nana had not been welcome either.

*****

Nana now had the love of their niece and their nephew. Arthenia wanted Zaire and Najma to know the truth.

Recently, she'd learned that Najma was in a boarding school in Mountain Crest. She decided to visit Najma there if Nana kept turning her down.

She also knew about Etembi who was the principal at Mountain Crest School for Girls. She wasn't sure whether Etembi had a hand in Najma's admission. She wondered whether he and Nana had managed to sort out their love issues.

Arthenia had often wondered about the fact that love had turned out sour for all of them.

Akusa, their youngest sister, had gone around coveting her sisters' lovers and ended up dead.

Elima had lost her mind because of unreturned love.

Arthenia herself had lost the only man she'd ever loved to her sister Akusa. She'd also had to kill them both, as directed by Ploutus.

Nana, who had walked into their misfortune by default, was now lonely, her lover miles away, without a family at all.

*****

In Arthenia's eyes, all four of them seemed to have been under a nasty spell. She'd often wondered if Afula's mother had had a hand in their misfortune . . .

She dismissed the thought. She was a scientist. She would not allow spirits and sorcery to affect her life and -thoughts.

The only logical way would be to fix the mistakes they had made in the past and to continue their father's good deeds to the people of Riverside.

She wasn't sure if Nana knew that she was the one responsible for Akusa's death. She had wanted to talk to her and explain her pain. She had wanted to reveal to her that Akusa had gotten pregnant by Ploutus, yet she knew he was Elima's man.

Arthenia hoped that if Nana would give her audience, she would be able to explain why she had killed Akusa.

Arthenia remembered the day as if it was a minute ago.

She'd walked into her sister's house at Lakeside, dressed like a servant; she'd served her meals for an entire day, and Akusa had never realized who she was.

Her sister had been so full of herself, shouting orders at her like she did with the rest of the servants, enjoying the house she, Arthenia, had helped her lover build. He'd promised to refund Arthenia everything he'd owed her for the home once his business started thriving.

They were to be married, but when Akusa showed up, he ditched her and ran off with Akusa.

When he'd married Akusa instead, Arthenia was shattered.

On that fateful day, Arthenia had dropped extracts from foxglove—her favorite flowers—in their wine glasses and had watched the two lovers grip their faulty hearts to death. She had then sneaked out of the house unnoticed after reclaiming the documents of her property.

She was willing to give the house to Nana and move her out of Corner Street.

Arthenia felt she had lived with the guilt for so long, and somehow the burden was lifting. She was ready to do something good for her father's people, and she needed Nana's support. She needed to make peace with her only living relatives, including Zaire and Najma. She had decided that she was going reveal the truth first to Zaire, whom she had harmed first, then Najma.

She worried less about Nana, since she knew that once she told her about Etembi's whereabouts, Nana would easily forgive her.

Her only worry was Ploutus. She wanted her moves to be so smooth that he wouldn't suspect a thing. He was too dangerous, and she didn't want to put Zaire and Najma, who were directly connected to him, in danger. She would have to be careful with him.

She pushed back her leather seat, rolled over to her phone table, and dialed Ploutus's private number. It was off. That was very strange. His private number was never off. Her heart fluttered. She wondered if it was all about Nysa's death.

She dialed Ekesa's number and listened as the phone rang.

"Hey girl, how are you holding up?" She feigned concern when Ekesa answered.

"I'm on my way to Mountain Crest." Ekesa said. "Ploutus is in hospital."

She hung up before Arthenia could react.

Arthenia forced herself to remain calm.

She walked to her Lexus without notifying her servants and drove to the airport.

She was going to Mountain Crest.

WARD NINE

"The surgery was a success, Zaire," said Jotham. "But there are a few things that you need to know. Let's go to the doctor's office."

Zaire had not left the hospital since he'd arrived. News of Nysa's death was all over, and it was time to release Ploutus's news to the people as well.

He had arranged with the state spokesperson to explain to the media that Ploutus was too shocked to give a statement. He had also warned him about allowing Ekesa to comment until he had talked to her. He'd been informed that Ekesa was on her way, accompanied by Arthenia.

Zaire had tried to locate Barvo and Lorantu, to no avail. He needed them to clarify certain classified state matters.

Some of the closest delegates were already in the hospital, working on ensuring that there was no panic in the state.

Zaire had kept contact with Osanyin, who had sneaked back to his own state. Osanyin had helped to isolate the media in Mountain Crest.

Zaire wondered if he was going to manage holding up the state at that particular time. He had just been torn away from Nana's bosom by the call about his father being in danger. He had really wanted to rest that night. He was still digesting his father's declaration that he loved him. He was also wondering why his father had acknowledged him in public.

He had no idea what to do about Nysa's death. His surveillance on Nysa had led him to Lorantu.

He searched his heart for anger, but there was none. He could only find pity and fear. He needed his father to be okay. Zaire felt like he was not ready yet. It was not yet time for Ploutus to go. He was just starting to know his father.

Suddenly, Zaire regretted the plans of vengeance, and he silently prayed for Ploutus to be okay.

"Have a seat, Zaire," the neurosurgeon said, motioning both of them to a couch.

Fatigued, Zaire gratefully sank into the deep, fluffy couch. His friend gave him a look of reassurance.

"The surgery was successful," said the doctor. "The Statesman is out of danger. He'd hit his head pretty bad and his throat had also collapsed. There is only one problem. All his memories are gone and will require a detailed psychiatric stimulus to return."

Zaire looked at Jotham.

"I will have to confine him to Ward Nine for a period until we have helped him recover his memories," Jotham said, as if to answer the unspoken questions that Zaire had.

"What do you mean, Ward Nine?" Zaire asked. "Can't you do that at home?"

"No, Zaire," replied Jotham. "He needs to be closely monitored."

There was a knock at the door. It was a bodyguard announcing Ekesa's arrival.

"Bring her here," said Zaire. "She needs to hear this."

He buried his head in his hands and slowly rubbed his temples. His head was exploding. He couldn't figure out what to do. He had to talk to the state spokesperson urgently. If Ploutus had no memory, then his position as a statesman would be in jeopardy. They had arranged for Ploutus's deputy to take over office in the meantime.

Things were moving so fast now, Zaire felt like he was losing grip.

For years, he had held West Valley and its affairs in the palms of his hands. He knew who went in and out. He knew everyone who mattered. He had Ploutus's deals executed faultlessly. He had never imagined that anything would be this hard for him to handle.

He felt as if his brain was deserting him.

He had no idea that Ploutus had gone to Bamboo.

He'd lost track of Nysa, and now she was dead. All the senior security team members had taken their own lives. How was he supposed to deal with Lorantu and Artemis?

Zaire was so lost in thoughts that he didn't notice when Ekesa walked in. His thoughts were rudely interrupted by her claws on his neck.

"What did you do to my husband, you bastard," she yelled. The doctors tried to calm her down. Eventually, she sank into a chair next to Zaire and broke down.

"They killed Nysa, Zaire." She finally said after calming down. "I know who did it."

For a moment, Zaire felt pity for her. She looked so fragile and weak.

"It was Lorantu and Artemis," she whispered and then broke down crying.

The room was silent for a moment. Zaire said nothing. He just stared at her, rubbing his neck. That was a huge allegation although Zaire knew there was some truth in it.

"What will I do without Ploutus by my side?" she asked him when he didn't respond.

"He isn't dead," replied Zaire, straightening his collar. "The surgery was successful. He just lost his memory, and we are moving him to Ward Nine for treatment."

"The doctor will brief you," he continued. "Then, you will release a press statement. I will send you an email containing exactly what you should say. If you mess this up, I will leave the castle, and you will be on your own. I am so tired already."

Zaire could not believe his own words. He felt like the whole world was on his shoulders.

He stood up to leave.

"Are we going to move the Statesman after the Press conference or before?" asked Ploutus's personal assistant.

"Arrange for Ekesa to release her statement," Zaire replied. "She will announce that we will move him closer to home. I will be back in time to make arrangements for him to be moved."

He walked out.

Jotham followed him.

"Where are you going?" Jotham asked.

"To see Najma," he replied.

"I am driving," said Jotham. "Come with me in my car."

They had not noticed Arthenia standing by the door.

"Zaire," she asked. "What happened to the Statesman?"

"Please keep an eye on Ekesa," Zaire said to Arthenia, intentionally avoiding her question. "Help her compose herself when releasing the statement that I will email her. I will talk to you when I get back."

Zaire and Jotham walked to Jotham's car and drove to Mountain Crest School for Girls.

GODS AND GODDESSES

Arthenia walked with Ekesa out of doctor's room. They were shown to a private room for makeup and prepping. Ekesa had left home in a hurry, not considering that she might be required to appear publicly. Arthenia could tell that she was weighed down heavily by how her shoulders slumped beneath her neck. She looked paler than usual and had dark shadows beneath her troubled eyes.

"Hey girl," said Arthenia gaily, tying to pep Ekesa up. "I will need a makeup boost too if I am going to be by your side during the release of the media statement. Don't want to be seen on TV looking like a gecko . . ." She laughed at her own joke.

"I am so glad you are here, Arthenia," said Ekesa, eyes getting teary. "I really need your support right now.

Arthenia sat down beside her, giving her hand a little squeeze.

"There is too much tragedy around me this week," said Ekesa. "I hope Ploutus really is okay.

"Has Zaire sent you the speech?" Asked Arthenia, trying to extinguish the pity party talk.

"Yes, replied Ekesa, exhausted. The P.A is working on fixing a teleprompter in one of the rooms in the hospital. I like how Zaire has covered up the issue. But I'm sure Ploutus was into something nasty when the accident happened."

Arthenia read in Ekesa's eyes that she was tired of living behind the mask of seeming perfection. Arthenia herself was tired. She wondered why the world thought it was easy being positioned at the top of the ladder.

"I suggest you read it as it is. Don't change anything," Arthenia cautioned softly.

"I won't change anything," promised Ekesa. "He's actually covered Ploutus's tracks of the weekend and has blamed his condition on Nysa's death. You know that makes it better since the rumor about Nysa not being Ploutus's child was just dying down."

Ekesa gasped when she mentioned Nysa.

"Those brutes killed my daughter Arthenia."

She continued whispering, but remained careful, using code language.

"Who?" Arthenia's eyes opened wide with her mouth in a whisper.

"The 'blue room' duo," Ekesa said using the code name for Artemis's brothel.

"Are you sure?" asked Arthenia.

"Yes!" confirmed Ekesa. "Nysa had 'powder' overdose in her system. She was allergic to many things, my girl. And the postmortem also showed that she was molested. The prints were 'blue.'"

Her voice trailed off.

"Those perverts!" exclaimed Arthenia. "I'd always known that the couple is up to no good, constantly getting into illegal stuff! Just thinking that the 'female blue' was our friend, disgusts me. I'm worried about the relationship 'the male blue' has with the 'capital'. What are you going to do?"

"I don't know. I am a bit concerned about the 'black letters,' " Ekesa whispered. They have already sent in a blackmail note to the 'capital'. I hope Zaire will be able to handle it once I show him. They're lucky that the 'capital' chambers are now under repair. The scans are unable to recall the 'recordings.' He would have cleared them out like vermin."

"Let's talk about it on our way home," replied Arthenia when she noticed that the PA was walking toward them. "I have something to tell you too."

The PA announced that the media people were ready for the press conference and requested the ladies to join them shortly.

Ekesa was surprisingly composed when Arthenia walked her to the makeshift studio. Arthenia kept throwing glances at her friend and was impressed by Ekesa's composure. All along, she'd had her pegged as a lucky bimbo and not much conversant with political manipulations.

Arthenia had underrated Ekesa.

Arthenia now knew that she'd been wrong about Ekesa all along. She was a survivor. Arthenia was not going to let her go. She was willing to sacrifice the truth to gain Ekesa's trust and support to win back her father's land and end Barvo, fake gold and all.

Ekesa was Arthenia's first step towards office, and Arthenia planned on making it firm and strong to hold the fleet that was to go on top of her.

When Ekesa finished reading her statement, she announced that the Statesman was in stable condition and was being moved back to West Valley within an hour or two. The media followed Ekesa to the recovery ward where Ploutus slept and took a few pictures of her by his side.

"Girl, that was awesome!" Arthenia congratulated her friend when they were finally alone.

"I don't know. But I have to be strong. My daughter's death will be in vain if I go down the drain like my brother," Ekesa said matter-of-factly.

Arthenia nodded in agreement. She was pleasantly surprised by the new person that Ekesa had suddenly become.

THE RE-UNION

Nana stared at the television, and her jaw dropped, her eyes wide with shock.

"Arthenia!" She exclaimed. She had not seen her sister in years.

The news anchor called her Arthenia Akitube of Riverside.

Since when did she use the tribal name? There was something fishy about her, especially since Nana knew very well that Arthenia had never used her tribal name, even in school.

What had changed?

Why was she letting the media announce that she was from Riverside? That was so strange of Arthenia.

Arthenia on television . . . the spitting image of their late father . . . the chief.

Her handsome features, accentuated by her short hair in a boyish cut, her khaki peddle pusher shorts that lightly tightened around her firm hips, and her cream-colored blouse with long chiffon sleeves that exposed her well-toned arms; these all created the impression of a solid person who had her act well together.

Nana had never paid attention to Arthenia's looks, but today she did, studying her appearance without missing anything. She wondered if Arthenia remembered her.

Nana recalled with bitterness the day that she'd gone to Arthenia's house, requesting help for Elima.

"I would take you in anytime, Nana, not Elima," Arthenia said plainly. Pain in her voice and her eyes. "Elima is father's favorite, and she'd let him down. Papa is dying because of her. Helping her will be betraying father. He has never loved me, but I will not risk losing his blessings because of Elima."

Nana remembered their childhood days, when they would walk to the river: Arthenia, Akusa, Elima, and herself. Elima had their mother's lovely features. She the tallest among the girls with the most curvaceous body.

Arthenia had always been boyish, having developed late. She had a darker tone of voice and started her period late, even though she was the eldest.

Akusa was a combination of beautiful and plain. She kept her friends closer than her sisters and coveted her sisters' stuff. She stole from their sisal wardrobes and unhooked shoes whenever the owner was not around. She was also the cheerful, fun-loving one. She laughed a lot, and it was impossible to stay. Nana wondered why anyone would even want her dead. The announcement that Akusa had been poisoned by an unknown person came as a shock to all.

Elima had been sick at the time, and the news had devastated her even more. Elima had missed the burial under the doctor's instructions, and Nana had had to hurry and get back to keep an eye on Elima.

Nana remembered that Arthenia had refused to even view the body before it was burnt and its ashes thrown in the river.

This was a custom in dealing with those who had been killed. The spirit of the deceased would thereafter be in every glass of water the killers drank, so that it would make them sick and eventually have the killed person avenged.

When the news of Akusa's death reached her, Nana had been was torn between grieving for her and wondering whose man she'd stolen this time. The last time she'd seen her, Akusa looked pregnant. Later, she'd heard that Akusa had delivered a healthy baby boy, named it after their father, and given it up for adoption. And then, years later, she'd been found dead in the arms of a man.

Nana wondered who the man was since nobody had ever heard of him or where he came from.

Later, it was said that he'd come from a different state and that his people had collected his body for rituals.

As custom required, Akusa had been buried hurriedly, without a ceremony.

She'd just ceased to exist, forgotten immediately.

Nobody had talked about her after her ashes had been thrown into the water. Nobody had fallen ill or had died from water disease. No one had drowned.

*****

Nana, sitting in her late sister's favorite couch, watched her only living sister; her face plastered in a plastic smile, sitting next to the Statesman's wife, who was reading from a teleprompter. She knew that there was no truth in what the State's First Lady was reading. For some reason, she hoped Zaire was not behind the fabrication.

She wondered how long he would put his life at risk for the man who claimed to be his father.

To date, she had not been able to figure out how Ploutus could have been Zaire's father. She couldn't grasp when he could have sired a son older than Najma, yet all the time he had been in love with Elima.

Poor Elima . . .

Nana's memories brought her so much sadness that she felt tears well up in her eyes.

They had declared that the Statesman would be flown back to Valley View from Mountain Crest. Nana hoped that Zaire would stop by. For a reason she didn't understand, she worried about him.

She felt certain that the dark cloud around his head involved something deeper than cleaning up after Ploutus. She hoped it would go away soon.

Nana knew how important Zaire was to Najma and how it would tear her to pieces, should anything happen to him.

That evening, she knelt down for the first time in many years and prayed for Zaire earnestly. She didn't understand how God worked, but she did believe that there was a Supreme Being that controlled what happened in the Universe. She'd seen people testify, saying that they had received miracles.

She had no idea who He was, but she hoped God didn't have any favorites. She made a point of asking Najma to take her to church when she came back for holiday.

Nana had not had a chance to call Najma at her school to say hello to her since she left. Zaire had told her that she was in safe hands. He had avoided taking her to Najma's school, and when she asked why, she could see a lie forming in his eyes, exactly like when she'd asked about the doctor at Ward Nine.

She'd wanted to know why Zaire trusted the young doctor with Najma so much . . . but when his eyes twinkled, she'd quickly changed the subject. She hated lies and was not willing to take some from a boy old enough to call her 'Mother.'

As she switched off the lights in the living room, and before lighting up the verandah, she heard a car pulling up closer to the house.

At first, she thought it was Zaire but peeped to confirm anyway.

There was a white sedan parked near the house. A woman got out of the car.

Nana flipped the switch back on since the woman was walking towards the door. Her form looked familiar, but she had a scarf around her head as if she was hiding from something.

Nana anticipated a knock. When the woman didn't knock again, Nana thought she would walk away, so she quickly opened the door.

Arthenia was in the doorway with a look on her boyish face that Nana could not describe.

Najma couldn't concentrate during physics class. Her eyes were stuck on the window, and her thoughts were in the clouds.

She had gotten used to the bouts of misty weather and the cloudy skies of Mountain Crest. She had not seen the sun in months, and she missed feeling its rays caress her skin.

Mountain Crest was hilly and green. The hills were covered in trees and shrubs.

Each town and market was on a hill. The state capital was on the largest hill—Katana, as she'd later discovered.

Katana Hills also housed her new school and most of the amenities in the capital. Despite the mist and clouds that would sometimes descend upon the whole school, making the air too thick to breathe, Najma loved the deep green panorama of the hilly folds. She enjoyed sitting outside her classroom on the balcony, reading a novel or magazine, distracted by the wavy mounds of green that formed a spectacular background.

Presently, she was particularly comparing her life to the thick dark layers of cotton-like clouds.

Her life had always been cloudy. There had never been beauty, truth, or transparency. It had always been tragedy after tragedy.

Her eyes welled up, her chest tightened, and she felt her throat block. She needed to get out of class before she got into trouble. Quickly rising from her seat, she walked to the physics teacher's desk and asked for permission to go out. One look at her made up the teacher's mind to let her go.

Najma walked through the mist, her eyes blinded by tears, her throat constricted by anger. She felt her heart pound as she walked to the principal's office.

"Did you know all about it?" she wanted to know. "Did you know he was your son?"

"What about Nana? Did you ever think about her?"

"How can you go on with your life as though nothing happened?"

"Your son just showed up, broken, and you are okay? How?"

She sat down, her shoulders shaking with sobs.

The alarmed Mr. Etembi rose from his seat and walked to the door, locking it. He didn't want anyone walking in or eavesdropping.

"You need to calm down Najma," he said.

"How do you suppose I should I calm down?" she asked, pressing out the words through her teeth. "All these lies! Please tell me you didn't know it all."

"I wasn't aware that I had a son," he said. "I thought I had a daughter. Ploutus played us all . . ."

"Just stop right there," she said, raising her voice. "I don't care about your relationship with Ploutus."

"Did you know who killed my mom? On that day at the market square, you were there. "Did you do it? Did he send you to do it?"

Mr. Etembi was visibly shaking. She could tell he was keeping something from her. She could see his lips quivering. His eyes darted around like a snake's. She hated him. She hated Zaire for bringing her here. She hated Nana for letting Zaire bring her here.

"Does Nana know you are here?" she suddenly asked.

"No," he responded.

"So, you lied to her too? Does she know about Jotham?"

"Maybe by now she does," he replied. "Zaire swore to tell her the truth."

She covered her face with her hands and cried some more. She was angry and bitter. She felt betrayed and didn't know whom to trust anymore. She'd known all along that Jotham was Nana and Etembi's son, but she hadn't bothered to find out how it came to be. It hurt her that Nana had suffered so much pain thinking she had given birth to a rainbow baby girl, yet she'd had a son. It broke her heart more that that son was Jotham.

Looking at Etembi, she felt disgusted. Zaire had also mentioned that Nana was her mother's sister. That they had two other sisters. That should be Zaire's mother and another one who's existence she had no idea about. Something was not adding up.

If Zaire is my brother, she thought, his mother and mine are sisters, but who is our father? I need to talk to Zaire. How is he holding up his step sister's death and the Statesman's illness at the same time?

"I need permission to go home for a week, sir," she said. "I can't be here, like this. I don't feel too well."

"I understand," he replied, trying to reason with her. "But examinations are around the corner. You will soon be out of here for good. Just hold on a little longer."

"I won't be able to do well in those exams unless I see Nana and I get answers from Zaire," she insisted, standing up. "I don't care about exams right now."

"I will have to call your brother now," he said, his voice shaking in fright. "I'd have to hear his thoughts before I let you go."

She suddenly had a look he had never seen on an eighteen-year-old. She looked ferocious.

"No!" she yelled. "You can't call him.! I don't want him spinning another lie before I arrive. I will call him myself," she said and walked out of the office.

The secretary rushed after her with a leave-out tab and a printout for a train ticket minutes later.

"Najma," she said, trying to converse with her before handing her the envelope, "you don't have to act angrily. Just stay calm. Everything will be okay."

Najma said nothing. She'd had enough. All she wanted was to talk to Nana and Zaire.

The train left Mountain Crest Capital almost immediately after she got in. In two hours' time, she was in West Valley Capital.

*****

There was news all over about the death of the Statesman's daughter. The Statesman himself was hospitalized at Ward Nine. The news wasn't new to her. Zaire and Jotham had talked about it when they came visiting. Zaire had looked anxious. His mind kept going on tangents, and she'd had to jolt him back to reality more than once.

"I am so scared, Najma," he had said.

That caught her by surprise. He was never sacred. She didn't know this side of Zaire. Zaire had always had answers for all problems. His own, as well as the State's. He acted as Ploutus's brain, and she knew it.

"I am weaving huge lies now for the state, and they might bite me in the ass," he confessed dejectedly. For once, he admitted to covering up for the capital.

She'd wanted to throw her arms around him and tell him everything was going to be okay, but Jotham held her back. Jotham was angry. She could see it in his eyes. There were veins on his forehead and his arm muscles twitched.

"All these years, Zaire, you have been my friend," Jotham said angrily. "You never said anything, so why now?"

"I needed all the facts, Ham!" Zaire said. "Without the facts, I couldn't say anything. How could I give you an incomplete story? Wouldn't that have made you even angrier?"

Najma noticed that his voice was thinner than usual. There was fear all over his face. He looked ragged and tired.

"You need to calm down, Jotham," Najma tried to advise him. "This is a school, and you can't just walk into somebody's office and announce that you are their son."

"I know," he replied, angrier now. "But I'm curious. I want to see the evil man, and you know what? I'm going to walk into that office right now and announce that I am his son. The imbecile who made my mother suffer needs to start paying. The idiot who thought I didn't deserve to be alive should face his moment of truth"

"Ham, relax," Zaire reasoned. "You don't even know who your mother is. How can you be sure that she suffered?"

"Okay!" replied Jotham. "Since you know everything about everyone, why don't you tell me, right now, who my mother is?"

He wanted to pounce on Zaire. The sarcasm in his voice warned Zaire to keep silent.

Najma sat between them pensively. She prayed that nothing would go wrong with the discussion. She hated that Zaire had chosen to come to her school to solve the mess. He should have done it somewhere else.

"I'm sorry, Najma," said Zaire. "You shouldn't be part of this. But I thought of you first. If father goes down, so do I. I wanted to ensure that you will be safe. I can't trust anyone with you but Jotham."

Tears were brimming in his eyes.

The last time Najma saw Zaire cry was when her mother died. She'd never imagined that anything else would make him cry. He seemed to have reached the brink.

She decided there and then that he needed her to be there for him until the death of his step sister wasn't main news any longer and the Statesman has healed from his wounds.

Jotham, on the other hand, was torn between anger and appreciation for his friend. Najma clearly saw that he wanted to punch Zaire in the face at that moment but was struggling to keep his cool for her sake. He had stormed out of the car and walked to Mr. Etembi's office.

Zaire had followed him, while tow and Najma had stayed in the car. She didn't want to see the three men bringing down the roof on top of them all. Also, she knew that she couldn't bear seeing the two people she loved most of all tear at one another.

She silently prayed that things wouldn't get out of hand.

Twenty minutes later, when they walked out of the office, neither of the two said anything to the other. She didn't bother asking how things had turned out in the office. The results were written all over their faces.

She stepped out of the car, silently accepted her pocket money from Zaire and walked off to class. She didn't look back to see Jotham extend his arms to her. She didn't wait to see the anguish on his face. She didn't see them watch her until she'd disappeared into the building.

*****

As she walked through the streets of the capital, alone at last, she remembered the first time Zaire brought her over. She'd been bemused by the neat sharp rows of buildings, the fast-paced people, and the exotic pieces of goods offered for sale by hawkers.

She'd never been out of Corner Street. The capital looked like a completely new world to her.

Zaire had laughed at her naivety. He'd taken her to an ice-cream parlor, then to a four-star restaurant for lunch, and later to a bigger and better café than the one on Corner Street. She'd been so happy.

He'd walked holding her hand, guiding her every step and buying her everything she wanted, even though she'd protested.

Now she walked boldly, amazed at how fast she had grown. She held onto her school bag and slowly moved along the streets, looking for a phonebooth. She knew Mr. Etembi would've called Zaire, but she didn't want to see him immediately. She knew he was working on Nysa's funeral, and calling him would be adding to his troubles.

When she found a booth, she called Jotham instead.

He had gone to work and asked her to wait for him in a restaurant so that he could pick her up. She spotted one she hoped was cheap and sat in a corner away from prying eyes.

Jotham was in the Capital forty-five minutes later. He looked ragged and tired. She knew he wasn't okay.

When he walked toward where she sat, she stood up to receive him. He held her tightly for a noticeably long minute. She thought he was going to break down, but he didn't.

"I'm sorry about the other day," Najma said when they were seated. "I couldn't bear seeing the two of you fight,"

"Let's find a better place, Najma," He said. "We can have lunch, and then I will call Zaire to tell him I'm taking you to my house."

He said this with authority, and it was like the cloud on his face had just melted away. His eyes were bright again, and a smile was playing on his lips. She thought that the veins that had crisscrossed his forehead when he walked in had just vanished.

"Is everything Okay, Najma?"

His question startled her. She didn't notice that he was staring at her.

"Yes," she whispered, almost choking on the word. It was so unlike her. She never lost control over her feelings, but with Jotham, it was impossible to keep calm. His eyes penetrated her soul and saw the deepest parts of her being.

"I'm sorry," he said. "I can't sit here. It's too public, and you're in a school uniform."

"I don't mind at all," she said. It was just the first place I saw when you said I should wait for you. Besides, I don't really know places here. It's only my second time coming to the capital."

She immediately regretted disclosing how un-streetwise she was.

He didn't giggle or laugh at her. He reached out for her hand, and together they walked to his car. He opened the door and held it for her. Just before she got in, he grabbed her by the shoulders and looked into her eyes. Her heart stopped, and her mouth parted. Her breath was suddenly hot.

"I am so happy you came, Najma." he said, emotion naked in his voice and eyes. "Thank you."

She looked down, staring at her school shoes. When he let go of her, she quickly sunk into the passenger's seat, strapped on the seat belt, and leaned back heavily. Her throat was very dry, and her heart was racing.

LOVE

Zaire didn't show up at Jotham's that night. They had stayed up late, talking and sharing snippets of their lives. Zaire had not told Jotham that Nana was his mother, so Najma did. He wasn't shocked. Najma didn't know why he'd been separated from his mother at birth; Jotham didn't push any further. He nodded and looked at her intensively when she talked, until she squirmed under his gaze.

"Are you even listening to me?" she asked, laughing.

"You are beautiful, Najma," he said. "I really like you. If I had to find out that we are related and that I can't be with you in the manner that I want to, I doubt I will be able to survive it."

His eyes were so intense that she trembled. He scanned her face, inch by inch, not blinking, breathing steadily but heavily.

"In what way do you want to be with me?" she whispered.

He took both her hands in his and surveyed her fingers. His eyes caressed her bare arms that flowed from a sleeveless silk dress. He had bought her some exchange clothes from the Capital to ease her out of school uniform. His eyes moved to her neck and rested on her face once more.

"Najma, from the first time I saw you, with your mother at Ward Nine, I immediately knew it was you I'd been waiting for. You were a child then, but I promised myself to wait for you. I have watched you grow and turn into a magnificent young woman. I want to spend the rest of my life with you."

His voice was so deep that it made her tremble. Her eyes didn't leave his, despite the fact that his burrowed deeply into hers. She wanted to see beyond the intensity of desire. She wanted to see beyond the fire. She wanted to reach his skull and know what was in his mind.

"I am too young for you," she said after a while.

"I know. But I'll wait for you," he promised. "I will wait until you feel that you are ready. I will wait till kingdom comes, if I have to . . ."

"Please don't make promises," Najma cut him short and suddenly stood up. She didn't want the conversation to go on. It was too soon for her to make any final decisions.

She loved him. She knew it. However, she had no idea what love was. She couldn't define what was going on in her heart. She'd never experienced this kind of love that brought pleasure and pain at the same time. This love scared her . . .

"I will help Kuti fix dinner," she said as she walked to his kitchen.

"Will you be my date tomorrow at Nysa's memorial service?" he asked. "Please come with me?"

The words caught her before she disappeared into passage. It was more of a plea than a request.

She turned and looked at him.

"I will," she replied. "But for Zaire. "She was his stepsister, and I must be there for him."

She smiled at the hint of jealousy on his face.

Kuti was lovely company in the kitchen. The room was meticulously arranged.

The pantry was filled with shelves containing groceries on one side and a wall-to-wall refrigerator on the other side. Inside the refrigerator was an array of vegetables, fruits, drinks, and other foods. The cabinets on the third wall, facing the entrance, were stacked with polished china and cutlery.

Against a wall on a countertop in the kitchen, there were a coffee machine, a juicer, a toaster, and various other small kitchen appliances. On the other side of the room was a massive oven next to a state-of-the-art cooking hob, above which there was an extractor via which all cooking fumes and smells were led through the roof and out the house.

"What are you preparing?" Najma asked when she walked in, hoping to break the ice with Kuti.

"Doctor asked me to make fish fillets, roasted potatoes, and some gravy sauce, Madam," replied Kuti, smiling. "He said it is your favorite, Madam."

"He asked you?" Najma feigned surprise. Kuti was probably her same age, or just a year or two older, but Najma found it hard to socialize with her.

In Kuti's eyes, she was Jotham's girlfriend. Kuti called her 'Madam,' a title which she felt was a bit heavy for her.

"Please don't call me Madam, Kuti. Call me Najma, okay?"

Kuti nodded. She opened the fridge to get tomatoes, lettuce, kale, celery, cucumber, cilantro leaves, and bell peppers.

"Let me help with the salad, please," Najma said.

Kuti nodded, handing Najma knives, chopping boards, Kalamata olives, feta cheese, spiced olive oil, lemon juice, and honey.

"You may choose which of these go in the salad," she exclaimed.

Najma nodded, handing the olives and feta cheese back to Kuti.

We already have plenty. Thanks Kuti," she said.

She spent the next few minutes chopping up the veggies.

"Doctor also likes cinnamon in his salad," Kuti whispered, handing her a cinnamon stick.

Najma nodded, smiling. She began to grate the cinnamon stick onto the chopped veggies. She added a little spiced olive oil, lemon juice, and a few drops of honey.

"Perfect," Kuti said, watching her. "Doctor really loves you. No madam has come to this house since I moved in two years ago."

Najma smiled. Kuti was an interesting girl.

She liked her.

She liked her nosy innocence.

She liked how she called Jotham 'Doctor' and whispered when she talked about him. It showed how much she respected him. It gave her, Najma, confidence in the house too.

For a moment, she wished her mother was around so that she could ask her guidance about what was expected of her as a girlfriend. She just knew that she had to be too careful about getting too close to Jotham and needed to master the art of playing hard to get every time.

So far, she had done that well. She intended to keep him intrigued.

Dinner was ready and Kuti went to set the table for two.

Jotham walked into the kitchen and stood behind Najma as she tidied up the sink area.

"Kuti says you make a salad like an expert chef," he said, surprising her. He was standing too close when she turned to face him. Their eyes met for a moment; he reached out to her, picked up her wet hands and brought them to his face. She felt the coarse beard that were sprouting from a past-due shave.

"Can I kiss you?" he asked. "Please Najma?"

Suddenly, her face was flushed. She looked down.

She'd never seen or heard people ask if they could kiss another. That was completely new to her new and she was clueless as to how she should reply. She'd never even kissed a boy, let alone a man. A few minutes before, she'd literally fled from him. Now, all she wanted was to be in his arms. Her eyes moved from his face to his lips. She moved her hands from his face and locked them behind his neck. He was much taller than her so she had to stand on her toes to reach him.

His hands rode down her arms, down her back, pulled her closer to him and settled on the small of her back. He lowered his head and slightly and touched her lips with his own. He waited for a second to see how she would respond. She closed her eyes and slightly parted her lips in an invitation. He gently kissed her on both her lips, noticed the inexperienced fumbling with her own mouth, and smiled to himself, relieved, knowing she had no idea how to kiss a man. He was the first man she'd ever kissed.

Her face was calm, her eyes closed, her mouth slightly swollen when he let go off her. He knew he had to restrain himself before things got out of hand. He was not going to push her into anything that she wasn't ready for.

"Doctor, here is the camera," Kuti said, startling them. They pulled apart quickly and Najma turned back to the sink. Her knees were feeble and her face was flushed.

She didn't want to look at him or Kuti.

She didn't notice when Jotham left the room with the camera.

She didn't see Kuti coming and going, carrying food to the table.

"Mada—I mean Najma, the sink is clean already," Kuti said giggling. "You have been wiping it for like twenty minutes now!"

Najma turned to Kuti, avoiding her eyes.

"Is the table ready?" she asked, her voice trembling.

"Doctor is waiting for you," replied Kuti, walking closer to her. "Was it your first?" asked Kuti in a whisper.

Najma blushed.

"Yes," said Kuti. I can see it was your first! You did okay. Just don't be too shy. You need to show him you are no baby," she went on.

Najma was shocked. How could she possibly know?

"With my first, I almost fainted. But I'm used to it n—"

Najma broke into laughter at this point. She couldn't believe she was discussing kissing in the kitchen with her boyfriend's servant.

The laughter eased the tension.

"Just walk in there and talk about other things," advised Kuti.

Everything will be okay. You'll see," Kuti continued. "He'll be your boyfriend. You are so lucky."

Kuti smiled.

"Why?" Najma asked laughing.

"You are very beautiful. And Doctor is very handsome. Hope I will be here long enough to take care of your babies . . ."

With that, Kuti disappeared into the pantry leaving Najma in stiches.

Najma walked to the dining lounge and found Jotham staring into the camera.

"Let me see the photo," she said.

"No, not now," he said, standing up to pull out a chair for her. "You will see it sometime in the future . . ."

Dinner was mainly silent with dots of smiles and blushes.

When they were done, Najma excused herself and requested to be allowed to go to bed early. Jotham asked Kuti to show Najma to her room.

GODS AND GODDESSES– The Royal Funeral

The mood was somber. The choir sung melancholically. The air was heavily tainted by a pungent odor. A dark cloud hung over the castle grounds where the funeral was taking place. There were no special decorations—just chairs for the people, stools for water, and a small dais for speakers. There was no need for a tent, since the clouds formed a barrier, keeping the sun from shining.

Najma's eyes found Zaire, detached from the rest of the family. He hadn't sat down for even a minute. He was on call, walking onto and off of the lawn to answer phone calls and welcome arriving delegates.

The Statesman sat next to his wife, his head still bandaged.

A bodyguard and nurse stood behind him. It had been announced that he would be present for a short while and then be flown back to hospital.

His face was grey and swollen, his eyes relaying no emotion. When he tried to move in his seat, only the nurse attended to him. His wife acted like the man next to her was non-existent. She looked pale and tired; her hands tightly clasped. She kept adjusting her position in her seat.

His presence, Najma thought, is clearly to show the State that he is alive and well—that even though his brain was damaged, he's still significant."

He looks as if he has no idea what is happening.

But . . . am I mistaken or is he following the proceedings closely? Is that even possible, considering the severity of his injuries?

And isn't it weird that his wife hasn't even looked at him yet? Could it be that they are in a silent conflict with one another? Why is she ignoring him?

Zaire threw a glance at Najma, but she looked away when their eyes met.

He was in a black tuxedo, a cream silk shirt and a black tie, just like the Statesman.

For the first time, Najma noticed that there was a striking resemblance between them. Zaire was only taller and more athletic because he worked out. Their faces were molded in the same way. She wondered if Zaire was really adopted, but immediately dumped the idea that he may be the Statesman's real son. She couldn't fathom how Ploutus could be Zaire's father since that would mean he was her father too.

Jotham silently sat beside her, his fingers locked in hers. Before they sat down, he'd shown her around the castle and introduced her to some of his acquaintances as a friend. She'd been nervous, but she smiled boldly, contributed to conversations, and tried to act like the mature ladies attending the funeral service.

Zaire had not said anything to them since he was busy, ensuring that things were running smoothly.

Najma wore a long, black lacy gown, semi-halter-neck. She'd selected very high heels to match Jotham's height and was wearing designer sunglasses that she'd bought on the way. A silver and diamond clutch bag completed her outfit.

Her face was lightly made up and Jotham had confirmed that she looked beautiful before they left his house.

Jotham wore a grey tuxedo with a black silk shirt and a white tie, accompanied by greyish-black cobra skin sharp shooter shoes. Najma thought that he looked different in a tux.

"Hey guys, thanks for coming," said Zaire. She didn't notice him walking towards them and was a bit startled.

"You two look lovely together," he said. "I need you to come and sit behind Mom and Dad, though. The nurse is not sure if dad is okay, and she needs your help. We don't want to cause a commotion, though. Please, Ham, come over with Najma?" Zaire requested.

Najma rose quickly and started to get out of the row. Jotham hesitated but followed her. Zaire walked behind her, smiling at Jotham in appreciation.

"Zaire, I'm really sorry I left school," she said when he caught up with her.

"We will talk after the service," he said, walking past her and moving ahead to show them where to sit.

Najma wondered why she hadn't noticed the empty seats behind the First Family. She saw the First Lady staring at her with malice in her eyes, so she smiled at her. Ekesa looked away after returning something like a twist of the lips, rather than a smile.

Jotham took her hand protectively when he sat down and gave the First Lady a warning look. He beckoned the nurse and instructed her to give the Statesman a certain drug, then attended to Najma again.

"This is so sad," Najma whispered to him.

"I know," replied Jotham. "She was so young."

"How old?" Najma asked.

"Twenty-four," Jotham said.

"An only child . . . I can only imagine their pain," she went on.

"Maybe for the first lady," he said. Important men in this State are known for sowing wild oats . . ."

Najma shook her head in disbelief. How could Jotham make such bitter remarks? She wondered if he had something against the royal family.

"They were smart to adopt Zaire," Najma said softly.

She didn't concentrate on the speeches by various officials, focusing more on their body language. Some seemed genuine, while others went up the podium to show off. Others attacked the royal family with their non-verbal cues or embraced them with their words. She was fascinated.

"Is this how rich people usually behave?" she asked when the service came to an end and everyone was walking to the dining lounge.

"How?" Jotham asked, smiling knowingly.

"Is this how superficial their relationships are?"

"What do you mean?" he asked.

"Those people were openly gloating over the family's misfortune. It is as if they are forced to be here. Look around you, Ham," she responded with exasperation.

"These folks are going through hard times, dear. Each one of them. They just hide behind affluence and money," Jotham responded, pulling her out of the way for a suited official to hurry pass.

"In that case, I would rather be poor," Najma resigned.

"It's okay to be rich," he said, directing her to a table for three. It's best is to keep your social circles small and remain private. Publicity destroys people. Half of those people I introduced you to don't know anything about me beyond my office. They are just my psychiatry clients. Period."

He somehow knew that Zaire was going to join them for lunch after supervising the motorcade to take Nysa's body back to the morgue.

The burial was to be conducted the following day, and it was announced that only family and close relatives would be allowed inside. Zaire would have to be present, and that meant she was going to see him the following day. She really wanted to spend some time with him, especially since they'd not talked yet and her time at home was limited. The Principal had only allowed her five days.

"Who was the lady seated beside the First Lady?" Najma asked when they finally settled down. "The one who helped her read the eulogy?"

She had asked for a non-alcoholic beverage, and he was having white sparkling wine.

"Oh, that one?" he said, pointing out Arthenia, who was sitting at the main table.

"Yes," replied Najma. "She seems quite close to the family."

"Yes, she is," confirmed Jotham. "Her name is Arthenia. She is running for the Riverside Village delegate post. She owns the largest pesticide and poisons manufacturing company across all four States. She is super rich."

"Wow," said Najma, sipping from her iced tea. "Pretty too. I have a feeling about her. I'm sure I've seen her somewhere. Not from a distance—kind of in a closer way."

She scanned the lounge, focusing on the royal table, trying to figure out where she'd seen the lady.

The First Lady wasn't talking at all. Seated to the right of the First Lady, the familiar woman was addressing a matron who sat to her right. The two of them looked as though they were immersed in a heated conversation. Najma felt sympathy for the First Lady.

"Come on, sweetheart. You are staring," Jotham distracted her.

"I couldn't help it," Najma replied. "I was just wondering why all those women are plastered around the First Lady, yet none of them connects with her," she said.

"You're going to make a great psychiatrist, darling. You're a natural," he said, smiling.

"What has that got to do with anything?" she asked.

"Everything, baby," he replied with a warm smile. You read people like scripts."

"Well, you know," she replied, "that is what I have done my entire life. Read people. I had nobody to talk to except my mom . . . and Nana sometimes, so I've learned to observe."

"And that is what I love most about you." Ham said, his eyes locked on hers. "You are quiet but deep."

Zaire joined them shortly after lunch was served.

Najma was having Maryland Chicken and spiced fries, some vegetable salad, and a glass of fresh juice.

Jotham was having baked wild boar, pasta, and fried fruit. He was on his second glass of wine.

Zaire joined them, carrying a plate of roast goat meat and some red wine.

"How is everything?" Najma asked as soon as he was seated.

"Fairly decent," Zaire sighed. Dad's been flown back to Ward Nine already, and Nysa's body is back at the morgue. Mom is well composed, considering everything."

"With Arthenia by her side, she will be fine," Jotham said.

"Yes," replied Zaire. "She's been very helpful."

"I wonder why Arthenia looks so familiar," Najma said, looking at Zaire.

"You never know. She may very well be. This family has proven to be quite industrious," said Jotham, a hint of sarcasm in his voice.

"Not here, bro, please," Zaire cut him short.

"I'm sorry, bro," Jotham answered slightly accentuating the word 'bro.'

"How are you, Najma? Did you see Nana?" Zaire asked.

"You mean my mom?" Jotham asked.

Zaire's eyes widened.

"Yeah, I know. She told me," Jotham said, gesturing at Najma.

"Really?" Zaire asked, eyeing Najma.

"I'm sorry, bro," she replied. "I couldn't keep the truth from him any longer. Besides, we needed to know if we are related. Just in case . . ."

"You are not related in any way," Zaire said sullenly. "And you promised to keep it a secret, Najma."

"I am sorry," Najma said sadly. "I just hate where all these bits of truth are headed. It feels like there is so much pain waiting to be unleashed."

"Zaire, how are you?" Chimed Arthenia. "Who is this beautiful lady? Hey Doctor!"

They didn't notice Arthenia walking to their table.

"Hey Arthenia," greeted Zaire. "This is Najma."

Zaire stood up, hoping to pull Arthenia away from the table. However, she formidably rooted herself to the floor and extended her hand to Najma.

"I never thought you were this grown already," Arthenia exclaimed. "Shouldn't you be in school? Nana told me you are at Mountain Crest?"

Najma was visibly shocked. She couldn't believe her ears. The woman in front of her spoke in her mother's voice. She opened her mouth to say something, but her lips were dry.

Zaire was equally stunned.

Jotham were ready to pounce on anyone who hurt Najma. His fingers were tightly locked into Najma's and the more Arthenia spoke the tighter he locked them.

"Arthenia," he said. "Let's focus on the lunch please." He looked at Arthenia in a manner that suggested she should leave.

"It's okay," She replied. "I was just excited to see my niece. She looks exactly like Elima. I don't know . . ." Arthenia's voice trembled slightly. There was an awkward silence. She excused herself and walked away."

Najma was frozen. She didn't touch her food again. Her eyes were fixed on the sparkling glasses on the table. She wanted to say something to kill the odd silence, but her mind was blank.

"I'm so sorry about everything, Najma." said Zaire. "I hope I'll clear it all up before it spirals out of control." He reached out for her hand, but Jotham refused to release it. She didn't try to get to him either. Instead, she just sat and stared blankly.

"Take me home please," she finally said, having found her voice.

Jotham nodded in agreement. The two walked out in silence, Ham holding her hand like both of their lives depended on it.

"Drop her at her house, Ham," Zaire said, following them. "Nana wanted to see her."

Jotham nodded and Zaire went back inside.

"Don't be so hard on him," Jotham said. "I think he's losing it all himself. It's not easy being him."

He started the engine, and they drove out of the castle compound.

"I deserve to know the whole truth," she said.

This time, she allowed her tears to flow freely.

Ploutus was in a VIP room—the same room that Elima had been put in when she'd been unwell. He stared blankly.

He could see her all over the room.

He heard her voice. Her laughter.

He smelled her perfume.

She was all over the brick walls.

Sometimes, the whitewashed walls closed in on him.

He saw them shrinking, squeezing him between the layered bricks like they were about to crush him.

Elima's face was all over the walls.

She laughed her infectious, innocent laughter like that of a little girl—the laughter that made him fall in love with her.

She'd always laughed at everything he said.

She'd laughed when he told her he wanted her to be his girlfriend; when he'd brought her gifts; when he'd asked her to marry him. When she'd broken the news that she was expecting his child, she'd laughed so hard that she'd cried afterwards.

Ploutus had never understood why Elima laughed so much. But then, when he'd told her that he'd decided to marry Ekesa, Elima's streams of laughter had dried up. Her eyes had grown dark, then wet. Her mouth had quivered. Her beautiful gapped teeth had become hidden behind the bitter downturned curve of her once laughing lips. The woman who'd stood before him that afternoon was a different person altogether.

"Sir, your medicine is ready," said a voice.

He turned toward the nurse and smiled.

"Can you see her?" he asked the startled nurse. She's all over the room. She's here."

The nurse was visibly frightened. Tablets knocked against each other in the small container she carried. She handed him the drugs with trembling hands and quickly left the room.

He knew she was going to call the doctor. When she disappeared through the door, Ploutus smiled, then broke into laughter. He laughed so hard that his head hurt.

He shoved the tablets into a container under his bed and gently lay his head on the pillow.

"He says Elima is in the room!"

The nurse's high-pitched voice reached him through the walls. He pretended to be sleeping when the doctor walked in.

Jotham took his temperature and blood pressure, then told the nurse to leave them alone. She was clearly frightened.

"How is your head today?" Jotham asked.

"Fine," replied Ploutus, shrugging. "Some slight pain. I saw you with my daughter yesterday."

Jotham was not surprised. He had suspected that Ploutus had requested Zaire to ask Najma and himself to sit near the Statesman. He'd pretended to be unwell to catch Jotham's attention. Jotham had noticed that he'd focused more on Najma all the time.

"What you did yesterday was so risky," Jotham said.

"I know," said Ploutus. "But I needed to see my girl. She is so beautiful. She looks just like her mother. I could not help but notice that when I saw you two walk in."

"Listen, if we are going to work together, I need you to act sick," Jotham warned him. Actually, you are sick. You have no memory. Stop talking about Elima."

"I can't," said Ploutus. "I see her all over this room. She talks to me and laughs. Sometimes, she threatens me. I'm not lying. She's always in this room."

For a moment, Jotham thought the Statesman was truly losing his mind—that he couldn't trust the man's sanity. He regretted having made a deal with him.

But then, Ploutus looked as though he was telling the truth. Was fate, indeed, catching up to him? Could he really be insane?

If that's the case, thought Jotham, how will I explain to Zaire that I'd made a deal with his father behind his back? The fact that Ploutus is Najma's father complicates matters. I cannot risk exposing myself. This secret will have to go to the grave with me, if need be.

"Sir," he said, "we have to be very careful. "Your being in this facility is risky enough with the other patients present. We need to hurry the process of moving them so that I can fully own this place. Then we can carry out our business without the interference of the larger hospital."

"You are too ambitious, young man," said Ploutus, his lips twitching with anger. "I know you are in love with my daughter, and you will need my blessing. In fact, Elima thinks that you are a perfect match for Najma, and I cannot argue with that. You should be grateful for that. I will sign the hospital agreement when I see it fit, so don't push your luck. We will operate as I direct. I've paid you for that, remember?"

Jotham remained silent.

"My head hurts. Get me some of those strong pain killers!" Ploutus demanded.

"Too risky," warned Jotham. You cannot use them more than twice a week."

He regretted having gotten himself into dealings with Ploutus.

"Just bring them!" Ploutus ordered.

"They're too expensive," replied Jotham. "The administrator will notice when they reduce. Perhaps we could buy some for you?"

"Just go get them, son!" Ploutus yelled. "I hate repeating myself. And next time you walk through that door, bring Najma with you."

Jotham left the room. He was so angry that he didn't notice the bodyguards standing outside the ward. He didn't notice that they'd been changed already. He wanted to be done with Ploutus.

Perhaps I need to talk to Zaire, he thought. Wonder if he'll believe me if I tell him his father is faking illness to get to his enemies. Would he believe me if I told him I had conspired with Ploutus and two other officials to get the doctor at Mountain Crest to sign a report that Ploutus had lost his memories and needed to recover at Ward Nine? Perhaps it's time to test my hypnosis skills . . .

His head was exploding with thoughts. He felt frustrated. He wondered what Najma would do if she found out what he had done. He wondered if she would ever forgive him.

"Where is my daughter now?" Ploutus asked him when he returned with morphine tablets.

"I dropped her at her house at Corner yesterday evening." Jotham answered.

"My friend," said Ploutus. "Cooperate with me, and I'll see to it that you have her—even immediately when she finishes her exams. She's old enough. I need to see her. Elima wants to see her. She will crush my head if you don't bring Najma. If you cross me, I'll take Najma away and have you frozen in a minute."

The drug was already working on Ploutus. Jotham contemplated silencing him at that moment and reporting that he'd died during medication, but decided against it. It would be too risky. Besides, with the secrets that Zaire kept, he doubted Zaire would protect him if this thing backfired. Lately, Zaire behaved as if Ploutus was the best thing since candyfloss. Jotham doubted Zaire still wanted to carry out the revenge he'd been planning for years. Besides, the postmortem would indicate that Ploutus had morphine in his system. That would put Jotham's license as a doctor at risk.

He hoped what Ploutus planned would end soon, so he could get the basis for his private practice in good time. Jotham also hoped that Ploutus would let him be with Najma. He couldn't stand the thought of being away from her. He felt like her life was in danger, especially since she was related to Ploutus. He suspected Arthenia's interest in Najma was not genuine since Ekesa was her best friend. He also doubted if Ploutus would risk announcing her as his daughter publicly. What if she were to discover that Ploutus had killed her mother? Would Ploutus spare her if she decided to sue him? This was getting much too complicated. At the end of the day, he was too exhausted to visit Najma as he had promised her the previous day. He wondered if Zaire would be available for a beer but decided against asking. He could no longer risk getting loose-tongued with Zaire.

He could only go to one place . . .

MOTHER MEETS SON . . .

Nana wasn't expecting anyone that afternoon. Najma had gone to meet Zaire at Market Square. She wondered who could be knocking at that time of day. They couldn't be back so soon. Zaire had said he would buy Najma lunch and would only be back for dinner.

Could it be Arthenia? She thought. I hope it's not her. I don't have any patience for her today.

Arthenia had visited a few weeks back, and it had felt like a poke in Nana's sour sores. She had come to mock her, hiding behind the goodwill of their home village. Arthenia never cared about anyone. She was talking about going back home to run the village affairs just like their father did. How could she? In Nana's eyes, Arthenia had no idea what life in Riverside looked like. Did she think it was all about banana forests and mango trees? Was she still stuck in the days of walking down the steep slopes that led to the pure crystal-clear water of the river? Was she still delusional, convinced that the people would care about her royal blood?

No one in Riverside cared about the Late Chief or his set of loser daughters. They had their own troubles with the rich, man-loving gold-maker who was poisoning the river. Even the rain was acidic already. Bananas became rotten before they could ripen. No trucks came from the capital to collect farm produce. The villagers were going hungry.

Witches were out every night, seeking innocent souls to sacrifice to the spirits to help them get rid of the rich gold-maker. They were angry—not only at his toxic industry but also at the trail of perfume he left behind wherever he went, making their children sneeze. As if toxic water wasn't enough already.

She unbolted the main door and walked onto the verandah. She'd not locked the verandah door so she pushed it aside, in time to see the doctor walking away.

"Hello, Doctor!" she said merrily. "Sorry I took too long. Come on in!"

Something about the doctor reminded her of her youth. He was so tall and well mannered—his smile so familiar. She stared at him as he walked back smiling.

"I'm sorry," she said. "I was having a siesta. It's so hot here, and an old woman like me can slip away to slumber, even on her feet. Come in!"

"Thank you," he said, stepping out of his shoes and into the living room.

"Najma just left with Zaire," she said. "They'll be back in the evening. I wasn't expecting anyone."

"It's okay," Jotham said awkwardly. His voice was trembling, and he hated it. He'd rehearsed all day what he was going to say to Nana, but now his thoughts deserted him. He looked at the bubbly woman, all happy and charming. He wondered if she'd recognized him. Zaire had said they were separated at birth. Could she remember?

"I'm sorry for barging in," he said, attempting to smile. "I was not looking for Najma, though."

"Zaire . . ." Nana started.

"Not Zaire," he interrupted. His eyes were fixed on her face. He wanted to fly into her chubby arms. He wanted to be cuddled so he could cry. He felt so alone and depressed. His life was in danger, and all he wanted was a motherly hug.

"I came to see you," he blurted out.

"Me?" she asked plainly, her smile vanishing. "What for?"

"I just needed your hug," he blurted out again. He immediately regretted saying that. She might have misinterpreted the whole thing. When she stood up, he opened his mouth to apologize, rising up to leave. However, she gathered him in her arms and embraced him warmly. He was rigid at first, but then he relaxed in her arms. He felt his chest tighten and a sob escaped his mouth.

"Mother," he gasped.

She just held him and said nothing. The warmth of her body reached out to him and warmed his trembling body. He felt like a three-year-old boy.

"Mother . . . he is going to kill me," he sobbed on.

She still didn't say anything. She led him to sit and sat next to him, holding both his hands. She looked him squarely in the face, scrutinizing his features.

"Son," she asked carefully, watching his eyes. "Who is your father?"

"I just met him the other day," Jotham answered without hesitation. He is the principal of Najma's school.

"What is his name?" she asked again, this time deliberately slowly. Her eyes were fixed on Jotham's face.

"Etembi," he said. "That's what Zaire called him."

This time, she looked away. The glitter in her eyes suddenly disappeared. Her mouth parted to say something, but she kept silent.

"I'm so sorry," he stammered. "I shouldn't have come . . ."

"It's okay," she said after a while. "Where is your mother?"

"I don't know," he said without thinking.

She raised an eyebrow to suggest she did not understand.

"I was raised in an orphanage." He said. "That's where I met Zaire. But now . . ." His voice trailed off.

"But now what?" she asked.

"You don't know?" he asked in return.

"Know what?" she asked, her mouth twisting in a quiver.

"Mother," he whispered desperately. He hated what he was doing to her—hated that he couldn't bring himself to tell her everything. In his moment of suffering and pain, he had finally found his mother—the one he had thought was dead all along.

Next to him sat a woman who had believed she'd given birth to a rainbow baby girl; a woman who mourned the loss of a baby and a boyfriend at the same time; a woman who had lost almost everybody whom she loved; a woman who had nothing to live for, except Najma. How could he break the news to her?

"Are you messing with my head, Doctor?" she asked, this time her voice trembling and her eyes welling up.

"I'm sorry," he said. "I have to go . . ."

Suddenly, there was a knock at the door.

They looked at each other.

"Did you leave someone in the car?" she asked sternly.

"No" he responded, shaking his head.

Nana went to the door and opened it. Arthenia walked into the house without Nana inviting her in.

"I knew I could find you here, Doctor," she said breathlessly.

"What's wrong?" Nana and Jotham asked in unison.

"Where is Zaire?" Arthenia asked. "We need him urgently."

"Who is we?" Jotham asked.

Nana nodded in agreement, her hands akimbo.

"I went to the hospital," explained Arthenia. "I mean Ward Nine, to see Ploutus. He wired me."

"How?" Jotham wanted to know. "I left him sleeping!"

"That's the problem," she said. "It was a set up. Someone used his phone to call me. Some delegates are going to release a media statement, claiming that Ploutus is pretending to be sick, to earn sympathy votes for his third term. There is talks about re-writing the constitution in the capital . . ."

"Mother, we need to find Zaire." Jotham turned to Nana. "Where did they go?"

"I am not your mother!" Nana said angrily.

"Yes, you are," Arthenia and Jotham said in unison.

"You know?" Jotham turned to Arthenia.

"Yes," she answered boldly, then turned to the bewildered Nana. "Now, if you don't mind, tell us where Zaire is."

It was more of an order.

"At the café at Market Square," Nana said.

Arthenia and Jotham ran out of the house, leaving Nana torn between following them and digesting what they had just disclosed.

GODS AND GODDESSES – Leveling the Blue Room

Artemis, Lorantu, Jerry, and Barvo sat around a mahogany map-shaped table. Each had a half-filled glass in front of them.

They were in a private bar complex that belonged to one of Barvo's friends, and the place was exclusively meant for people like him and Jerry.

It was located in a gorge, tucked into the caves, and only a few people knew about it. The cottage in which they sat in was large enough for four people, but most of the cottages in the bar complex could only contain two.

There were erotic gay pictures all over the walls.

The huge glass windows let a breeze into the cottage, causing it to be chilly, but the musky warmth of male perspiration dulled the chill. There was also the sweet aroma of nature, emitted by the fern and moss that surrounded the premises, separating it from the rocky walls of the gorge.

The table was a chiseled-in map of Lakeside. The wooden couches on which they sat were curved in such a way as to resemble a man's bare chest.

Barvo held a brown smokeless cigar in his left hand while pouring Scotch into a glass with the right. When he wasn't pouring whisky, he used his right hand to caress Jerry's left thigh ever so gently.

Jerry's face was grey with fear. Every time he tried to speak, his lips only quivered and stuck back together.

"I would never let anything happen to you, my love," Barvo said, drawing hard on his cigar.

"Those beasts almost killed me," said Jerry's with a trembling voice. "They had a gun to my head and a knife to my throat . . ."

Artemis was clearly disgusted by the two. She gulped her martini so quickly that Lorantu had to take the glass away from her lips forcefully. He planted a sudden kiss on her lips to block her protests.

"You can't afford to get drunk now if you are going to be the next First Lady," he said, agitated. "You look awful already. It's just a few hours till midnight, when we'll release our statement to the media."

They had a plan of releasing the recorded evidence, showing Ploutus talking to Jotham. The recording would indicate that he was not sick and was using the mental facility to run his affairs privately. Arthenia had confirmed about two hours ago that Ploutus was actually faking amnesia.

They also wanted to portray Ploutus as a brute who blackmailed people and killed them afterwards. In the recording, Ploutus was threatening to silence Jotham if he dared to double-cross him.

Lorantu was on the brink of declaring himself a candidate for the next election and calling upon the delegates who had the power to elect a Statesman among themselves in case of an emergency, to select him. He had bought a few men and women in senior positions to support him, and some had willingly joined his circle. He had plans to make Barvo a delegate for any village he wished to have as well.

"Sorry, darling," said Artemis, "but I hate what we are doing. Ekesa is my friend . . ."

"No, she is not!" exclaimed Lorantu. "You killed her daughter, remember? If she gets a better footing than we do, we all go down. They won't spare our lives. Can't you see?"

His voice escalated to way above the room, echoing amongst the deep brown mosaic walls of the bar.

"I did not kill Nysa. You did," she said, looking at him in disgust. "You drugged her and raped her!"

Lorantu grabbed her neck and squeezed it, making her squeak like a rat.

"If you ever repeat that," he growled, "I will snap this thin neck of yours and send you back into the village where you came from. You are such an ungrateful bitch!"

"Oh, no," said Jerry in a weak voice. "I hate violence."

He looked like he was about to cry.

"Would you mind your business?" Barvo snapped at him. "If there is nothing better to do with your mouth, just get down and shove this thing down your throat."

"Don't talk to me like that!" Jerry said, rising up.

"Then mind your own business!" said Barvo.

Jerry started to move out of his seat.

And where do you think you're going?" Barvo wanted to know, pulling Jerry down roughly.

Jerry stood up, swiftly this time, picked up a glass of scotch and flung it into Barvo's flaming eyes.

"Ungrateful bastard!" Barvo roared, rubbing his eyes, which were stinging because of the alcohol.

"All I ever did was love you!" Jerry said angrily. "I've always cleaned up after you. Been your eyes on the ground, but this is it! I'm done!"

He began to walk away. Barvo grabbed his hand, but Jerry managed to wiggle out of his grip.

Artemis and Lorantu had stopped fighting and Lorantu was now watching Barvo and Jerry.

Artemis's eyes were on the door, silently hoping that someone would walk in before it was too late.

"Jerry," said Lorantu, pulling out a pistol. "If you walk through that door, I . . . will . . . shoot you . . ." Jerry stopped in his tracks when he heard Artemis and Barvo gasp together. He slowly turned around, finding himself standing face to face with Lorantu's pistol.

"I dare you to shoot me," Jerry said, his eyes fixed on Lorantu.

"I will if you push me," warned Lorantu, his voice lower than usual. "What has gotten into you?"

"What has gotten into *me*?" Exclaimed Jerry. "Really? Just look at your woman! She is trembling like a leaf in the wind, undoubtedly in fear of you! What makes the two of you think that you can use us as you please? We are the most loyal . . . actually, the *only* loyal people you have had for years. But how do you repay us? With threats and treating us like we are pieces of trash. I am tired."

"Put that thing away, Lorantu," said Barvo. "We can't be fighting when we are about to release a statement in just a couple of hours."

"You are not going to release any statement," Artemis said.

The two men turned around at once, looking at Artemis.

"What do you mean, woman?" Lorantu asked.

"We cannot allow West Valley to be in the hands of a brute like you."

"You traffic people who should be voting for you."

"How many young girls have died in your hands? You wouldn't think twice before you shot me in the mouth. The same mouth that has sung you praises, given you pleasure, and warned you when things were going under. That stops now. Right now, I am willing to go to jail, but I will not live to see the day you become Statesman Lorantu. Over my dead body!"

Artemis was breathless when she finished her tirade.

"Is this some kind of conspiracy?" Barvo asked, first eyeing Jerry, then Artemis.

"Call it whatever you want," replied Jerry, but it stops tonight."

A waiter walked into the room, carrying a bottle of whisky and two clean glasses.

"Did you call for more drinks, Lorantu?" Barvo asked.

"Nope. You?" Lorantu replied.

Barvo shook his head in denial.

"This is my treat," said Artemis, standing up. Lorantu tried to grab her, but a sudden pistol shot stopped him.

The cottage door was wide open. Another waiter walked in with a pistol in the air.

"If you lay your hands on that woman again, I am going to plaster these disgusting walls in your brains and intestines!"

The waiter's voice boomed across the room. There were two more men in black and white. They strode in and locked the cottage door.

The waiter who'd brought in the whiskey stepped back, directing Artemis and Jerry to the door. He searched them for recorded tapes, then slightly opened the cottage door to let them out.

"We have them, sir," one of the men said on the phone. "We let the ladies walk. Zaire will deal with them."

Lorantu and Barvo were bundled up, their mouths taped. A few men, who'd heard the commotion from the nearest cottages, peeped through their door.

"It's going to be nasty, boys," one suited man shouted at no one in particular, gyrating his hips suggestively. The peeping men smiled knowingly and went back to their drinks and partners.

WARD NINE – Father Meets Daughter

In Ploutus's Room

Ploutus watched eagerly as Zaire, Jotham, and Najma walked along the corridor towards his room. He was excited to see Najma. He whispered to Elima, asking her to come and see their daughter.

"Who are you talking to?" Jotham asked when the trio walked in.

"How dare you take my daughter to that criminal dungeon, Zaire?" Ploutus thundered back.

Zaire and Jotham exchanged a look of surprise.

Zaire took Najma's hand and squeezed it slightly. A nurse was just a step or two behind them. When she heard the Statesman shout angrily, she ran back through the door. A bodyguard grabbed her before she could disappear into the corridor.

Jotham looked through the window quickly, in time to see the nurse disappear into the next room with the bodyguard.

Outside Ploutus's Room

The bodyguard tightly held the nurse who tried to wiggle herself loose. He directed her toward another room. He showed her a gun that was mounted with a silencer. The nurse stopped squirming and bit her lower lip in silence.

In the Bodyguard's Room

"Someone talked to people about the Statesman," the bodyguard said, his hand tightening around the nurse's arm.

"I don't know what you are talking about," said the nurse, her lips quivering and tears running down her cheeks. "Let me go or I'll scream!"

The bodyguard pushed her into a room and locked the door behind him. Inside the room, Lorantu and Barvo sat on beds, dressed as patients.

"Does this jog your memory?" the bodyguard sneered.

"Don't hurt her, please," said Lorantu, trying to stand up. "My daughter is innocent."

His hands and feet were fastened to the bed.

"Dad!" the nurse almost screamed. "When did you get here? You promised we would be safe."

Lorantu couldn't look at her. His eyes were on the bodyguard, pleading in every way he knew.

"I will answer all the questions. Zaire has the tapes of my confessions. Please let my daughter go," Lorantu pleaded.

"Do you know what this is?" the bodyguard asked the frightened girl, handing her three bottles of liquid.

In Ploutus's Room

Zaire tried calming Ploutus down.

"This is not Nysa," said Zaire. "This is my friend. You haven't met her before," Zaire said.

"Stop playing with my head, Zaire!" Ploutus said, his mouth frothing in anger.

"Sir, you need to calm down," Jotham said, his face feigning concern. "Nysa isn't here. We buried your daughter a few days ago. This is not your daughter."

"Sweetheart," said Jotham. "Maybe you should step out a little. The Statesman is confusing you with his late daughter. You know he is unwell," Jotham said to Najma.

Najma stood there, her eyes fixed on the Statesman. His face looked exactly like that of Zaire. She wondered why Zaire and Jotham insisted that she come to Ward Nine with them, yet now they were trying to make her leave.

"It's okay," she said, moving closer to Ploutus's bed. "Perhaps the statesman needs me,"

She took his hand, looking into his angry eyes. Jotham stood to her left and Zaire to her right.

"My daughter . . ."

Ploutus choked on his tears. Suddenly, he was wailing.

For a moment, neither Zaire nor Jotham knew what to do.

They just stood there, watching Najma stroke Ploutus's head, whispering.

She told him it was okay; that his daughter Nysa was in a better place; that he should focus on his recovery so that he could get out of hospital; that his people were waiting for him to get better so that he could out of Ward Nine.

This would be the only intimate moment Najma would have with her father in her lifetime. It would be a cherished memory.

"My daughter . . ." Ploutus murmured again.

"Dad," said Zaire. "We need to get her out of here."

Ploutus shot him an angry look . . .

In the Bodyguard's Room

The nurse looked at the tiny glass bottles that the bodyguard had handed to her, and her eyes widened when she read the labels.

"These are highly dangerous!" she exclaimed "How did you get these?"

"None of your business," replied the bodyguard, closing in on her. "The question should rather be: what should I do with them?" He grabbed her by the waist and pulled her to himself. For a few seconds, she was breathless.

Barvo observed silently and Lorantu continued begging.

"Do you know what your father does for a living?" the bodyguard asked the nurse.

"He is a businessman," she answered quickly.

"What kind of business?" the bodyguard whispered in her ear.

"I don't know," the nurse said.

The bodyguard pushed her away and stretched out his hand for a bottle.

Lorantu was now weeping, pleading with the bodyguard to spare his daughter's life.

"She's the only child I have. Please!" he sobbed.

He promised the bodyguard money.

"Your father abducts young girls like you," said the bodyguard.

"I don't believe you!" she yelled.

"And then, he lures them into drugged sex," he said, eyeing the three bottles, "selling them off as sex toys when he's done with them."

The nurse gasped, her face slowly turning into a mask of disgust—even hatred. She looked at her father, who was struggling to get out of the restraining apron.

In Ploutus's Room

Najma was getting suspicious.

Zaire was acting weird.

Had he not been the one who begged her to come with him and Jotham to see the Statesman?

Why was he insisting that they go? If anything, Jotham had said that Nana needed some alone time after the news that he'd broken to her.

Arthenia had also suggested that they should give her time to recover—that there was a chance for her to help out with a patient.

And Jotham and Zaire were already bundling her out?

"I don't have to go now. I will stay with the Statesman," Najma said.

"Not in this condition, dear," said Jotham, working on a drug table. "He is hallucinating right now, and it is dangerous for his recovery. We need to give him medicine so that he can sleep."

"What is that?" yelled Ploutus. "What are you mixing? Do you want to kill me? Don't do this! You are messing with the wrong person, young man . . ."

Ploutus was now in a panic. He yelled, calling for his bodyguards.

But the bodyguards were not outside his room, so they couldn't hear him. They were watching out for the nurse's business, as instructed by Zaire.

Najma tried to calm him down. He was twisting and turning in his bed. Thank God there were rubber restrains on him. If it were pieces of cloth, he would have broken them easily.

"Don't let him inject me, Zaire!" Ploutus shouted. "Don't trust this doctor. He is killing me. He's a quack. I'm not mad. I have all my memory. I just pretended to get some things done!"

Jotham sunk a syringe into Ploutus's neck. He suddenly went limp.

"Will he be okay?" Najma asked after they removed the rubber restraints and covered him.

His face was now peaceful.

"Yes," replied Jotham. "I just gave him something to calm him down."

"We need to get you out of here, Najma," said Zaire. "Go with Jotham to his place. I will pick you up later. I have something to attend to."

Jotham recorded some things in a file, put them in a drawer, locked it, and then took Najma's hand. They walked out together, while Zaire stayed behind for a while.

In Jotham's Car

"I'm not sure, but I think the Statesman said my mother's name," said Najma. Did you hear it too?"

"No," he said, feigning surprise. "How could he possibly know her name?"

Najma shook her head and focused on the road.

"Perhaps, I should go back to school now," she said after a while. "I think you guys will be okay."

"But . . . you need to have a talk with Zaire, first," replied Jotham. "There are lots of things you need to understand before going back."

"You're right," she responded. "But after meeting Arthenia and discovering that she is my aunt, I feel that she's connected to the Statesman in a closer way. This is just too much for me. I need to focus on my studies. It's better that I don't know the rest. At least for now."

Najma's eyes were on the road. Jotham drove with one hand and held hers in the other.

"I wish there was something I could do," he said.

In the Bodyguard's Room

The Bodyguard broke the seals of the three bottles and gave a bottle each to Lorantu, his daughter, and Barvo. He ordered them to drink the contents, cocking a pistol. The nurse and Barvo drank on command, but he had to force the contents down Lorantu's throat, threatening to shoot him if he dared to spit.

"Now, gentlemen," he said, shifting his gaze between Lorantu and Barvo. "You will be found in the morning, soaking in your own shit. Orderlies will clean you up, then assign you to different wards where you will start your medication."

"What about my daughter?" Lorantu asked, his face contorted with pain.

"This one is coming with me," he replied. My friends and I will show her what you do to other people's children and when we are done, we will organize a decent burial for her. Just like Nysa's."

With that, he swept the nurse off her folding legs and carried her out of the room as though she were a baby.

The loud fart that Barvo released silenced Lorantu's muffled screams of protest.

"Is it done?" asked Zaire when the bodyguard came out of the room and locked the door.

"Yes, it is." He responded.

"Don't leave a messy trail behind," Zaire said indicating the nurse in the bodyguard's arms. "I've dropped her resignation at the administrator's desk. Make sure she never comes back."

The bodyguard nodded.

"Guards will be changed tonight," said Zaire. When you receive your pay at midnight, leave the state and never come back if you value your life. Clear?"

Zaire whispered the last word in an ominous tone of voice.

"I know how it works, Zaire," the bodyguard who carried the nurse said.

This particular bodyguard had been a close ally to Zaire, and together they had cleaned up a great many messes. However, he'd requested to be let off the hook, and Zaire had granted it. Zaire knew that Ploutus would never approve, but then, he was in no position to protest. Zaire and Jotham were going to turn his subterfuge of amnesia into a reality . . .

Outside Ward Nine

As he walked to his car, Zaire wondered if his plan worked out. Jotham had confided in him that Ploutus was pretending. He had prevented a situation by silencing the whistle blowers, Barvo and Lorantu, who were planning a state coup. He had sent word to their supporters, using a harsh hushed signal, and all had pulled out in fear.

Jerry was already on a plane to Lakeside, and Artemis had requested to be allowed to see Ekesa before she left. All he still had to do was get Ekesa to announce an early election via Ploutus's deputy and the state spokesperson.

Ploutus had no idea that Zaire, Jotham, and Arthenia were already working together. They had agreed to keep him in Ward Nine as long as possible. Zaire had no problem with Arthenia and her plans but wasn't sure whether she deserved to be a delegate.

He had no bitterness towards her for killing his mother. After all, Akusa had dumped him in an orphanage and never cared how he turned out. Arthenia was paying for her own sins already. She had a terminal illness and wasn't sure if she was going to live long enough to correct her mistakes. There was no need of punishing her; nature had done it for Zaire and for all the people that she'd harmed. He wished Riverside had a better candidate, though.

He pulled out a notebook and made a 'to do' list:

Reveal to Najma the necessary truth

Consult with Nana about Arthenia and her illness

Clear Ward Nine to be a private hospice for Jotham

See Ekesa and help her organize a statement on behalf of Ploutus

Bring in Osanyin for questioning

Move out of the Castle

He circled the last one, then leaned back in the driver's seat and closed his eyes. He longed for the day all his governance troubles would be something of the past.

Father Cruz's voice came to him clearly and loudly: West Valley will need you more in a suit than in a priestly gown. Just don't let it darken your pure soul.

Zaire wondered if he even still had a soul.

GODS AND GODDESES - Moment of Truth

Artemis looked around her.

She'd released all the girls that were waiting to be shipped to Mountain Crest. She'd cleared all those who'd worked in her brothels and had paid them their dues. She'd given them back their passports and some money to start a business back home.

What used to be home to her was now quiet and empty. She'd requested workers to drain the swimming pools, take whatever they liked, and vacate the servants' quarters.

As she stood in her house on her way out, the memories of how she'd come here, played in her mind like a movie. She remembered how frightened she'd been.

Lorantu had taken her away from the village when she was only fifteen.

Her father had died and her mother had deserted her to run off with her lover. She'd been so helpless at the time.

Lorantu had been looking for girls to work in his hotel in the capital. The woman who'd been helping him had begged him to take her with them.

She'd been so petite, Lorantu had been reluctant to comply.

"What could I do with her?" He'd barked at the woman. She's too small, for Pete's sake!"

"I can clean, sir." Artemis had said, trying to impress him. "Or I can look after babies."

He'd just looked at her pensively.

"My daughter needs a playmate," he'd finally said.

Artemis remembered how she had marveled at the big house, excitedly shrieking while clapping her hands. Lorantu's daughter had liked her so much that Lorantu was moved. He'd agreed to let her stay.

Then one day, after two years of free food, shelter, and clothing, Lorantu had come home from his business and had forced himself into her. She'd whimpered in pain, but after a few months of regularly being treated that way, she'd become used to it. He'd found someone to teach her how to act in bed and dress like a big girl. He'd overhauled her wardrobe. He'd also found a doctor who'd removed her womb so that she could never conceive.

His daughter went to a boarding school and she'd never seen her friend again.

She'd never questioned him . . .

It was his house.

His money.

His daughter.

His hotels, bars, drugs, cigars . . .

. . . and she became his . . .

. . . just like the many objects he'd owned.

*****

As she walked to the door of the house that she'd lived in for over twenty years—the only home she could remember—tears ran down her cheeks. She had no idea where she was going. She knew she could buy a home and start over. Zaïre had given her another chance. He had saved her from Lorantu.

Pulling her suitcase in one hand and her clutch bag, containing her passport, in the other, she made a decision: the legacy of the Blue Room would die. No girl would have to face what she'd had to go through, ever again . . .

She knew that Lorantu had enough petrol stored in the house to blow up a small island.

She took her luggage to the new car she had bought for her journey, drove it off the premises, and parked at a safe distance.

She took a box of matches from the cubbyhole and went back to the house.

She took a container of petrol, ran upstairs to Lorantus's study and emptied the container on the floor and over his desk and computer.

She struck a match and dropped it on Lorantus's desk.

She watched until the blue and orange tongues of fire began to consume the computer.

Then, she began to run.

She had to get out before the fire reached the main supply of petrol. She had to avoid the explosion that would inevitably follow.

Outside, she ran to her car, got in, and sped away, just in time. When she was about one hundred meters from the house, she heard a massive blast. What had once been the source of so much pain and suffering for so many young people had finally ended.

Artemis felt a surge of relief flowing through her entire being—body, soul, and spirit.

She drove until she reached the capital and filled up her tank.

I have to stop at the Ploutus Castle first to see Ekesa, Thought Artemis. I doubt she'll even want to look at me, but I have to ask for her forgiveness in person.

When the tank was full and she'd paid for the petrol, Artemis went to a café to eat and have something to drink. She remained pensive for a while.

What a weird feeling, she thought. I'm finally free! It's almost impossible to believe! Perhaps Zaire was right. Perhaps it would be better to drop her a note. That way, she won't be able to kill me for what I've done to her daughter.

She ate her food, paid the waiter, and went back to her car. She got in, started the engine, and drove away.

A note won't do it, either, she thought. I'm going to write my story, publish it, and send Ekesa a copy. Maybe she will forgive me when she reads it.

With that, she turned the nose of the car toward the Plateau Highlands. She decided to settle where there was nobody that knew who she was. She opted not to see Ekesa. Wounds would heal—Ekesa's as well as her own. When she'd published her story, Ekesa might be ready to forgive her. As for restoring their friendship?

I don't think that will ever be possible, she thought. However, time will tell . . .

She'd made a three-course buffet.

There was a bowl of spiced ox-tail soup, tiny buttered cinnamon scones and scoops of homemade jam.

She had roasted some boar steaks, fried fish, and chicken wings and -drumsticks.

A whole bowl of vegetable rice and a bowl of traditionally crushed millet completed the main course.

An attractive fruit salad tower, made with papaws, oranges and pineapples, was served as dessert. Mango and banana smoothies rounded off the final course.

Finally, for after the meal, pancakes soaked in honey waited to be washed down with bitter espresso.

Nana was in a jubilant mood. Najma was also in high spirits. Zaire had gone to Mountain Crest with Jotham to bring Etembi. Arthenia was on her way. It was going to be a huge reunion.

Najma looked at Nana and realized that she was distant. "Everything okay?" she asked.

"I don't know. My heart is so calm. I have never felt like this before," Nana answered.

"I know you're scared," Najma said.

"No, I'm not," replied Nana. "I've seen Etembi before. He'd just never told me we had a son, and that's what I want him to clarify. He was by my side when your mother died. I could never have handled it alone," Nana said.

"You kept him from us." Najma said, sulking.

It didn't matter anymore. Many things had happened in just one week, and Najma was exhausted. It felt as if her life was starting over. There had been so many lies, but now the truth had prevailed.

She knew that Nana was her mother's stepsister and that Arthenia was her mother's biological sister. She also knew that Zaire's mother was her mother's sister.

Knowing that she could have a comfortable relationship with Jotham because they were not related was another breath of fresh air.

Jotham was happy to have his mom back; Zaire helped to clear Nana's doubts by retrieving the hospital documents to confirm that she'd delivered a baby boy. Nana was so excited about her son who'd grown up in an orphanage and had turned out so well. He was now a doctor.

Najma wasn't sure about Etembi and if it was okay to have him in their family circles.

"Do you still love him?" Najma asked suddenly. Nana dropped the spoon she was wiping.

"Who?" she asked.

"Etembi," replied Najma. "Do you still love him?"

"I don't know, my girl," said Nana. "Perhaps he is married. He kept the truth away from me for years. I doubt I can trust him."

Nana was surprised by how mature Najma had become.

"What if he isn't married?" persisted Najma. "Would you get back together with him?"

"Oh, you nosy girl!" mocked Nana. Go switch off the coffee maker."

There were knocks at the door. It had to be Zaire and the rest.

Jotham stood at the door, carrying a bottle of wine. Behind him were Etembi and Arthenia.

Zaire was still in the car, talking on the phone.

Najma received the wine from Jotham and put it on the table.

She showed the guests to the living room and they all sat down. Nana came to the living room, and Najma noticed how her face beamed when she saw Etembi.

There was a stiff exchange between Nana and Arthenia. Jotham received a warm hug.

"You can call later, bro!" Najma called to Zaire. "The food is getting cold!"

He locked the door and walked towards her. They hugged tightly and walked into the house, hand in hand.

"Najma, you look just like your mother," Arthenia said.

"Everybody tells me," replied Najma. "She was so beautiful."

She served some scones and soup for herself and Zaire.

"If you are serving your brother, who will serve me?" Jotham asked, his brow twisted.

"I am not your servant . . ." Najma responded with a cheeky smile.

"Hard-headed I see," Etembi said in his booming voice after his second sip of wine. "My son will have a nut to crack in this one,"

The mood was lively and cheerful. Everyone talked about everything.

Zaire's phone rang.

"Will you switch off that thing so that we can eat?" Nana said.

"My movers," replied Zaire. "They wanted to know which room to decorate for Najma." I'm moving out of the castle and Najma is coming with me to my new house."

"What?" exclaimed everyone except Etembi.

"I requested him to allow me to buy this house for Nana," explained Etembi. That is, of course, if Najma would allow me . . ."

"But . . . I was going to offer Nana my Lakeside house," said Arthenia. "The one that Akusa had stolen from me so long ago. It is closer to Jotham . . ."

"Whaaaaaaaat!" Nana, Najma and Jotham chorused.

"No! No!" protested Nana. "Did any one of you bother asking me what I want? Who told you I will accept any of those?" Her tone was firm and serious. There was a thick silence around the table.

"Come on, guys," said Najma. "Please, let's not complicate what should be a wonderful reunion dinner. I'm beginning to think that our family is cursed."

"I can't wait to finish school so that I can finally make my own decisions," she continued.

"Girl," said Arthenia, "making your own decision will never happen as for long as those long fingers of his are locked in yours as always."

She gestured to Jotham's hand, which was seeking Najma's beneath the table.

Everyone burst into laughter.

Najma blushed and pulled away from Jotham.

"I am serious though," continued Arthenia. "Someone will have to take over my estates when I die. The doctors reckon I have less than five years. I can't donate everything to Riverside. I hoped Nana . . ."

"Why don't we cross that bridge when we get there, please," Nana cut Arthenia short.

"And one last thing: I am leaving Mountain Crest School for Girls next year. I want to stay home with my girl, if she'll let me," Etembi said.

Nana's eyes dropped to her plate.

"You have a wife and a daughter?" Nana asked softly.

"Are you jealous?" He played with his spoon.

"Of course not," Nana replied quickly, sending the company into laughter once again.

"You are my girl, Nana. Always," he said.

It was Nana's turn to blush.

WARD NINE – Rounding Up Criminals

Ploutus sat up in his bed, wondering whether what Jotham was telling him was the truth.

It had been weeks now, and Elima came to his room frequently, asking him to take his life so that they could be together.

He tried explaining it to Jotham, who kept telling him he was losing his mind.

Was he really losing his mind? Every time he argued with him, Jotham injected with something that made him sleep. He wanted to get out of Ward Nine. He had to do something before the whole thing turned on him.

But what was left for him outside? His son had found out the whole truth and was working on getting him the punishment he deserved.

Maybe Cosmos had been right. Zaire *was* going to be his downfall.

"Get me out of here, Jotham," Ploutus begged. "Tell the world that I'm okay. I will sign the documents for you to own this facility."

"I already own this place. Zaire did it for me," Jotham said.

"How could he?!" exclaimed Ploutus. "Is he betraying me? His own father . . ."

"I see you are getting agitated," said Jotham, picking up a syringe. "You need your medicine."

"No," begged Ploutus. "Please don't. I'm not insane. I'm okay. I have my memories."

"No, you don't," said Jotham, approaching him with the injection. "You are not Ploutus. You are just my patient. We can give you another name if you don't remember your name."

Ploutus knew fighting would be futile.

Maybe I'm not Ploutus, he thought. Maybe he's right.

Maybe I was never a Statesman.

Elima, I need your help.

Help me, Elima.

Elima! Help me! Get me out of here!

Elima: Slice your wrists, Ploutus. Join me. Together we can watch over our daughter.

Ploutus: I am so scared. I don't want to die.

Elima: Since when are you scared? You are Ploutus. Ploutus is a god. Gods are never scared.

Ploutus: Please stay with me. Don't go, Elima.

As Ploutus sunk deeper into his conversation with the nonexistent Elima, Jotham recorded him. He needed evidence to show the delegates that Ploutus had lost his mind. They were deliberating on making the Deputy Statesman the Statesman, but there wasn't sufficient evidence that Ploutus would not recover soon.

Jotham had gotten the evidence. Those who supported Ploutus in the capital would not argue with the diagnosis of a senior psychiatrist with such evidence.

Barvo and Lorantu were already in their place at the hospital. Lorantu's supporters tried to create some scandals, but Zaire threatened to inform the public about his abductions and sex trade. He also had a video of the two soaked in their own vomit and diarrhea.

When Lorantu's house and estate went up in flames, he'd completely lost his mind. He screamed the whole night and it took at least three male nurses to sedate him.

Barvo was in a worse state. Apparently, his immunity had been compromised by the chemicals of his fake gold endeavor, and was taking the conditions at the hospital badly. His body erupted with wounds, and he smelled like a dead body. He had to be separated from Lorantu and was kept in isolation.

Jotham walked around, taking down notes about his patients. He loved his job. He enjoyed helping people get mentally stable. But he loathed the fact that he had to use the facility to keep the three men from facing charges. He did it for Zaire, because he was his best friend and Ploutus was his father. And there was Najma. She had yet to discover that Ploutus was her father. That worried Jotham. *How will she react?* wondered Jotham. *What if I lost her for keeping the truth from her?*

But she never hated Zaire for keeping all those things from her.

But I'm not her brother. She has no obligation toward me. I just hope she'll understand.

He made a mental note to call her later in the evening to see how she was doing. He thanked God that his father, Etembi, hadn't quit yet. He could talk to her any time via him.

His phone rung. It was Zaire.

"Hello, bro!" Zaire said when he answered the phone.

"I hate it when you call me that," groaned Jotham. "What do you want me to do this time?" Jotham asked.

"It is Osanyin," replied Zaire. "He needs asylum and I cannot think about a better place than your facility. His state has overthrown him. Can you make him insane for me?"

There was a long pause. Jotham had had enough. He wanted his facility to help people with mental health issues . . . not harbor state criminals and those in exile.

"Hello. Bro, please," Zaire begged.

Jotham didn't know what to say.

"It will be the last one, I promise," Zaire continued.

"I am booking him in," said Jotham. "But please let it be the last. Unless, next time, it's you." Jotham hung up and went to prepare a bed for Osanyin in Ploutus's room.

COATING BITTER PILLS WITH HONEY

Nana removed the curtains from the window in Najma's bedroom. She missed her. She wondered how her life would be without Najma.

But then, Etembi was coming back. He'd visited twice already, and the house smelled of his cologne.

She smiled at her naughty thought.

Nana had refused to take Arthenia's house. She didn't want to live her life being afraid of Akusa's ghost.

She packed Najma's bags to be moved to Zaire's house at the Capital. She had plans of changing the bedroom for when Jotham would visit. She was happy that her son was in love with who could have been her daughter.

She picked up a framed picture of Jesus from Najma's study stable and looked at it. "I now believe that you exist," she said. "You brought back my son and my husband. My daughter will remain in my family. Arthenia is fighting for the villagers. Zaire turned out so well. You are real. Thank you."

There were tears in her eyes. Etembi had confirmed that Najma was going to do her exams well.

When they talked to Najma on the phone, she was excited about finishing school.

Zaire had also confirmed that Ekesa had accepted his leaving the Castle.

Ekesa had released a statement confirming that Ploutus was in no position to rule. His Deputy has taken over until someone else was elected.

Zaire did not have to take care of state affairs any longer, unless he was really needed. He was running one of his father's oil companies, and the rest of the property was being managed by the State and Ekesa.

Nana wondered if Zaire was planning to settle down soon.

She made a mental note of asking him if he was seeing anyone. She wondered why it bothered her that Zaire was not in a hurry to find a good woman for himself. She remembered the picture in her hands and looked into the eyes of the Jesus illustration once more.

"Please bring a good, calm, and loving woman into Zaire's life," she prayed. "He deserves better."

She took the picture to her own bedroom and packed the rest of the stuff. When she was done, she called Zaire to come for them.

Zaire walked through the door a few hours later in a happy mood.

"I am so excited today," he said. "I have finally settled in my new home, and Najma will be joining me as soon as she finishes her exams."

He sat down, drinking a glass of cold juice.

"How is your father doing?" Nana asked. She knew that over-excitement was not good. She needed to dampen his spirits a little.

"Not so well," he said. "Jotham is working on him, though."

"And," Zaire added, sarcastically, "His best friend joined him from Mountain Crest yesterday."

"What do you mean?' Nana asked.

"Osanyin," he replied, laughing. "The former Statesman of Mountain Crest."

"What? Is he . . ." Nana asked, gesturing by pointing her forefinger to her head.

"Not really," he remarked. "Just running away from a real prison to a mental prison."

Nana hated where the conversation was going. It seemed that Zaire was still using Jotham to do his dirty work . . .

"Zaire," said Nana. "As a mother I am warning you. Please stop doing this dirty work. And don't get Jotham involved . . ."

"Come on, Nana," Zaire interrupted. "I have a past. I can't run away from it. And Jotham is an adult. He will know if something can get him in trouble. Trust me, it is the last one."

"You haven't told Najma yet that Ploutus is her father," Nana said flatly.

"I don't have to," said Zaire, standing up. "He will confess it to her himself. Remember, she is coming to work in Ward Nine when she finishes her exams."

Nana sighed, frustrated. She hoped her gut was wrong for once. There was something awful laced in his excitement. She wondered what it was.

"Nana, don't worry about Ploutus and Najma. Najma has swallowed so many bitter pills already. This one is coated in honey. Her greatest adversary is facing judgment already. Don't you see?" Zaire babbled on.

"May God forgive you, son," she said. "The man you are talking about is still your father."

Zaire opened his mouth to say something, but Nana raised her hand to shut stop him. She silently helped him carry Najma's luggage to the car.

She then held him in her arms with a heavy heart, and bid him farewell.

Zaire drove off whistling.

He didn't hear Nana asking him to drive carefully.

He didn't notice that there was a funny smell in his car.

He sped out of Corner Street toward the Capital.

He tried slowing down when a motorist tried to overtake him, but the brake pedal sat solidly. It didn't budge.

The car sped down the unkempt valleys of Valley View. He panicked.

Had someone messed with his brakes? Who could it be?

He tried swerving the car to get it off the road so it could slow down. It didn't slow.

His only option was to ram into a tree and hope that he'd survive. For the first time in many years, he looked up and saw the face of Father Cruz in the clouds.

"Forgive me, father," he said. "My soul got darkened, and now I'm gonna die."

His car hit the tree, the airbag knocking him unconscious.

*****

Zaire woke up in hospital, unable to move. Najma, Jotham, Nana and Etembi were standing at his bed.

"He's awake," said Etembi, watching Zaire closely.

"Where am I?" Zaire wanted to know.

"You're in the hospital at Mountain Crest," said Jotham.

"You were very lucky," said Etembi. "I was on my way to Nana when I saw your car crash. I was just in time to pull you out, drag you to my car and drive away. The car exploded seconds later. You wouldn't have made it.

I took you straight to Jotham's facility. He stabilized you and ordered a helicopter to fly you to Mountain Crest.

"Thank you, guys," said Zaire, looking Etembi and Jotham.

He then looked at Nana and Najma,

"I'm sorry," he said with tears in his eyes, looking at Nana and Najma. "I'm thankful for the fact that I can say this to you."

Tears began to run down both ladies' cheeks.

"I'm sorry," he said again, looking at Nana. "I'm sorry that I was such an insensitive brat. Many times, you've tried to bring me back to my senses, but all I could think about was my revenge. And I'm sorry for keeping quiet about Ham and Etembi."

"I'm sorry," he said again, looking at Najma. "Sorry for all the lies and that I delayed telling you the truth for such a long time."

"Etembi," he said. "I'm sorry for taking so long to let you know that you have a son. I should've done that the moment I found out."

"Ham," he said, looking at Jotham. "You are the best friend ever. I'm sorry for using you to do my dirty work. Thank you for not reporting me to the police. I'm sorry for keeping quiet about who your parents are. That was unforgivable.

Finally, he addressed them all together.

"Could you guys ever forgive me?" he asked.

"Well," said Najma. "What about . . ."

But Jotham silenced her by placing his finger on her lips.

"After everything you've said, we cannot help but forgive you," he said.

"Right, guys?" he prompted, looking at the other three in turn.

They all nodded their agreement.

Suddenly, someone rang a bell.

"Visiting hours are over," said the nurse.

After greeting Zaire, they all left for home.

Najma's exam was about to begin, so she went back to school with Etembi.

Jotham and Nana went back to Corner.

Two months later, Zaire was discharged. He was flown home, where Najma was waiting to attend to her brother. He still found it difficult to move around, given the multiple injuries he'd suffered, but it was improving a little bit each day. He was thankful that he had a sister to look after him.

Little Elima walked down the runway. She was taller than most of the babies that were displaying her mother's designs. She had a bright smile, and the pink baby gown that she was wearing cast colorful rays on her face, making it glitter. She kept smiling like her mother had shown her the previous night. There were cheers and claps throughout the hall.

At the end of the stage, she turned around and put her tiny hand on her waist then twisted it in pose.

Najma gasped. She hadn't taught her daughter that. She met little Elima on the walkway, clapping as the master of ceremonies announced her name as the chief designer of ELINAJ BABY CLOTHES.

Her heart was overflowing with joy. Jotham was shouting her name loudest, and she could hear his voice. She wondered if her pregnancy made her extra sensitive. Little Ham kicked in her belly. She wondered if he also felt her joy.

It had been three years since they had buried Ploutus. It was during her internship as a psychiatrist in Ward Nine that he had confessed to her that he was her father. She remembered the pain that seared her heart when he'd confessed that he'd killed her mother to perform election rituals.

Her fellow interns had thought he was hallucinating, but she'd known that it was the truth. She'd never felt so much sorrow as she did on that day. She was sad that Zaire had been the cause of most of it. She felt like everyone had betrayed her—even Nana and Jotham. She'd confronted Jotham, and it was during their fight that

Little Elima had kicked for the first time. As she shouted at Jotham, the baby kicked again, flooding her heart with so much sorrow because she hadn't even known that she was pregnant.

Two days after his confession, Ploutus had slit his wrists. He was found drenched in his own blood the following day. Najma had buried her father two days after she'd actually formally met him.

She'd stopped college to nurse her pregnancy. Jotham had to hurry marrying her. They wedded in a private family ceremony officiated by Zaire's friend from the seminary. Zaire could not do it himself, since he had not yet been ordained. But Jotham had the pleasure of having his best friend as his best man, and Zaire's fiancée did Najma the honor of being her bridesmaid.

As she mounted the podium to make her remarks about her designs, she scanned the room for Zaire. He was seated next to Jotham and a smile lit up his face. Beside him sat his beautiful bride-to-be nurse.

He had joined the seminary as soon as he'd recovered sufficiently from his injuries.

He still managed the oil company, but a large percentage of its proceedings went to orphanages and to building churches in Valley View.

Suddenly, he became aware that his sister was looking at him. He waved at her and smiled.

THE END